PRAISE FOR
WRECKERS' KEY

"A kick-butt, female salvage-boat captain, two gorgeous men and a gruesome murder along Florida's sunny coast keep the pages turning on this excellent mystery."
— *Romantic Times*

"Suspenseful . . . vivid."
—South Florida *Sun-Sentinel*

"Kling, noted for brilliantly rendering the world of South Florida's teeming waters in her Seychelle Sullivan novels, does it again. . . . *Wreckers' Key* sails to its surprising conclusion."
—*The Sanford Herald*

"Kling knows boats and she knows South Florida and she's learned how to ratchet up the suspense with each new book in her entertaining series."
—Crime by Collins

"Action-packed and suspenseful . . . This series gets better with each book."
—Over My Dead Body

Also by Christine Kling

Surface Tension
Cross Current
Bitter End

WRECKERS' KEY

A Novel of Suspense

Christine Kling

BALLANTINE BOOKS • NEW YORK

Wreckers' Key is a work of fiction. Names, characters, places, and incidents are the products of the author's imagination or are used fictitiously. Any resemblance to actual events, locales, or persons, living or dead, is entirely coincidental.

2008 Ballantine Books Mass Market Edition

Copyright © 2007 by Christine Kling

All rights reserved.

Published in the United States by Ballantine Books, an imprint of The Random House Publishing Group, a division of Random House, Inc., New York.

BALLANTINE and colophon are registered trademarks of Random House, Inc.

Originally published in hardcover in the United States by Ballantine Books, an imprint of The Random House Publishing Group, a division of Random House, Inc., in 2007.

ISBN 978-0-345-47906-8

Cover design: Carl D. Galian
Cover photograph: © Alamy

Printed in the United States of America

www.ballantinebooks.com

OPM 9 8 7 6 5 4 3 2 1

In memory of my father,
who first taught me to sail

ACKNOWLEDGMENTS

I would like to thank the following people for all their support and assistance: Mark Tavani, my editor, who rocks; Judith Weber, my agent; Laura Jorstad, my copyeditor; Fred Rea—who can now be called the Car Guy; Captain Bruce Amlicke, S/V *Wild Matilde,* for all his ideas and then some; Captain Mark Haskins of the S/V *Liahona* for his insight into salvage; Captain Ken Bloemker, S/V *Thalia,* for helping me birth the idea; Captain Kelton Joyner, S/V *Isle of Escape,* for tales of corporate layoffs; Captain John Verdon, S/V *Imagine,* for letting me borrow his house; Kathleen Ginestra for her knowledge of Fort Lauderdale—the town and the people; Cindy Gray for her expertise in windsurfing; Mary Barrett, who gave me the title; Melanie Neale and Mike Jastrzebski of the Bluewater Writers' Group; and finally, to my mother, Pat, and to my son, Tim, both of whom taught me what motherhood is all about.

I

"WE hit the reef so hard, I'm surprised no one was killed," Nestor said. "I keep dreaming about it, you know? Hearing the sound of the hull crunching across the coral and then Kent's screams when his arm broke." He rubbed his hand across his eyes like he was trying to wipe away the vision. "This situation scares me, Seychelle. My whole career's on the line here."

I couldn't disagree. When you put a multimillion-dollar yacht on the reef on her maiden voyage, your reputation as a captain is toast. I was there to help with the salvage of the boat, but I wasn't sure what I could do to salvage Nestor's career.

Catalina Frias reached across the table, took her husband's hand, and focused her large brown eyes on his face. She didn't say anything for several seconds, but there was a sense of intimacy in that moment that was stronger than if she'd grabbed him and planted a wet one on him. "Hey, we are going to get through this, *mi amor*, okay?" Her soft voice was accented, but her English was perfect. She squeezed his hand, her other arm resting across the top of the belly that bulged beneath her pretty print maternity top.

I was sitting with the two of them at an outdoor table at the Two Friends Patio Restaurant on Front Street. I'd arrived in Key West late the afternoon before on my forty-six-foot aluminum tug *Gorda,* and when I called Nestor on the VHF, I told him I was too tired to come ashore after a four-day trip down from Lauderdale with only my dog as crew. I just wanted to drop the hook and collapse in my bunk, so we'd agreed to meet in the morning for Sunday brunch. Now here I was, sitting under a lush trellis of bougainvillea pushing scrambled eggs and sausage around my plate, my appetite gone.

"Nestor, this is the first time I've taken *Gorda* this far from home. I wouldn't do this for just anybody, you know."

When he smiled that boyish smile so full of gratitude, my heart ached for him. He was in a hell of a spot.

"*Gracias, amiga.* I can't lose this job," he said, the backs of his fingers caressing his wife's belly. "Not now, with the baby coming in just a few weeks."

I'd known Nestor much longer than his wife had, and I loved him like a brother. There was a time when maybe that love could have gone another way, but the attraction that might have been had turned into an abiding friendship. He really was one of the good guys. He'd showed up on the docks just before Red died, and afterward, when I started running *Gorda* on my own and several of the captains were bad-mouthing the only female captain in the towing business, he always stood up for me. I'd watched him work his way up the waterfront, going from being a captain on the Water Taxi to running the charter fishing boat *My Way,* until now, finally, he'd gotten his big break about four months ago, as the captain of a luxury power yacht. The *Power Play* was a newly commissioned Sunseeker 94 owned by a local resident millionaire, Ted Berger. Berger had made his money in dot-com-related businesses, and when he'd sold out, he'd bought several South Florida TV stations and sports teams.

"Do you think Berger's going to can you?"

"I don't know. Maybe. He hasn't said anything yet. Seychelle, this was the first passage I'd made as captain. Other than a couple of sea trials to work on the engines, we hadn't really taken her out yet. He told me when he hired me to commission the yacht that he wanted her down here in Key West for Race Week, but then he decided to install new flat-screen TVs in all the staterooms, then a new sound system, and we were late getting out of the yard. The festivities down here had already started, and the boss was itching to come down and party. Otherwise, we wouldn't have been going so fast in a squall."

"You hit that reef going almost twenty knots in a rain squall?"

"I know it sounds bad, Seychelle. Especially to someone like you. But let's face it—you haven't exactly embraced the electronics age. Do you even *have* a GPS on that tugboat of yours?"

"Nestor, what I do is not the point here."

"Sey, you don't even own a cell phone."

"Okay, already."

"See, the *Power Play* is loaded with every bit of electronic equipment imaginable. Berger spared no expense. The man is really into toys, and there are backups for the backups. So what we were doing is running on instruments, the same way commercial pilots do with planes full of hundreds of passengers. The autopilot is tied in to one of three separate GPS systems. We were in Hawk's Channel, and everything had been working great up to that point. I was on the bridge myself because I knew we were nearing the entrance to Key West Harbor. All the instruments showed us more than half a mile from any obstructions when *bam*! We ran right up onto these rocks off West Washerwoman Shoal. The impact knocked Kent off his feet, and when he tried to break his fall, the bone just snapped—came right out through his skin." Nestor shuddered at the memory. He'd already told me it had been a nasty compound fracture.

Nobody said anything for several long seconds while we all saw it happen in our minds, saw the big ninety-four-footer come to a grinding halt on the rocks, the men on the bridge thrown off their feet, the screams and the blood. Nestor grasped the Saint Christopher's medal he wore around his neck and kissed the face of the saint.

"So, Nestor," I said, "what do you think happened?"

My friend looked at his wife for a moment, as though unsure if he should say what he was thinking. It was amazing to watch how the two of them communicated, saying so much in a glance or a touch.

"Seychelle," Nestor started, after a quick look around the dining patio to see if anyone was listening to our conversation. Satisfied, he leaned closer and lowered his voice. "I've spent a lot of time with Ted Berger these past weeks, and I wouldn't put anything past him. He calls himself the Other Ted, as though he's in the same league as Turner. But he'd do anything to get there. *Ruthless* is the word that comes to mind." Nestor lifted his shoulders and bobbed his head once, like a bow. "Okay, maybe you have to be that way to get the kind of money he has, but lately, with the start-up of this girls' hockey league and buying this boat, I think he's overextended himself. He wants out of this boat deal and now he seems more pissed over the fact that he's getting hit with a big salvage claim than over the business of wrecking her in the first place."

"Wait a minute. Are you saying you think Berger tried to wreck his own boat?" I tried hard to keep the disbelief out of my voice.

"Jesus," he said, swiveling his head to look around the empty patio. "Not so loud, Sey. I don't have any proof—yet. But it just doesn't make sense otherwise. The only way this could have happened is if the equipment malfunctioned somehow. And I'm just saying that Ted Berger would have been better off with the insurance company cashing him out of an investment that had got out of hand."

"Nestor, I'm finding this kind of hard to believe."

"You'd understand if you could have heard him while we were in the boatyard. He was constantly complaining about how much things cost. He had no idea what he was getting into when he bought a yacht that size."

"I suppose it makes sense in a way. If he'd just put the boat up for sale, it would have signaled to people that he was in financial trouble."

"Exactly. And he has the background—he *made* his money in electronics. I'm going to have a buddy of mine check out the equipment on the boat and see if he can find evidence it's been tampered with. Get him to come down before we take off to head back up north. I don't intend to take the fall for Ted Berger's financial problems."

At that moment Nestor's eyes flicked to the right and focused on something outside the restaurant. The skin across his cheeks grew taut and his eyes narrowed for only a second before his face broke into a huge, forced grin. He lifted his hand and waved.

I twisted in my seat, glanced over my shoulder. A white-haired man wearing a loud red-and-blue Hawaiian shirt was standing on the sidewalk in front of the restaurant. He waved, and then went in the front door, clearly headed for us out on the patio. An instant later he appeared in the side door, and his voice boomed, "Good morning," causing the other diners' heads to turn. When he reached our table, he placed both his hands on Catalina's shoulders then bent and kissed her on the cheek. He said, "Our mommy-to-be looks more glowingly beautiful every time I see her."

Catalina's body had gone still at his touch, her only movement turning her face away as he kissed her, so his mouth wound up kissing her hair.

Nestor stood and shook hands with the man. Either he hadn't noticed or he was choosing to ignore his wife's discomfort. "Good morning," he said as he pumped the man's hand. Then he turned to me. "Seychelle, I'd like to introduce you to Ted Berger."

I started to stand, but Berger waved me back down. "So you're the tugboat captain," he said as he seated himself in the fourth chair at the table and waggled a coffee mug at the waitress. "I kind of expected a hag with a corncob pipe." He cocked his head to one side and looked at me from head to as much as he could see above the table. "You're definitely not a hag."

The Tugboat Annie jokes had grown old about the second month after I inherited Sullivan Towing and Salvage from my father. That was more than three years ago.

"I'm just here to do the job you hired me for, Mr. Berger."

He threw his hands in the air in mock surrender. "Oh my, I've offended her. Very businesslike of you, Miss Sullivan. Or should I call you Captain?"

"Seychelle is fine," I said. Up close, I realized that the man's white hair was deceptive. He wasn't as old as I'd originally thought. His face and neck looked like they belonged to a man not yet out of his forties. He was a couple of inches shorter than me, maybe five foot eight, and his forced joviality and loud clothes made him appear to be overcompensating for something.

"Okay. Seychelle, then. Interesting name."

I got ready to go into the usual explanation, but he beat me to it. "Named after the islands in the Indian Ocean, I assume."

"Pretty good. Not many people recognize the name."

"Trust me, Ted, Sey's a lot better off than her brothers," Nestor said.

"Oh?" Berger asked, his eyebrows lifting into the lock of white hair that had fallen on his forehead.

I nodded. "Madagascar and Pitcairn."

"Oh dear," he said, laughing. "Parents *can* be cruel. So, Seychelle, Nestor tells me he'd rather have you tow the boat up to Lauderdale than any of that scum over at Ocean Towing."

"Ted, I may have exchanged a few harsh words with those guys, but I didn't call them scum," Nestor said.

"Well, I'll call them that!" He turned to me. "Do you know what they're trying to charge me for getting the *Power Play* off that reef and into Robbie's Marina on Stock Island?"

"I can imagine. Nestor told me it took them almost twelve hours to get her free."

"They're goddamn pirates!"

"No, sir, actually, they probably saved the boat and saved the insurance company a bundle. They'd rather pay the yard bill and salvage than suffer a total loss."

He rolled his eyes and turned away from me.

Out in the street, a tall man with stringy shoulder-length hair, wearing nothing but swim trunks, was trying to untangle the leash of his mangy German shepherd from around his legs and the pedals of his beach bike. He was mumbling to himself. Our table was situated so close to the street, we couldn't help but overhear the string of obscenities and incomprehensible answers he was giving to the voices he apparently heard in his head.

When Berger spoke again, he continued staring out at

the man on the street. I wasn't sure if he was talking to himself or to us. "I like things that are new and shiny. No matter what, *now* the *Power Play* is going to be a repaired vessel." He turned and focused his eyes on mine. "And I don't like patched-up shit."

I smiled, refusing to look away. "Well, welcome to boats, Mr. Berger. If you're not running them, you're working on them. As I understand it, the hull wasn't even holed. You've just got damage to rudders, stabilizers, props, and the like," I said. "You know, I wouldn't think of it as a patched-up boat. I'd say Nestor was just breaking her in."

He tightened one cheek in a half smile. "That's one way of looking at it." His tone told me it would not be his view. "So you're going to help our boy here get the boat back to Lauderdale where they can make proper repairs?"

I didn't like the way he called Nestor *our boy.* "Sure am."

Nestor said, "The guys at Robbie's have put a temporary epoxy patch on the deep scratches in the hull. It will have to be faired and painted later; they just didn't like the bare glass underwater. One prop was a total loss and the other is slightly damaged, but usable. Rudders were totaled. There was some structural damage to interior bulkheads, and some issues that will need to be addressed up in Lauderdale. I just want these guys to get her in shape for the trip north. It'll be close, but I'll bet we could launch tomorrow."

"That sounds good to me," I said. "The sooner, the better."

Berger pushed back his chair and stood. He looked down at Catalina. "You gonna get this guy to show you around Key West, relax a little bit? Beautiful woman like you comes down to be with her man—he should show you off. Seems he spends all his time in that boatyard."

"I told her I was going to be busy," Nestor said. "And I didn't like the idea of her riding the bus in her condition, but she insisted."

"My husband says *my condition* like pregnancy is an illness," Catalina said to me. She was ignoring Berger's comments. "Having babies is natural. Stop worrying." She reached for his hand again. "I have been trying to talk him into doing a little windsurfing," she said. "I would like to see him relax, have a little fun. He is very good, you know. When he was in his teens, he was the national windsurfing champion in the Dominican Republic."

"Listen to your wife, Nestor. She's a smart, stand-by-your-man kind of woman. Makes me wonder what she sees in a guy like you." He punched Nestor in the arm hard enough to rock him back in his chair. "So, how soon do you two think the boat will be ready to head north?"

"We've got a good-weather window coming up, and I'd like to leave as soon as possible," I said. "Nestor and I were just starting to discuss our departure plans when you arrived."

"Really?" he said. "You looked so serious. And secretive. Like my crew here was plotting a mutiny."

Nestor and I both must have shown our surprise. Berger laughed and punched Nestor in the arm again, harder. "Just kidding, buddy."

II

"**D**o you think he overheard what we were saying about him?"

We watched his back as he disappeared up the street.

"He would've been hard to miss if he'd been lingering around in that shirt," I said, but I couldn't rule it out. I thought about the man on the street with his dog earlier, and how we'd overheard every word he uttered. "I really don't like that guy."

"He's not usually such a jerk," Nestor said, rubbing his upper arm where Berger had punched him.

Catalina looked at her husband and raised her eyebrows.

"He's not that bad," he said, lifting his hands, palms upward as if he were a weight lifter. "Okay, you're right. And if he did have a hand in putting that boat on the stones, then he's a major asshole."

Nestor put his elbows on the table and leaned his forehead against his clasped hands. He was muttering what sounded like curses in Spanish. Then he raised his head and looked at his wife. "Berger heard or he didn't. He'll fire me or he won't. In the meantime, I need to get Jorge down here to look at the boat. I'll call him tonight, see if he can come down tomorrow. Time to go on the defensive."

He reached for her hand and they sat there for several

seconds, not talking. Once again I felt like an intruder just sitting there.

Nestor had met Catalina two years earlier when he'd returned to his hometown in the Dominican Republic after his father was admitted to a hospital, near death. The young, chocolate-skinned woman of mixed race had been his father's favorite nurse. After the funeral, Nestor returned to Fort Lauderdale and the two started an e-mail correspondence that ended with a marriage proposal six months later. They made a striking couple with matching heads of black hair, yet so different in their body types. Tall, slender Nestor had his Spanish ancestors' olive skin and sharp features, while Catalina's beauty came from the lushness of her African lips, carved cheekbones, and a figure that even when pregnant evoked desire in men and women—the women desiring to look half that good. Being around them made me a believer in marriage. Maybe it wasn't something that would ever work for me, but for these two, their union made them better, stronger, wiser. I envied them that.

And now I could understand Nestor wanting to believe that the grounding wasn't his fault. It could, probably would, ruin his chances of ever moving up, of getting the highest-paying jobs on the megayachts. Gossip spread like the wind on the waterfront. But I knew how quickly things could change when a yacht was traveling at a speed like twenty knots. Only a few seconds of inattention could result in disaster. Obviously, Nestor *wanted* to believe this wasn't his fault.

We paid the bill and rose to leave. On the sidewalk, I embraced Catalina and smiled at her. "Berger was right about one thing. You look great."

She lowered her eyes, embarrassed by the flattery. She really had no idea how lovely she was. "I feel great." She took my hand in hers. "Why don't you come back with us to the yacht? There is not much else to do. We have movies, computers—many toys." She elbowed her husband in the ribs. "And we can send him off windsurfing while we have an afternoon for the girls."

"Thanks, but not this afternoon. I haven't been down to Key West in a while, and I want to wander around—been cooped up on the boat too long on the trip down."

"So tell me, why did you make this trip alone?" Catalina asked. "Where's that wonderful man of yours?"

I winced at the possessive term. While B.J. and I were lovers, we continued to take things one day at a time. Thing is, I was the one balking at commitment. Catalina had met B.J. once, and he had made his usual impression. Women were drawn to him like iron particles to a magnet. It usually took more than a brush-off to shake them loose. I think it was something about his long, sleek black hair and part-Samoan heritage that made him seem like a tall, brown island king. We all just wanted to picture him wearing nothing but green leaves.

"B.J. was busy," I said, not really wanting to explain at what, "and I couldn't find a good deckhand on such short notice. Besides, the autopilot did most of the steering. I've had some stuff going on in my life, and I needed the time alone. I enjoyed it. The light has been spectacular. Gave me time to do some thinking, and I got some great photos of scenes I hope to paint when I get back."

Catalina wouldn't let it be. "He is busy at what?"

Geez, these people were Latins. Machismo and all that. I knew how they were going to react. But I needed to say it as though it didn't bother me. "My friend Molly asked B.J. to take some classes with her. They're studying to be midwives."

Nestor burst out laughing and pretended to bury his face in his wife's hair. He was standing behind her, his arms casually wrapped around her waist, and he patted her swollen belly like a tom-tom. "Sorry," he said when he caught his breath. "I just never heard of a man wanting to be a midwife—or do you call it a midhusband?" His face was turning red as he held his breath trying not to laugh again.

"Well," I said, "If you think about it, it fits right in with his fascination with shiatsu and aikido and all that enlightenment and Eastern religion stuff. Besides, B.J. is very secure in his masculinity. He's really interested in this, and he—"

This time they both exploded with laughter.

"You guys, stop it. I know how it sounds. I think he's really doing it for Molly. Geez, I don't know what to think."

"Have you checked to see if he's still got cojones?" Nestor asked.

"*Mi amor,*" Catalina said, a playful huskiness coming into her voice, "this man—there is no question. He is beautiful. Perhaps, too beautiful."

"You know, you're not making this any easier on me."

"Maybe you should call him to come down to Key West," Nestor said. "There are lots of bars on Duval Street he might like."

"Okay, you two, you go ahead and yuk it up." I hitched my bag up over my shoulder. "I'll see you both later."

IN fact, I thought, as I headed back toward Schooner Wharf to admire the charter yachts of Key West, it had been good to see Nestor laughing like that, even if it was at my expense. The young man had sounded so somber when I'd received his first phone call. He was in a pretty bad spot, and he might find himself having to look for another line of work after this.

Maybe I should join him, I thought, as I walked down Greene Street, shoving my hands deep in the pockets of my sweatshirt. I had done a job recently that was now hanging over me like a threatening storm, only I didn't know how to prepare for this one. That's what had made me so quick to say yes to the opportunity to leave Fort Lauderdale for a while. My career just might be in need of salvage, too.

There's a reason why I normally don't try to pick up distress calls on channel sixteen, I thought, as I settled onto a bench to watch the activity in Key West Bight Marina. There was once a time, back when my dad first built *Gorda* and he was one of only a couple of guys in the business, that he would answer every call that came up on the radio. But things had changed in recent years— changed drastically. As the yachts grew bigger and more expensive, the salvage and towing business became more lucrative, and dozens of companies had sprung up to try to cash in on the bonanza of idiots who could afford to buy boats but didn't have the sense to get any kind of training to run them. There was Sea Tow, Offshore Marine Towing, Cape Anne Towing, Ocean Towing, Big Tuna Salvage—the list went on and on.

Unlike cars, boats don't require a driver's license for personal use. Anybody can go buy a vessel that can run at speeds up to sixty and seventy miles an hour, then just jump in and turn the key. And the waters around South Florida have been chewing up boats for centuries. While Ted Berger had just been complaining about Ocean Towing, they weren't the only ones out there slapping boat owners with outrageous salvage claims. I'd heard from captains who'd applied for jobs with these outfits that it was company strategy to do anything they could to upgrade a job from a tow, which paid by the hour, to a salvage operation, which could result in an award of

20 to 40 percent of the value of the boat. Plus, they all needed the bucks to buy bigger and faster towboats and put up higher land-based VHF radio antennas. The end result? *Gorda* and I just couldn't compete.

And then there was that afternoon just over a month ago when I answered an emergency call and the boat sank and a child almost died. And now I was being sued for $1.3 million for damages and mental anguish.

The whole situation was causing me a fair amount of mental anguish of my own, so when Nestor Frias called and requested me to assist him with getting the damaged *Power Play* back up to Lauderdale, I didn't care if B.J. was off taking lessons in how to deliver babies. I grabbed at the chance to get out of town.

I stood up now, stretched, and told myself to stop whining. It was a sunny, crisp January day, I was in Key West, and I had lots of nerve to complain. There were thousands, probably millions of people all across America who hated their jobs at this very moment, and they weren't standing outside in the warm sun gazing through a sea of rigging in Key West Harbor. The seafood restaurant to my left was broadcasting Buffett's "Boat Drinks," and I was admiring the fleet of schooners at the docks in the boat basin tucked behind breakwaters. Some were smaller workboats like the *Wolf*, some more than a hundred feet like the *Western Union*—industrial-strength charter head boats built to carry crowds—and others were classics like that black-hulled, immaculately varnished schooner with the name *Hawkeye* written in gold leaf on her bow.

Okay, so you've been thinking about getting out of the boat business, but listen to yourself. What else do you think you could do?

I started to stroll back toward the dinghy dock on the waterfront, thinking I might stop off at the Schooner

Wharf Bar for a cold one before heading back out to the boat.

Paint. That's what I really wanted to do. Like my mother. She had been a fairly successful watercolor artist before she died. We spent many happy hours standing in front of the easel together, her warm body pressed to my back, her hand guiding mine. *Yes, that's it. Well done. You've really got a talent for this, darling.* Her work still graced the walls of some of the most prominent homes in Fort Lauderdale from the days when the galleries sought her work. And now I'd been invited to enter several paintings in the prestigious Las Olas Art Show, and at least one gallery was hinting at wanting to show my work. I knew the statistics, the very small number of people who actually made a living as artists, but maybe if I sold *Gorda,* I could use the money to take a year off just to paint. Just to see if I really had it.

"Seychelle?"

I turned my head in the direction of the distant shout. At first I didn't see anyone. Then, far down one of the Schooner Wharf piers, I saw a man stepping off the schooner I'd been admiring just a few minutes before. He came trotting up the dock toward me with an incredulous look on his face.

"Seychelle Sullivan? Is that really you?"

III

I WAS pretty sure I would have remembered this guy if I'd ever met him before. The fabric of his white T-shirt was stretched tight across his broad chest, and where the sleeves of the shirt had been cut off, his tanned biceps bulged as he half ran toward me, waving. His slim hips were encased in cargo shorts, and his thick brown hair was streaked with strands of sun-bleached gold. All in all, I was figuring it was my lucky day that he was running toward me, whoever the hell he was.

My face must have shown my confusion. He stopped about five feet away from me and smiled. "You don't remember me, do you?"

"Um, no. Are you sure we've met?" There was something about his eyes that was ringing bells somewhere deep in the recesses of my brain, but I couldn't nail down the connections.

He opened his mouth wide and laughed. His teeth were whiter than a puppy's and the look he was giving me, enthusiastically waiting to see if I would come up with his name, made me think that if he'd had a tail, it would have been wagging.

He dropped his head to his chest for a few seconds, as though giving up. Then he looked up, showing off those gorgeous teeth again, and said, "Ben. Remember? From high school? Ben Baker?"

"Benjamin Baker?" I said, my voice rising nearly an octave on his last name. "Oh my God, Glub? Have you ever changed!" When I'd called him his old childhood nickname, he'd dropped his eyes for a moment and his dazzling smile dimmed by just a few watts. I reached out for his shoulders and held him at arm's length. I knew I was babbling, but I couldn't believe it. "Look at you. Oh my God. You're gorgeous!"

As I walked around him, surveying the transformation from head to bare feet, he cocked his head sideways and watched me.

"Changed a little, huh?" he said.

"A little? Geez, I never would have recognized you."

Benjamin Baker had been one year ahead of me—in my brother Pit's class at Stranahan High. He was one of those nerdy boys, shaped like a pear with a wide ass and narrow shoulders. His mother always buzzed his hair short, making his head look even more pinlike in relation to his enormous butt. I used to think he would have made a good singing Country Bear in a Disney attraction.

Ben had been totally into marine science, though, and that was our connection. That and the fact that we lived in the same neighborhood, and Pit and I often had to save him from the cruel teasing of our older brother Maddy. I'd spent hours with Ben going over all the creatures he had in his slide collection and peering into the powerful microscope his mother had bought for him.

In high school, Ben had suffered from the triple curse—he'd had braces, acne, and glasses all at once. His face had been a red, bumpy field of scabs and pus, and if it hadn't been for the fact that he had the coolest hermit crabs as pets, I don't think I would have gone over to his house anymore.

"What happened to you?"

He laughed again in that openmouthed way that was so unlike anything he had ever done as a kid. He'd always been trying to disappear into the woodwork back then, hoping not to stand out so the other kids wouldn't tease him or beat him up as they did regularly. If he did laugh, he'd hold his hand in front of his mouth so you wouldn't see his braces.

"Hey, people change, you know? After high school, my dad wanted me to go to work for him at the car dealership, but you can guess how I felt about that." He stretched his closed mouth until his lips were so thin they nearly vanished.

Yes, I knew more than I wanted to know about the relationship between Ben and his father. The older Baker never passed up an opportunity to remind his son of just how much of a disappointment he was.

"Soon as I turned eighteen, I joined the Coast Guard. Got the braces off, got contact lenses, went to boot camp, and started eating right. Got away from my mother's cooking and discovered I liked working out. Within a couple of years, nobody from back in Lauderdale even recognized me. I passed people right on the street and they had no idea it was me."

"You know, I can believe it. You really look great. I am so happy for you, Ben," I said, and I meant it. But, there was something about seeing him again that made me remember moments in my childhood when I hadn't been the person I wanted to be. I'd never teased Ben like so many of the girls had. Any teasing was always just between us, as a friend. But there had been times, many of them, when I'd seen other kids being really mean to him, and he had looked at me with those sad eyes, beseeching me to do something. I was a scared kid, too, and I hadn't stepped forward to defend my friend. I wasn't proud of those moments. "What are you doing here in Key West?"

"I live here," he said. "See that black-hulled schooner back there, *Hawkeye*? She's my boat. I live aboard and do sunset charters and snorkeling cruises, that sort of thing."

"I always thought you'd become a marine scientist."

"Yeah, well, that *was* what I wanted to be when I was a kid. But after I joined the Coast Guard and started spending all that time on boats, I just couldn't face going back to school. Whenever the guard would make me go in for training, it just brought back all those memories of high school—and they weren't particularly good memories."

I nodded. "I can understand that."

"I spent a year stationed on a cutter here in Key West, and I really liked it. Decided this was the place I'd return to when I got out of the service."

"How are your folks?"

"My dad's still the same." He lifted his shoulders and spread his hands wide. "We don't talk. My mom died about a year ago."

"Oh, Ben. I'm so sorry to hear that." Ben's father owned Baker Ford, a large dealership on Federal Highway in Fort Lauderdale. I was always afraid of Mr. Baker when I went to Ben's house as a little girl, and Ben literally shook when his dad called his name. His mother was a soft-spoken woman, but she was a society type, Junior League and Garden Club and all, keeping herself busy and out of the house. When we were kids, Ben used to come over when his parents were fighting, and though I never saw his mother wearing dark glasses or anything like that, I'd known it was pretty bad. There was always an air of barely suppressed violence in that house.

"I heard about your dad," he said. "I read the local boating magazines, and I saw a couple of articles about him when he died." He shook his head. "I really liked

Red. I wish I'd had the opportunity to sit and listen to some more of his stories. Too late now, I guess. So, you've taken over the business?"

"Geez, Ben, you sure know a hell of a lot more about me than I do about you."

His lips stretched wide again, this time showing those teeth, but I noticed that the smile didn't quite reach his eyes. "Wasn't it always that way?" he said.

I'd always suspected Ben had liked me more than I'd liked him. Not like a boyfriend–girlfriend kind of thing, but he had always wanted to have a friend who shared his love of the sea and all things marine. I came closest to that of the people he knew, but I already had a best friend in Molly. She lived next door to me, and we were fast friends right up through high school. Ben yearned for a friendship like I had with Molly, but few kids wanted anything to do with him. "That's quite a boat you have there," I said, trying to change the subject. "I was admiring it earlier. You sure do keep her in great condition."

"Thanks. I work at it. She's a special boat, a real Alden, designed and built in 1922."

"How big is she?"

"Seventy-five feet overall, but only fifty-nine on deck. The problem for around here is that she draws seven feet. That's no good here in the Keys. The water's a little thin. The guy who owned her before me did all the restoration work, but it's still a full-time job keeping her in shape. I renamed her after my great-great-grandfather."

"Oh yeah?"

"According to my granddad, the original Benjamin Baker was a captain here in Key West in the late nineteenth century. He had a wrecking schooner named the *Rapid*. I've named my fishing boat after his schooner, and my schooner is named after the man himself—his nickname was Hawkeye. He salvaged over forty wrecks in twenty years."

"I love learning about the history of this place. Makes me feel like I'm a part of this long line of Florida salvers. Last time I was here in Key West, I went to that Wreckers' Museum in Old Town."

"Yeah, they've got pictures of old Hawkeye in there. And I agree with you about the history. That's a big part of what I like about living here. This town cherishes its history. In fact, today's the first race of the Wreckers' Cup series. I'm getting the boat ready now for a charter. We're going to race. If you're not doing anything, you're welcome to come along."

"The Wreckers' Cup?"

"Actually, what they win is a bottle of Captain Morgan rum and a night's bar tab at the Schooner Wharf Bar. We race out to Sand Key Light. It's only seven and a half miles. It's really a lark of a race—like a reenactment of the heyday of the wrecking business here in Key West. You know, back when the wrecking schooners would race out to the reef, hoping to arrive at a new wreck first so the skipper would become Wreck Master. Most of the charter boats go if the weather's right. People wear costumes, and there are all sorts of shenanigans that go on. It's lots of fun."

I shook my head. "That sounds tempting, but I'm here on business and I've got to get back to my boat."

"You're here on *Gorda*?"

"Yeah, a friend of mine asked me to help tow his boat back to Lauderdale."

"What happened?"

"He put her aground not too far outside the Key West Harbor entrance. He was driving this ninety-some-footer at speed in a squall," I said, shaking my head.

"I heard about that," Ben said. "I was listening to the

VHF when he called for a towboat. It's pretty well marked out there. What happened?"

"To hear him tell it, it wasn't his fault. He thinks there was some kind of problem with his navigation equipment. He's got this friend who's a super hotshot in electronics coming down to check it out. He's determined to go to court if he has to. He's that kind of guy—stubborn and determined to clear his name. I think the world of this guy—I've known him for years, and it's breaking my heart to see him in trouble like this. But if you ask me, his friend is making the trip for nothing. Nestor just needs to own up to it and try to get beyond it. These young captains rely too much on electronics."

Ben nodded. "I know exactly what you mean. I saw it all the time during my years in the service."

At that point we both grew quiet. I figured we'd just about exhausted the Nestor topic and damned if I knew what else to say to him. This man, in whose company I'd spent thousands of hours as a kid, now made me feel extremely self-conscious. I kept sneaking looks at him, seeing the eyes of that fat boy in the handsome face of this man.

"Look," I started to say just at the same time he started to speak. We both stopped, then laughed, then started to speak at the same time again. "Hold it," I said, raising my hand like a traffic cop. "I'll go first. I've really got to be going."

"Right," he said, "That's what I was starting to say, too. My charter guests are due here any minute, and I've still got a few chores to take care of on the boat."

"Well, this was really a weird coincidence running into you on the dock in Key West."

"Yup. Small world, eh?"

"It was great seeing you again, Ben."

"Same here," he said.

I waited, hoping he was going to offer an invitation for a drink or dinner later, but none came.

"You take care of yourself, Seychelle. See you around." He strode off down the pier back to his shiny black schooner.

I watched him for a few seconds. Man, I thought, and he had a nice ass, too. Given that the male in my life was off with one of my best friends studying childbirth, a big tall handsome boatman with a nice ass looked pretty damn good to me about now.

I turned and made my way down the dock. I didn't want him to see me watching him with the sort of weird fascination I felt. Once I'd realized it was Ben, I could see the resemblance, but I wouldn't have recognized him on the street in a million years. Old Glub, the biggest nerd in high school, had turned into some great-looking guy who owned a spectacular classic boat. Now, that's one I never would have bet on.

BACK at the dinghy dock in front of the Turtle Kraals Restaurant, I pushed aside the crowd of small boats to pull in my little inflatable. Now that I was here in Key West, I wished I had my Boston Whaler with me, but I'd decided against towing it all those miles. The inflatable fit inside the aft deck box along with the little six-horse Nissan outboard, but it made for a wet ride going back and forth to the anchorage out off Christmas Tree Island in these strong winter winds. The outboard was running really ragged, and though she eventually warmed up and smoothed out, the popping and sputtering continued. If I wasn't hauling any cargo and the water was fairly flat, I could get it up onto a plane, but today wasn't going to be one of those days.

The wind was blowing out of the west at fifteen to eighteen knots, and I was motoring right into a nasty chop. The small waves broke over the pontoons, drenching my pants and forcing me to throttle down to an agonizingly slow pace.

By the time I got to the boat, my black Lab, Abaco, was leaping for joy and trying to crawl down into the dinghy with me. I kept a piece of Astroturf tied to a length of line on deck for emergencies, but she hated to use it. She'd get this guilty look and slink off to the foredeck in shame whenever nature forced her to relieve herself on board. I never wanted to put her through that. She needed to get to shore quickly, but all I could think about was getting aboard and getting out of my now wet clothes.

There were dozens of boats flanking the west side of Christmas Tree Island anchored along the edge of the Northwest Channel, the best route for heading to the Dry Tortugas. Most were cruising sailboats, although there was one big classic motor yacht at the opposite end of the anchorage that I'd heard this morning belonged to some Danish heiress. A giant brown dog, hard to tell what breed from this distance, strolled the decks and barked at boats that came too close. I'd yet to see anyone aboard take that dog ashore, I thought as I hurried below to change.

When I stepped out of the deckhouse about twenty minutes later, I saw a parade of schooners charging past, hard on the wind, making for the outer channel. There must have been nearly a dozen of them, from the smallest—a little 30-some-footer with gaff-rigged tanbark sails—to the grand 130-foot *Western Union,* Key West's own flagship. They all had full sails flying and were having to tack their way out of the harbor, not an easy feat with all those gaffs and topsails and square sails. They had just crossed the starting line off the beam of my tug, and *Hawkeye* was in the lead. I could see costumed characters on nearly all the boats, eye patches, head scarves, and striped pantaloons marking the piratelike gear most of the crews sported. Abaco startled when a loud boom and a puff of smoke heralded a cannon shot from the schooner *Wolf*. The wharf ashore was lined with spectators, and, like good Floridians, a few of them hit the dirt at the sound of the gunfire, while the rest laughed and pointed at the picturesque boats pretending to battle for first rights to the wreck. The *Appledore* responded with another cannon shot as she attempted to overtake the *Western Union*, and the tourist charter guests on the big schooner responded with applause.

Over on *Hawkeye*, though, there was no sign of the usual Key West craziness—no costumed blokes hanging from the rigging waving mugs of grog. I reached into the wheelhouse and pulled out my binoculars. Through them, I watched Ben at the wheel, hunched forward, as though urging his boat on. He wore a yellow foul-weather jacket and a dark baseball cap pulled low over his face so I couldn't really even see his profile. He nodded once, then spun the wheel around to execute a near-perfect tack. He had a young kid crewing for him, cranking on the winches. His charter guests sat huddled around the front of the oval cockpit watching the two men handle the big schooner with almost graceful precision. The Wreckers' Race wasn't really much of a race, but it appeared Ben Baker took competition of any kind very seriously.

THAT afternoon, I took my dog ashore on the little spoil island and threw sticks down the narrow beach so she could run and splash into the water. She sometimes found it torture out on the boat—surrounded by all that water and not allowed to jump in. She was a Lab, after all. Australian pines and palmettos grew so thick in the center of the island that when I threw her stick inland, she disappeared into the bush. I called her name; the third time, when I was starting to feel just a little worried, I saw a flock of doves take wing and Abaco charging out of the brush, the stick in her mouth and her eyes alight with mischief.

When we got back to the boat, I had a long list of projects waiting. I soon found myself dismantling the accumulator in my freshwater pressure system, which was leaking and causing the pump to tick over several times an hour and keeping me awake through the quiet hours of the night. I kept the radio on, as usual, tuned to channel sixteen, listening to the chatter of the racers and the fishermen and the charter boat captains. Late in the afternoon, I heard the shouts and laughter, the rush of water and creak of rigging, as the schooners returned from their race to Sand Key. I stepped out on deck to see *Hawkeye* sail by very close to *Gorda,* and her captain swept off his baseball hat and bowed to me like a swashbuckling hero as they passed.

"Cute," I said aloud, even though he was out of earshot. "Very cute." And I meant it. "Now that the competition is over, he can relax and have fun. Boy, has he changed."

Abaco looked up at me and cocked her head.

"Never mind, girl. I'm just talking to myself," I said as I watched Ben work the foredeck, furling sails. I found myself hoping he would glance my way again. There was something about the way he sailed and worked his boat that spoke of his love of the sea, and *that* I found even more attractive than his great ass.

I laughed out loud. Ben Baker? What was I thinking?

I watched the sailboats motoring and sailing back to the marina, all in a hurry now for the best part of racing—the party in the bar. Through the boats, I could see the crowd gathering for the nightly sunset celebration on Mallory

Pier. The various street performers were erecting their high wires or setting up perches for their performing cats and dogs. The vendors were open and selling their piña coladas, carved coconuts, and shell necklaces, and though the sun wouldn't set for another hour or so, the pier was already packed with tourists.

I left the rail and returned to clean up and put away my tools in preparation for the afternoon's first beer. I was just reaching for an iced Corona when I heard the panic in the voice that seemed to explode from the radio.

"Mayday, mayday, mayday! Attention all vessels in Key West Harbor. There's an overdue windsurfer from the Casa Marina beach rentals. Anybody who can help search, please assist."

IV

I IMMEDIATELY thought of Nestor. Had Catalina convinced him to go windsurfing after all? I looked at the clock. It was four forty-five. The sun would set at five thirty. After sundown, there would be maybe another thirty minutes in which a downed windsurfing sail might be visible in the light of the waning dusk. After that, forget it. The missing person would spend the night at sea, in the water, and at this time of year that probably meant death. I was sitting by the radio, listening to the Key West Coast Guard marine operator quizzing the kid from the beach rental about the possible location of the missing windsurfer, when I started hearing boat engines.

Out on deck, the scene before me was remarkable. There were charter fishing skiffs, muscle boats, big sportfishermen, sailboats, and runabouts of all kinds charging out the channel. They were all headed toward Sand Key, the place the kid at the windsurfer rental shack had said his customer was headed for. One thing I had to say about the boating community: when someone was in a jam, they came together. It was kind of like the old days, really. The scene playing out was more reminiscent of the onetime wreckers than their namesake race had been.

I was considering lifting the anchor and heading out on *Gorda* when I spotted a white-hulled center-console runabout coming at me from the other side—out of the north. The operator was waving at me. I waved back, and when he turned to approach my boat, I saw the name T/T POWER PLAY in blue paint on the bow. It was the tender to the big Sunseeker, and I now recognized the man standing at the helm. As he drew close, Ted Berger shouted, "I could use another set of eyes. Want to come?"

"Sure," I shouted back. In less than a minute, I'd grabbed my rain jacket off the hook inside the wheelhouse, slipped the strap for my binoculars over my head, closed up *Gorda,* and jumped aboard Berger's boat. Abaco whined, pleading to come along, but I told her to stay. Somehow I didn't think Berger would appreciate dog hair all over his immaculate tender.

Ted pushed the throttle forward and the big two-hundred-horse four-stroke Honda engine pushed the boat up onto an easy plane. We probably wouldn't be able to hold that speed once we hit the open ocean outside, but for now he was eating up the water in a way my little tug would never manage.

"I was on my way back from fishing Bluefish Channel when I heard," he shouted. As we came out from behind Sunset Key, Berger whistled. "Damn. Look at all the boats."

He was right. There must have been at least thirty boats all steaming out toward Sand Key.

On the center console of Berger's boat, he pointed to the large-screen color GPS chart plotter, which displayed a chart of the Key West entrance channel out to Sand Key Light.

"I'm not going to head out toward Eastern Dry Rocks. Looks like all the others are already working that area. Let's start from the midpoint channel markers and work a search pattern east from there," Ted hollered over the roar of the outboard. "You keep watch on the starboard side, I'll watch the port."

"Sounds good to me."

I alternated searching with the naked eye and peering through the glasses. The breeze was dying down a bit, but the wind waves were still confused and choppy. Patchy gray clouds had blown in from the west and now covered the sun and half the horizon. The sea reflected the colorless sky; it was difficult enough to make out the channel markers, much less spot a small sail floating on the surface of the water.

My watch told me the sun had just set when I checked it, but the clouds had hidden the event. We had been searching for what seemed like hours and were now due south of Key West, over a mile offshore from Smathers Beach. The radio had been depressingly quiet except for the Coast Guard operator, who was continuing to seek information from the young man on the beach. He worked at the rental shack at the Casa Marina Resort and when his client, who'd rented the windsurfer for two hours, hadn't returned by three PM, the kid went out in his Boston Whaler to search for the man. He'd had no luck. When he realized darkness was fast approaching, he decided to get on the radio and call for help.

My eyes kept playing tricks on me. I would think I saw something, then when I blinked or tried to steady the binoculars, I'd look back and it would be gone. In fact, it was never there in the first place. That was why I didn't believe it the first time I saw the flash of yellow in the water. When I squeezed my eyes shut that time, I thought it had disappeared, but then the patch of yellow rose again on a choppy swell.

"Over there," I shouted, pointing with my right arm while I held the glasses in one hand, keeping my eyes fastened on that spot of color. "I saw something in the water." I shifted my position, swinging my arm around as Berger turned the boat. I couldn't take my eyes off that spot.

At first, the wet suit was indistinguishable from the dark water. The sail was blue with a small horizontal stripe of yellow, and it wasn't until we were nearly on top of him that I realized a man's shadowy form lay facedown and half submerged across the sail. I knew before we pulled alongside and I touched his cold wrist to feel for a pulse that it was Nestor and he was dead.

V

"**O**H, great," Berger said and rubbed his hand across his mouth. "Shit."

I couldn't look at him. I kept my eyes on the horizon like a seasick person who feared she was going to vomit. The idling outboard filled the boat with fumes, but it was neither that nor the sight of Nestor that made me feel ill. It had been Berger's voice. He'd sounded about as emotionless as the computerized voice that reads the NOAA weather on the Coast Guard radio.

We got a line onto the windsurfer's boom and stood by waiting for the Coast Guard to arrive on the scene. Berger and I didn't say much as the last streaks of light evaporated from the western sky and a few stars began to blink between the swift-moving clouds overhead. I moved up to the bow of the open runabout and sat on the padded seat that ran in front of the center console. I thought about Catalina and how fresh and alive and in love they had been that morning at breakfast. I didn't want to break down and bawl in front of this asshole, but I felt like my chest and throat were pulled in so tight and hard that I was going to suffocate if I didn't let it out. I wanted to hit something and scream curses at the stars. At nature. At fate. At God. Why Nestor? I pulled my knees to my chest and gritted my teeth, but when I pictured Nestor smiling behind Catalina, his arms wrapped around her waist and patting the bulge that would be their child, I couldn't hold it in any longer. I let go.

When the Coast Guard arrived in their forty-foot utility boat, I dried my eyes on the backs of my hands and handed the young crewman a bow line. Ted had taken out his spotlight and was shining it on the windsurfer and sail so the Coasties would know to come alongside on the other side of his boat. His spot cast a stark light on the bright sail and the neoprene-clad body, which I could now see was tangled in the lines from his mast and harness. A young man in a blue uniform wearing a bulky life jacket leaned over the rail of the Coast Guard boat and took several flash photos of the body. At first, I was offended, thinking he was just taking souvenir shots, but then when they hoisted the body aboard, Nestor's head turned, and I saw the discolored and swollen contusion at his temple. I realized the photos would likely be needed as forensic evidence.

It was a somber procession that headed back into the harbor. We'd been told the police would be waiting and that they would want to talk to us. We were to follow the Coast Guard to their dock, so Berger cruised back slowly in the big boat's wake.

"So what do you think happened?" Berger asked.

I didn't look at him. I kept my eyes on the white stern light of the Coast Guard boat. I was angry and embarrassed that this stranger had seen me sobbing, had witnessed that raw grief. I couldn't wait to get off his boat and away from him. "I don't know. Maybe a strong gust, maybe it flung him headfirst into the mast, knocked him unconscious, then he drowned?" I turned to look at Ted's profile. "What do you think?"

He was nodding slowly, mulling over my theory. "What you said sounds about right to me. I think that's it," he said as though it were up to him.

I watched the lights of the hotels and condos at what used to be the old Truman Annex. There had been many times when I wished I could turn back time, but now I just kept thinking that maybe if I had done something differently—if I had gone back to the *Power Play* with them and we had watched movies all afternoon, or something, anything. If I had just done something different, Nestor would be alive. Much as I wanted to get away from Berger, I started up another conversation to quiet the accusations in my mind. "It's a good thing you decided to search farther east. We were the only boat over there. Never would have found him before nightfall if not for you."

He shrugged, "It was just a hunch."

IT was almost eight o'clock by the time we were finished with the Key West detective who questioned us about how and where and why we'd found the body. His name was Lassiter, and while he was built like a bodybuilder above the waist, he had one of the most extreme cases of bowleggedness I'd ever seen. He wore his iron-gray hair in a crew cut, and I would have had an easier time picturing him in the tight clothes of a motorcycle cop than in the ill-fitting suit and tie that he kept tugging at.

"I don't understand it," he said. "Why the hell anyone would think it's entertaining to go out on a little bitty board when it's storming. I'm from Nebraska."

"Have you been in Key West long?" I asked.

"Long enough."

"Because that wasn't really a storm," I said. "Just our usual strong winter winds."

He shrugged. "Been here about twenty-two years. That don't change how I think, though. Wind's blowing like it was today, I don't go out in the water. Fact, I never go out in the water. Hate the water. I don't even know how to swim."

I wondered briefly why he had come here and stayed on in this place that was surrounded by water, but I didn't ask. I felt tired, too weak to really care about this cop and his chatter. I took the card he offered with his cell phone number scrawled in black ink on the back and said good night. I had an errand to see to, an errand I dreaded.

BERGER offered to run me back out to my boat since I didn't have my dinghy ashore, but I told him no thanks and assured him I would find a way back to my boat later. Once out on Caroline Street, I flagged a cab and gave the driver the name of the Stock Island boatyard where the *Power Play* was hauled out. The yard watchman let me through with a look of sympathy. Word traveled fast in these islands. I suspected he already knew the skipper of the *Power Play* was dead.

The boat looked like a debutant in a bikers' bar, propped up in the dirt among the shrimpers and fishing boats that made up the rest of Robbie's clientele. Bright lights illuminated several boats where workmen continued their jobs in the dark. I stood in the shadows a moment, wondering if she knew yet. If not, I was about to destroy her world.

I climbed the wooden ladder propped against the aft swim step and called out to see if I could raise anyone. The young man and woman who peered down from the bridge deck identified themselves as Drew and Debbie, the mate and stewardess, and they invited me into the main salon saying they would be right down.

The Sunseeker is really a production yacht, if you can call any vessel that sells for more than five million dollars such a thing. The layout is pretty standard on all of them, and I had towed one up the river before. There wasn't anything particularly outstanding on Ted's yacht from my point of view. There was the usual bar just aft of the inside steering station, the round table booth up by the windshield, and the opulent salon aft before exiting onto the dining deck area. The sleeping cabins were belowdecks, the crew aft, the captain's cabin below the galley. The formal dining table was exactly the same as the one on the other boat I'd towed, and this one had the same doryshaped coffee table. So much for the thought that you'd get anything very special for your five million. It was up to the buyer to customize, and aside from the huge flatscreen monitors on almost every bulkhead, it looked like Berger hadn't paid much attention to the furnishings.

Yes, Drew said, when he and Debbie arrived in the salon wearing matching navy shorts and white Polos with the name POWER PLAY stitched over the pockets. They had all heard it on the radio. Catalina had been napping in her cabin. Here, at the interior steering station, Drew and Debbie had been working together, trying to get the bloodstains from Kent's injury on the reef out of the upholstery. Drew explained that Kent had been the original mate, injured on the trip down from Fort Lauderdale. The compound fracture had pierced his skin, and the carpet and upholstery were badly stained.

"It was so gross," Debbie said, wrinkling her little nose.

When they heard the call on the VHF radio, they explained, both had immediately thought of Nestor, but they'd just stood there, as though riveted to the deck, staring at the radio, waiting for their fears to be proven wrong, unaware that Catalina had been standing behind them, leaning against the bar for support. It wasn't until Ted Berger's voice broke in on the Coast Guard transmission to announce that he'd found the windsurfer and the body of a man he recognized that Catalina cried out and ran for her stateroom where she'd been ever since, locked inside.

I tapped lightly on the stateroom door. "Hey, Cat, it's me, Seychelle. Open up, okay?"

Silence.

"Catalina, I want to see you. I know what you're going through. Believe me, I do."

Silence.

"Cat, please." I put my ear to the door. "I loved Nestor. I'm hurting, too."

The lock clicked and the door swung inward. The stateroom was dark, but I could hear the sound of her clothes sliding against the upholstery as she lay back down on the bunk. As far as captain's cabins went, this was not one of the better ones. The inward-opening door barely cleared the bunk. From the little light that spilled through the doorway, I saw a lamp on a side table. I clicked it on.

She was on her side, her legs curled up, her hands hiding her face from the light. "It was him, wasn't it?" she whispered.

I tried to keep my voice strong but failed miserably. "Yes, it was. I saw him."

The small moan that came from the bed sounded like the weak cry of a child. That was followed by staccato, voiceless sobs. Her body shook, and I was afraid of what this kind of grief might do to the child she was carrying.

I rested my hand on her shoulder and tried to pat her in a soothing motion. But what I really wanted to do was throw something or hit someone. I wanted to scream.

"Catalina, is there anything I can do for you. Anything I can get?"

She didn't respond at first. It was as though she hadn't heard me speak. I was about to repeat my question when she pushed her body up into a sitting position and wiped her face on the pillow in her lap. After several ragged breaths, she whispered, "Tell me about it."

"There's not much to tell."

"Start at the beginning," she said, her voice stronger now. "Tell me everything that happened."

I eased my body down on the bunk next to her. Tired. I just felt so tired. People I loved kept dying, and there didn't seem to be any sense or reason to any of it. I'd heard the platitude about how only the good die young, and it wasn't true. That would imply that there was some sort of logic to who dies—and there was none. Others always chimed in that when it's your time, it's your time. Bullshit. I'd seen too many good people die senselessly, as well as those I considered downright evil. Death is as random as it gets.

"I was on *Gorda* late in the afternoon when I heard the first call on the VHF. I saw Ted Berger going by in the *Power Play*'s tender, and he invited me to help with the search. We saw that most of the rest of the others were headed out to Sand Key, so Berger suggested we search farther downwind and downcurrent. His hunch paid off."

Catalina buried her face in her hands and drew a deep breath. When she lifted her head, her face, aside from the puffiness around her eyes, looked as blank as a freshly swept sidewalk. "Tell me what he looked like," she said, her voice a monotone. "Tell me exactly what you saw."

I closed my eyes, and the image appeared as detailed as though I had captured it on film. I opened one eye. "Cat, are you sure you want to hear this?"

"Yes," she said, and her mouth was the only part of her that moved. Her body was so rigid, it looked as though she had been cast in concrete.

I nodded, pulled in a long breath, and closed my eyes again. The image was still there. "Okay. His body was facedown on the sail, his head half underwater, his face submerged. I knew immediately that he had to be dead. I didn't recognize the wet suit or the windsurfer, but from the hair and the shape, I was certain it was Nestor. I reached down, grabbed a corner of the sail, and pulled him to me. A piece of line was wrapped around his far arm and tangled in the harness he wore. I reached for the arm closer to me, and his skin felt cold. There was no pulse. He'd been like that for a while. Later, when the Coast Guard got there and lifted his face out of the water, I saw a big contusion on his temple. Here." I touched my head at my hairline. "I think he hit his head on the mast, was knocked unconscious, and then drowned."

Her spine stiffened and she turned her head, locked her eyes on mine. It was like looking down the twin shafts of an abandoned mine. "No," she said. She started shaking her head. "No, no, that's not possible."

"Cat, that's exactly what happened." I put my hand on her shoulder.

She shook off my hand and stood up. "No, that's not what I mean." She began to pace the cramped room, speaking to herself in Spanish, her hands gesturing wildly. I got the feeling she was speaking to Nestor.

"Catalina, come here, sit down." I patted the bunk beside me.

She spun around to face me. Her back was straight, her eyes flashed, and she looked like a very pregnant African warrior queen. "No, do not patronize me. What you are describing to me was not an accident. Someone killed my husband."

VI

B Y nine o'clock Monday morning, I'd already been into town to walk Abaco, grabbed coffee and some breakfast taquitos at the Turtle Kraals Restaurant, and I was back out on *Gorda* trying to whittle down a few more jobs off my to-do list. I hoped that immersing myself in some mundane tasks would allow me to take my mind off Nestor, but it wasn't working. I found myself throwing tools around and spouting tears over the least little problem. The starboard diesel tank had developed a small leak, and I was hanging upside down in the bilge with a flashlight trying to see the fitting where the hose exited the aluminum tank when I heard someone call my boat's name on the VHF.

"*Gorda, Gorda,* this is *Power Play.*"

With a shower of curses, I shimmied my body out of the crevice under the aft deck and headed up to the wheelhouse to answer the radio. I recognized the voice. It was the mate, Drew, the guy I'd met yesterday on the big yacht.

"I'm calling to give you a message," he said. "Mr. Berger has been trying to reach you. He sounded kind of pissed when he found out you didn't have a cell phone."

"The VHF works fine as far as I'm concerned."

"He's staying at the Hyatt. Told me to tell you to stop by his hotel this morning to discuss towing the boat back to Lauderdale."

"Thanks, Drew. I'll head in there soon as I clean up a little out here."

"From what I've seen of him, he expects people to jump when he says so."

"Well, I've never responded well to folks like that. I jump when I'm ready."

After we signed off, I went into the head to wash off the diesel and dirty bilgewater. I kept thinking about Catalina and her insistence last night that, based on my description of Nestor, someone must have arranged the body, entwining his hand in the lines.

"Seychelle," she'd said, "he is an amazing windsurfer. He could have turned pro and made money doing that, but he got it into his head that he wanted to captain big yachts and it was not possible to change his mind. He took me windsurfing a few times and taught me to stand up and sail a little in light winds. It just would not happen that he would get tangled with his uphaul rope or the harness line. Even I know enough to see that. If he really had been thrown into the mast by a gust, he would have been catapulted into the water and drifted clear of the sailboard. What you are describing to me sounds arranged—like a tableau. Somebody hit him in the head and then purposely tangled him in the lines of that windsurfer. They wanted to make it look like an accident, but they did not know what they were doing."

"But why?"

"You mean why kill him?"

"Well, yes, that too, but why try to make sure the body is found with the board? Why purposely tangle him in the lines?"

"I cannot answer that. I just know that someone did it."

"It's only that it's so hard to believe, Cat. Who'd want to kill Nestor? The guy couldn't have had an enemy in the world."

We had gone back and forth on it for several minutes, and I knew perfectly well the suspect she had in mind. A multimillionaire entrepreneur offing his boat captain? The very idea seemed so far-fetched that I left before she had the chance to say the name out loud.

AS I was tying up my dinghy to the dock in front of the Turtle Kraals Restaurant, the older waitress who had taken my order earlier that morning signaled me that she wanted to speak to me. I met her just inside the heavy wooden doors, and she handed me a piece of paper.

"Lucky for you, I grabbed the phone right after you left this morning. Your friend was asking if I'd seen this woman, and I knew right away it was you. Told her I'd keep an eye out for you. Says she needs to talk to you."

"Thanks, Glenda," I said, reading her name off the plastic badge she wore. "You got a pay phone around here?"

She pointed me toward the restrooms up by the bar.

Knowing full well that she'd bitch about it, I called Jeannie collect.

"Hey, it's me," I said when she answered.

"Calling collect? Don't you know how expensive that is? I've given up trying to get you to buy a cell phone, but you could at least buy a calling card."

"Nice to hear from you, Jeannie."

Jeannie Black was both my lawyer and one of my dearest friends. I suppose she would be categorized as a "plus-size" woman since her weight hovered close to three hundred pounds. I would also categorize her as the smartest woman I had ever known, and I measured her worth more by the size of her brain than the size of her ass.

"So what's up?" I asked her.

"It's about the lawsuit."

"You mean the guy with the Grady-White?"

"Seychelle, just how many people are suing you? Of

course, I meant him. The boat's name was *Seas the Day*—
you know, spelled *s-e-a-s*?"

"How original."

"I'd call it prophetic. I think the guy is trying to scam
you. Probably pulled the plug on his own boat."

"Really?"

"Yeah. I've been checking up on him. Last year he tried
to sue a McDonald's restaurant, claiming he'd found a
cockroach in his burger. Half a cockroach, that is."

"Why try to sue me? I don't have deep pockets like
Mickey D."

"Well, your name has been in the paper quite a bit
these past few years on some pretty big salvage jobs.
And besides what you've done, there's been a lot of press
for the salvage business in general. It makes all salvers
look like they're making out like modern-day pirates,
getting awards of twenty, thirty percent of these big
yachts. I'll bet this guy thinks you're worth millions."

"Maybe you'd better educate him then, Jeannie. Get
on the phone and talk to him. Explain it. Maybe he'll
drop the suit."

"Fat chance."

"Why?"

"Because even if you don't have superdeep pockets,
your insurance company does. You've got a mighty high
limit on your liability because you deal with these mil-
lionaires, and our friend Melvin Burke knows it."

"You'd know. That's the stuff I pay you to take care
of. Okay, so our friend Melvin isn't going to go away
anytime soon. Man, I'm really starting to hate this guy.
I can't believe he did this on purpose. He had his daughter along, and if he put her at risk like that for some con,
he's an even bigger dirtbag than I thought."

"It is looking that way."

"Shit. But I don't suppose that's what you called me to ask me about."

"In a way, it is. The news just keeps getting better. The bill for the insurance on your boat just arrived." I had a post office box for my business, and Jeannie was handling my mail during my absence. "They've nearly doubled your premiums. I'm sure it's a combination of all the recent hurricanes here in Florida and the increase in boating accidents. I thought I'd ask if you want me to check around, see if I could get you a better rate somewhere else. We don't have much time. The policy renewal date is only a couple of weeks away."

"Geez, Jeannie, almost double? Already it seems like I work a good week each month just to pay that bill. This business. Red must be rolling over in his grave."

"You had your father cremated, Seychelle."

"You know what I mean. It's not like the old days when he built *Gorda* and started the towing business. Back then, he wasn't getting ripped off every time he turned around—both by clients and by his insurance company. Hell, most of the time Red probably didn't even have insurance."

"Times have changed."

I exhaled into the receiver and didn't say anything for several seconds. I could hear Jeannie breathing on the other end of the line. "I know. There's too much change for me sometimes." I wanted to add, *and too much death*. Now it started again. Whenever someone died, there were the many days of having to tell people over and over what had happened. Both my parents, Elysia, Neal—and now I had to add Nestor to the list of those I had loved and lost. And I had to tell Jeannie without turning on the tears again. I was tired of tears. "Make the calls, Jeannie. See what you can do. But before we hang up, I've got to tell you about what's happening down here."

TED Berger's room at the Hyatt was bigger than my whole house. Granted, I live in a little converted boathouse and I don't normally frequent the homes or hotel rooms of the rich and famous. But just the living room of his suite could have held my whole combined living room/kitchen and the tiny bedroom that I called home. Berger was sitting at an ornate desk in front of a laptop computer. Over his shoulder was a fantastic view looking out over the harbor, and I could just make out *Gorda* anchored in the lee of Christmas Tree Island. She stood out among the many cruising sailboats.

Berger looked up over the top of a pair of half-glasses. "What the hell is wrong with you? How can anybody live today without a cell phone?"

I held my hands out in a gesture of surrender. "You want me to work for you, you take what you get."

"Goddammit," he said, whipping off his reading glasses and throwing them on the desk. Then he stopped, and his face broke into a smile. "Shit," he said. "It's been a while since anybody's talked to me like that. Sit down." He gestured to the small armchair on the opposite side of the window.

Berger was dressed in khaki pants and another nearly neon Hawaiian shirt. This one was electric blue and yellow. Brand-new leather boat shoes completed the outfit. He ran a hand down the side of his head, smoothing his trim white hair.

"Seychelle, what happened yesterday was a tragedy. No doubt about it. Nestor was a good kid. But we've got to press on. I called an agency up in Lauderdale and I've already hired a new captain. He's flying down tonight. I want you to meet him in the yard tomorrow."

"No problem," I said, but I thought that Ted Berger was a mighty cold son of a bitch. It hadn't even been twenty-four hours. "I assume you'll let Catalina Frias stay aboard until we get back to Lauderdale?"

He tapped his pen on the desk and didn't answer right away. His eyes were unfocused, staring at something only he could see, and a shadow of a smile played on his lips. I was preparing to walk out of his office if he said no. "I might be an asshole, but I'm not sending a widow home on the bus. Look, it'll take a day or so for the new captain to familiarize himself with the boat, and today's Monday. Do you think you could be ready to leave by Wednesday, Thursday at the latest?"

"I can leave whenever the weather permits. Right now the forecast is looking good for a midweek departure. A little front came through yesterday, and they're predicting a period of calm weather through the end of the week. But if something changes between now and then, weather-wise, I reserve the right to say whether or not we leave."

He laughed. "Damn. Do you always boss your clients around like this?"

"When it comes to moving boats around? Yes, I tell them what I expect them to do."

He shook his head. "Here I am stuck between you and Pinder."

When he saw the puzzled look on my face, he continued. "Neville Pinder is the asshole who owns Ocean Towing. I take it you've never met him?"

"No," I said, shaking my head. "Seen his boats around, but haven't had the pleasure."

"Pleasure!" he said. "Ha!"

"Ocean Towing's only been in business in Broward a little over a year, but when he came on the scene, he came on big. He's got lots of boats and lots of gear.

Can't miss those bright green boats of his. They're everywhere. He's not much into the New River business, though—he mostly works the emergency calls."

"I hate to think of what's going to happen to my insurance when I get out of this thing. He's trying to stick me for twenty percent of five million—in other words, a million bucks for just pulling her off the reef and towing her in."

"And he'll probably get close to it, too. That's not totally unreasonable."

"Not unreasonable? For towing the boat a couple of miles? It's fucking piracy!"

I sighed. People never understood the salvage business. "Mr. Berger, there is a huge cost difference between towing and salvage. Sometimes the line between the two isn't very clear, but in your case there was no question. Towing is paid for by the hour, but salvage is a different story. Maritime law states that in order for a case to be considered salvage, it must meet three criteria. First, the vessel has to be in peril. Your boat was sitting on an endangered reef, unable to move due to the damaged props, and the weather was worsening. Nestor agreed to it, so it was voluntary on all parts, and that's the second criteria. Finally, it must be successful. Salvage is a 'no cure–no pay' business, so if Ocean Towing worked for three days to get your boat off, then your boat sank when they pulled her into deep water, they would have been entitled to nothing."

"A million bucks for twelve hours' work is a far cry from nothing."

"But they risk getting nothing if they aren't successful. A salver can work for a week to free a grounded vessel, and if she sinks when he pulls her free, he gets zilch. It doesn't matter how many hours or days the salver put in. But if he is successful, he's entitled to a percentage of the value of the boat that he saved. See, you don't just pay for the hours that a salver puts in on your job. You pay to keep him in business, to have his boats there waiting and ready twenty-four hours a day so when you do need him, he's there. You pay for the radio gear that takes the call. You pay to have him go out and risk his boat and his life through the afternoon and into the dark hours, even when the weather is forecast to worsen. As I understand it, Ocean Towing deserves a fair claim. I don't know about twenty percent, but I'd say he might be looking to get several hundred thousand in this case."

"I'd say I'm in the wrong business, then."

"It doesn't look to me like you've done too bad for yourself," I said. "Besides, salvage awards like this are few and far between, but every time there's a big one, another half a dozen guys decide to jump into the business. It's growing very crowded out there. There are too many boats trying to make a living in this line of work and not enough big wrecks."

"Glad I could make a contribution," he said, rolling his eyes.

I laughed. "Look, I'll go have a talk with Pinder for you. See if I can convince him that this whole thing will stay out of arbitration if he's just willing to be a little more realistic. Then we'll get your boat safely back to Lauderdale, the insurance company will pay Ocean Towing, me, and the yard bill. And soon, you'll have your boat back good as new."

"Oh goody," he said.

VII

THE streets of downtown were jammed with tourists and it wasn't even eleven o'clock yet. Hordes of pale people in shorts and tank tops jostled their way past the shop windows on Duval Street. The weather had warmed up considerably from the day before, and though the temperatures were only bound for the low seventies, unlike the places most of them called home, here there was no snow in the forecast, so they were thrilled.

I kept thinking about what Berger had said—that Pinder was some kind of pirate or rip-off artist. That was what this business had come to. I'd made a career change several years ago from being a beach lifeguard to taking over my dad's salvage business. Back then I saw the two jobs as essentially the same thing—saving people's lives and property. It was getting paid to be a Good Samaritan. I was doing something clear and honorable that I could feel proud of. Today it had become a question of gear and equipment and electronics. I understood that cell phones and chart plotters and GPS could be wonderful tools, but I didn't trust them. First Nestor and now Berger—both had chastised me for not jumping into this electronic mess. The truth was, it had done neither of them any good in the end. The End. In fact, his wife believed that it was Nestor's reliance on these bits of metal and wire that had caused his end. Granted,

I did own a small GPS handheld, but I'd prefer a hand bearing compass, parallel rule, dividers, and paper chart any day.

Still, there was a huge difference between what I believed and what would help me make a living. Could I compete with my little tug? Probably not. How long would it be before the VHF radio went the way of adding machines, eight-track tapes, manual typewriters, records, videotapes, loran, wringer washing machines, hell, even steam engines? How long before a radio call was no longer the way of the salvage business? But I hated being lumped in with guys like Pinder who saw this industry as a way to build an empire and go for exorbitant claims. Maybe this was just another sign that it was time to think about a career change—again.

After nearly getting stepped on as I tried to look in a shop window, I ducked into Sloppy Joe's Bar, slid onto a stool, and ordered a draft beer. I was alone at the bar, but there were a couple of tables full of rowdy college-age guys. When the bartender, an older guy with a long gray ponytail, brought the plastic cup and set it in front of me, I asked if he had a phone book.

"No," he said, spreading his hands on the bar. "But what're you looking for?"

"How about the offices of Ocean Towing?"

He squinted at me. "What would a pretty girl like you want with that rat bag?"

"I take it you know Neville Pinder?"

The man reached deep into his pant pocket and produced a small container of Skoal tobacco. He opened the tin with one hand and took a pinch with the other. Once he had packed it firmly under his lower lip with his tongue, he started to speak. The bulge was apparent right there on his chin, but it didn't impact his speech in the least.

"Yeah, I known him." He reached his hand across the bar and I shook it. "Call me Sam," he said. "I've known him and his family awhile. First sailed over to the Abacos in '69. Neville—he's from there—was just a kid at the time. There's lots of Alburys' and Pinders and certain family names over there. Those families go way back. White Bahamians, Loyalists. First settled in the Bahamas around the time of the Revolutionary War. They wanted to stay loyal to the queen."

"I've read about that."

"Lots of Pinders come to Key West through the years. Probably six or eight families by that name here now, all with ties to the islands and none of 'em wanting to have much to do with our boy Neville. His family's on Man O' War Cay. Don't think Neville's been back to the islands in years now. They don't want him back. Family more or less kicked him out."

"Why's that?"

"He always was a troublemaker. Petty stuff. Stealing, public drunkenness, vandalism, mischief. Lots of those islands are dry, you know. They're religious people. They didn't take to Neville thinking that anybody's skiff should be his for a joyride just because he drank a few beers. That's how he got those scars."

"What scars?"

"On his right arm. He's missing a couple of fingers, too. Actually, it's kind of a funny story. Neville got drunk, stole this fella's boat, and went fishing in the middle of the night all by hisself. Caught a good-size barracuda, then, trying to take the treble hook out, he snagged his own arm with the hook, and the fish bit down on his hand. He ended up with a couple of furrows plowed down the skin of his arm. Doc had to amputate two of his fingers when the infection got so bad it almost killed him."

"So how does a guy like that end up head of a big company like Ocean Towing? I mean, hell, they've got boats and bases from Stuart to Key West."

"That is the question, isn't it? And you aren't the first person to ask it. There are a few of us old-timers around here, still living aboard our wooden boats out in the anchorage. Not many, that's for damn sure. Most cruisers now have mini Winnebago plastic boats with generators and microwaves and toaster ovens. But a few of us were around back in the '60s and '70s, and we remember when everybody knew everybody over in the islands and you couldn't get away with much."

"I know what you mean. I wasn't around back then, but I heard about those days from my dad."

"So somehow our friend Neville got himself some backing and now he's fleecing the yachties and super-yachts. The goddamn salvage people are even worse than the cruisers now. You get in trouble, you don't dare take a line from anybody. They're just out to steal your boat from you. Not everybody's got insurance, you know."

"What's the name of your boat?"

"The *Osprey*. She's a thirty-four-foot yawl."

"I'll keep an eye out for her." I dug into my bag for a card. "I'm on the tug *Gorda*," I added, handing him the card. "I'm one of the goddamn salvage people. Thanks for filling me in on Pinder."

He stared down at my card for a few seconds; then the only thing that shifted in his face was his eyes. They slid from the card back to me. "Sorry if I got kind of carried away there," he said.

I raised my hand to stop him from going further. "No apology necessary. Most of the time I refer to folks in my business the same way. Like you said—things are changing, and I don't like the changes any more than you do."

Down the bar the waitress hollered, "Sam, I got an order."

"Excuse me," he said and went down to mix her drinks.

I drained the last of my beer and dug in my bag for money. When Sam came back, he waved my money aside.

"This one's on me," he said. "I enjoyed talking to you. You want to find Neville, he has an office over on Fleming Street. Just head up Duval to Fleming, turn left, and you can't miss it. It's past Fausto's."

"Thanks, Sam," I said.

SAM had been right when he said I wouldn't be able to miss the offices of Ocean Towing. They painted all the boats in their fleet the same bright yellow-green color that some local fire engines had now adopted. I supposed it was the latest color to signify emergency services of some sort. The little office that stood in a block of attached offices was the only one painted that same blinding shade.

The receptionist who sat behind the desk in the front office of Ocean Towing was a very buxom young woman wearing a tie-dyed, gauzy skirt and a white tank top. She was braless, and I could see the outline through the thin fabric of the metal stud that pierced one nipple. It made me shiver. She had been working on the *New York Times* crossword puzzle when I came in, and it looked like it was nearly complete.

"Hi there, can I help you?" she asked. She sounded like Elmer Fudd. I wasn't sure why.

"Yeah, I'd like to speak to Mr. Pinder if he's available."

She frowned. "I don't know if he's available or not."

I understood then why her speech had sounded so strange. Her tongue was pierced, and she was trying to avoid touching the stud to the roof of her mouth.

"Do you think you could find out?"

"Sure." She got up and disappeared down the back hall.

The office had some threadbare chairs and a rack of brochures outlining the Ocean Towing fee-based towing plan, but little else. I grabbed one of the brochures, sat down on a worn chair, and had started to read when the girl reappeared.

"Sorry," she said and it sounded more like *sowy*. "I forgot. What's your name?"

"Seychelle Sullivan," I said. "Of Sullivan Towing and Salvage." I crossed the room and handed her a card.

She glanced at it, then spun and bounced back down the hall, swishing her skirt with her hand as she walked. From where I was now standing, I saw her enter the last door on the right. I didn't even have time to retake my seat before she poked her head out the door and said, "Come on back," waving her hand. I circled her desk and headed back to the door she held open for me.

Neville Pinder was seated behind his messy desk when I walked in, but he rose and came around it to shake my hand. To say he was a big man would have missed it by half. Pinder had to be about six foot five with the massive lumberjack-size hands and feet that would fit a man that tall. And he wasn't fat; just big. I guessed he was in his midforties, and though his hair was shaggy blond, his sideburns and mustache were streaked with gray and his brown leathery face was covered with a web of fine lines. He was wearing shorts and a yellow-green Ocean Towing T-shirt that showed the deep brown skin on his legs and forearms. This was a man who had spent most of his life outdoors.

When he extended his right hand, I saw the raised pink scar tissue that ran down his forearm in twin parallel lines. The hand itself was missing the pinkie and ring finger, but because his fingers were so huge, his grasp felt more than ample.

Once we'd finished with the handshakes and introductions, he offered his condolences about Nestor. His eyebrows peaked and the skin pulled tight around his pale green eyes, but he looked more like he was trying not to laugh.

"So I take it you know why I'm here in Key West." I wasn't there for niceties and I wanted Pinder to know it.

He pointed to one of the two metal folding chairs and returned to the black leather office chair where he'd been sitting when I walked in. "Yeah, the recently departed Captain Frias convinced his boss he should get you to tow the yacht back up to Fort Lauderdale instead of me."

I'd met white Bahamians before and always found their lilting accent disarming. With Pinder, though, it sounded overdone and pretentious.

"I take it you didn't like Nestor. You sure don't seem to show much respect."

"Neither did he. Asshole come in here talking trash to me and my partner, even gone so far as saying that I might be in on something with his boss."

I didn't say anything for several seconds. "The man's dead."

"So? Just because he went out and got himself killed don' change the fact that the man was bad-mouthing my business." Pinder leaned back in his chair and put his feet up on the corner of his desk. The flip-flops on his feet looked like somebody my size could use them as wakeboards.

I glanced around the office. For an operation that was making the big bucks on all these recent salvage claims, they weren't spending it on office décor. The desk was made of gray metal that matched the folding chairs and the four-drawer file cabinet in the corner. The only other item in the room was a calendar on the wall that showed a Key West schooner sailing past a flaming sunset.

"Do you know why Nestor recommended me?"

"I know that Ted Berger now thinks I'm ripping him off when I'm only asking for the industry standard here."

I had been prepared—after the stories Sam had told me and after seeing the flaky receptionist—for Pinder to be a total space cadet. I was surprised by his blunt reply. He knew *something* about salvage.

"Come on, if you've been in this business any amount of time, you know that's not true. There's no such thing as an industry standard in salvage. Sure, you can get an award of thirty to forty percent of the value of the small sailboat you keep from sinking, but with a multimillion-dollar yacht like this, you're looking at a much smaller percentage. Not ten, maybe not even five."

"There been salvage awards as high as six million," he said as he reached for a pack of Marlboro cigarettes and shook one out.

"That was when a friggin' oil tanker saved a fuel cylinder from the space shuttle, for Pete's sake. The *Power Play* wasn't even holed. You know, Pinder, it's guys like you who don't know what the hell they're doing who are giving this business a bad name. Learn a little more about the law, look at history."

He pawed through the papers on the desk until he found the lighter, then lit the cigarette. He blew a stream of smoke just to the left of my face. "I look at history every fuckin' day when I walk to the office. I look at these fancy old Victorian houses 'round this town built by poor Bahamian suckers for the rich wreckers. Yes, indeed. I've given it quite a bit of thought, and I made my decision concerning which group I'm goin' to belong to."

* * *

I stepped out into the sunlight and pulled the door shut behind me with a bang. I wanted that barrier between Pinder and me. I had harbored a naïve hope that somehow I would be able to put some sense into his head, get him to lower the amount he was asking for on the *Power Play* salvage. I had become a part of this job, and I didn't like being associated with this deal he was pushing for, which would undoubtedly get written up in the papers and talked about in all the waterfront bars. It wasn't as though Berger and his insurance company couldn't afford a big salvage award, but it was bad for this business as a whole, this business I had made my life.

Jamming my hands into the pockets of my jeans, I took off walking back down Fleming Street. At the corner I looked up, trying to decide what to do next, and I recognized the gray-haired, stooped man coming toward me in the crosswalk.

"Hey, Arlen," I called out, then waited for him to reach my side of the street. I embraced him with a swift air kiss past his cheek. "What are you doing here in Key West?"

Arlen Sparks had been a near neighbor of the house in which I grew up. As a kid, of course, I'd called him Mr. Sparks, but most of the adults, including my dad, had called him Sparky. I didn't realize until much later that it had to do with his profession as an electrical engineer and his ham radio hobby. The Shady Banks neighborhood had been a close-knit community where all the adults looked after all the kids, and as often as not Molly, Pit, and I were in someone else's yard or kitchen or garage. Sparks himself had been a crotchety fellow, balding and with a comb-over hairstyle that we kids found hysterical. He didn't know much about kids since he and his wife had never had any of their own, and we did our best to stay out of his way. He worked at a local research and tech firm called Motowave, and he would scowl at us on our bikes as he left in his big white sedan for work.

After our brief embrace, he mumbled a soft hello and said, "Wife and I have a house on a canal here."

Arlen's wife had been the favorite of the whole neighborhood. She was the children's librarian at the county facility just west of Shady Banks. On weekends, she'd invite us into her kitchen with offers of home baked brownies and then let us look at her collection of signed first editions of children's picture books from the 1930s and '40s.

"Really? I had no idea." I patted him on the shoulder. "You lucky dog. You must have bought it back when mere mortals could afford real estate in Key West."

He nodded. I hadn't seen him in several years, not since Red's memorial service, and I was surprised to see him look so old and tired. His shoulders hunched, the waist of his pants seemed to cut across his lower chest, and his head bent forward, his eyes cast down.

Twenty years ago, when I was only ten years old, I had thought the Sparkses were old. They'd probably been in their midforties then, which meant he was only in his sixties now. He looked at least ten years older.

"How's your wife?"

When he looked up, I saw raw fear in his eyes. "She's not good, I'm afraid. Sarah has been sick for a long time."

"I'm so sorry to hear that. I didn't know. What is it? What's wrong with her?"

"A few years back she found a lump," he said, lifting a hand and touching the side of his chest, under his arm. "They operated and she did chemo and everything was looking fine. We thought she'd beat it. We were thinking about moving down here to Key West permanently once I retired." As I'd noticed with many balding men, Arlen's eyebrows seemed even bushier, composed of long errant white strands. They bounced up and down as he talked. "But then, I got laid off." The eyebrows dropped down. "Last July."

"You're kidding. Just before you retired?"

He nodded. "And then in the fall, her cancer came back. I don't know if she can take this again. She's not strong. The doctors say they have this new treatment they want to try on her, but the benefits went with the job and we have no more supplemental insurance. Medicare won't cover it because it's experimental, and I can't afford it. That's what I'm doing here now. Going to put the house here on the market."

"Arlen, how can they do that to you? I don't understand. They can just drop you after you worked for them all those years?"

"It came as a surprise to me, too. Used to be you put in your time working for a big company like Motowave, and you retired with your pension and reasonable benefits for the rest of your life. Things have changed now. Big business doesn't think it owes anything to the workingman."

I hardly thought of Arlen Sparks as *the workingman*. He was more like the mad scientist. When we were kids, sometimes we'd go out to his Florida room where he had all his ham radio gear set up, and we'd watch him tinker with his soldering iron and circuit boards. Being kids, we'd start asking questions about what he was doing and what he did in his job at Motowave. Mrs. Sparks would usually come scurrying out of the kitchen, drying her hands on a dish towel, and shoo us back into the kitchen. There, she'd sit on a red vinyl chair and, speaking in a hushed voice, tell us that we were not to bother Mr. Sparks as the work he was doing was top secret and he wasn't allowed to talk about it. We believed it at first, but when we got to be teens we decided she'd been teasing us. Later I read in the paper that Motowave got many of its contracts from the Department of Defense, and I decided old Sparky might have been doing some 007 work after all.

When we parted, I promised him that I would drop in to visit them once I was back in Fort Lauderdale. I remembered all the times Mrs. Sparks had fed us sweets, listened to our problems, put Bactine and Band-Aids on skinned knees, and shared her love of books with us. Now she was back home gravely ill. We needed to step up, to return the gift of time and comfort. I wondered if Molly even knew—and she lived just down the street from them.

When I got to Fausto's market halfway up the block, I paused to look back at Arlen, and I was surprised to see him open the green door and walk into the offices of Ocean Towing. What the hell would he be doing there? He had said that his house was on a canal, so I supposed it wasn't such a stretch to assume he owned a boat here, too. I tried to picture him at the helm of a powerboat, his long strands of gray hair flying off his bald crown and trailing back in the wind. I shook my head. It was a ridiculous thought.

VIII

THE cabdriver dropped me off at the entrance to Robbie's boatyard, and as I walked the sandy track in the shadow of the rows of propped-up boats, I felt my pace slowing. I had to go see her. I couldn't stay away no matter how much I wanted to. Part of my reluctance was the usual shying away from the reminder of my own mortality. We all feel it when we see someone close to us through age or circumstance die unexpectedly. Nestor was about my age and a part of my waterfront world. But he had been more than that to me—hell, I'd once lusted after the body that now lay cold in the morgue. And seeing her was a visceral reminder of that loss. He had been vigorously alive yesterday at this time, and even though I had seen his body I still found myself struggling with the how and the why. How could anyone feel safe in a world that let someone as strong and alive as Nestor die? He was such a good, decent human being. When there were so many scumbags who lived long lives, you couldn't help but keep asking yourself why.

But I was also dreading this visit because I knew what she was likely to say. After last night, I knew it wasn't the *why* that was driving Catalina. She would begin again trying to convince me that someone had murdered her husband and that I should help her find and punish the *who*.

Thanks, but no thanks. First off, I wasn't convinced—as she was—that there was even anything to investigate. It seemed pretty clear to me that Nestor's death came at the end of a bad string of accidents. Watching his career go into the toilet had upset him so that he probably wasn't really paying proper attention on his windsurfer. I remembered how it had been blowing yesterday. Those big schooners had been charging through the water like ornery horses with the bit in their teeth, and it takes a fair amount of wind to get those big heavy boats moving like that. Out in the open ocean on a little sailboard, conditions would have been worse.

But she is alone now, I thought as I climbed the ladder to the *Power Play*'s deck. She will have things to see to, arrangements to make, and I am the only friend she has here.

There was no sign of either Drew or Debbie, but the door to the main salon was wide open, so I went on in. Down in the captain's cabin, I found Catalina lying on her bunk fully dressed, facing the bulkhead. I wondered if she was sleeping, but before I could cross the narrow cabin to check, she sat up and swung her feet off the bunk. I was amazed at her agility despite what looked like a basketball hanging on the front of her body. Her eyes were rimmed with red and her long black hair, which was usually tied back in a ponytail, now hung about her face like a frizzy halo.

"Hi," she said. "Thanks for coming by."

The way she said it sounded as though she hadn't expected me, and that made me feel like a real louse. Had I given her reason to have such low expectations of me? Probably. On the very day she lost her husband, I hadn't believed her.

I didn't want to ask her how she was. It would be a stupid question under the circumstances. But as I leaned against the door frame, I didn't know what else to say to her.

"Have you eaten anything today?"

"No," she said, stretching her arms wide and yawning. "I'm just not hungry. Besides, there is not much to eat on the boat. They cannot run the refrigeration when the boat is hauled out."

"Then let's go to town."

She reached for a slip of paper on the table next to the bunk. "Debbie brought this to me earlier. She said the police want to talk to me."

"That's normal."

"Debbie thinks I should get a lawyer, but I cannot afford one. I have not worked in several months, and we can only just pay our expenses with Nestor's paychecks. I don't even know how long I will be allowed to stay here on this boat. But I cannot take the bus back to Fort Lauderdale until I have taken care of my husband." She closed her eyes and turned her head to one side. I could see from the tension in her neck that she was fighting against her need to weep.

"Look, Cat, let's take things one at a time. You will be allowed to stay aboard this boat until we get back to Fort Lauderdale. I made sure of that. I talked to Berger."

At the sound of his name, the corners of her mouth dropped and she set her chin forward. I tried to ignore her reaction.

"As far as the cops go, I don't think you need a lawyer. They just want to talk to you. I'll go with you—but only if you promise we can stop for something to eat first. I'm starving."

She pushed herself up off the bunk. Her movements were graceful as a dancer's, but cautious, as though she thought her body might break if she moved too quickly. The child she carried was now the only tangible remains she had of her husband. She stroked her belly, smoothing the print blouse over the bulge.

"She has been kicking today. It is as though she is upset, like she knows something terrible happened."

I didn't know what to say to that. I'd never felt a baby kick. There had been a time when I felt a life within me—and I'd worked hard to ignore it. But that was different and in another time that I now did my best to forget. Anytime something happened that caused that memory to poke its little head out, I changed the subject and stuffed it back into the darkness of lost memories.

Catalina took the two steps to the head. With the door open, she quickly splashed water on her face.

"Do you know for sure it's a girl?" I asked.

"No, we decided to wait and be surprised." She paused, the hairbrush in midair, and stared at her own reflection. "Now . . ." She let her voice trail off, and I could see the muscles and bones of her jaw working under the skin. She smoothed the hair back and restrained it with a black clip. Her usually lush lips were stretched flat. Stepping back out into the cabin, she reached for a sweater that was hanging on a bulkhead hook. "Seychelle, I know you don't want me to talk about Nestor, about what I believe happened to him." She swung the sweater over her shoulders, the sleeves hanging down in front, and I noticed again just how lovely she was with her smooth brown skin. When she turned to look at me, her eyes were wet and glistening and there were dark red spots coloring her cheeks. "But right now, the only thing keeping me from breaking into pieces is the rage I feel at whoever killed my husband. I will find who did this to him," she said. "I will."

AS we walked through the boatyard parking lot, a small, mousy-looking woman climbed out of an older, dusty Toyota Corolla and walked toward us.

"Catalina Frias?" she asked.

"Yes, that is me," Cat said.

The woman had an oversize fabric shoulder bag bulging with its unseen contents, and she carried a notebook in her hand. She extended her hand and said, "My name is Theresa Banks. I write for the *Key West Citizen*. Could I speak to you for a minute?"

I did my best to steer Cat away from the reporter, but she shook her arm loose from my grip. "Yes, I will speak to you. This is about Nestor, correct?"

"Yes. My sympathies, ma'am, but I'm writing a story on the accident and I wanted to get a little more background material on your husband."

"This was no accident," she said. "Nestor was a champion windsurfer in the Dominican Republic. He was too skilled for such an accident."

I stepped between them. "Listen, Cat, right now Ted Berger is going to let you stay on the boat until we get you back to Lauderdale, but if you go talking to the papers like this—"

"Mrs. Frias, if you don't think it was an accident, what do you think happened out there?"

I spun around to face the reporter. "Please, show a little respect. This woman just lost her husband. She is not going to talk to you today."

I turned back to Catalina. "Come on. Let's get out of here."

Cat reached past my body, snagged the woman's offered business card, and stuffed it into her handbag.

We reached the street just as a city bus was passing in front of the yard, so we flagged it down and I tried to help Catalina aboard. She shooed my hands away and pulled herself up the steps with the handrails. I told the bus driver we were headed for the Key West police station and were looking for a good place to eat close by.

He dropped us off at Garrison Bight Marina with directions to Captain Runaground Harvey's Floating Restaurant. We ate without much talk, and I was trying to figure out what I could do to break through the tension when Cat asked for the check and hustled us out. She said she was in a hurry to get to the police station to see what they had discovered.

Through the window, we told the officer behind a desk that we were there to see Detective Lassiter. He called another officer, who ushered us inside to a small waiting room with a table and about half a dozen chairs. When he came in, Lassiter didn't seem any more comfortable in his coat and tie than he had the night before. He wore a look of perpetual irritation. Dropping the file folder onto the table, he sat down across from Catalina with a heavy sigh.

"Ms. Frias, I'm very sorry for your loss."

Cat nodded her acknowledgment of the detective's statement, but her straight-backed posture seemed to indicate she didn't quite believe it.

He folded his hands on the table in front of him. "The medical examiner has determined that the cause of death was an accidental drowning. The body can be released to you at any time now. By law, the hospital cannot keep the body there for longer than twenty-four hours, and we don't have an official coroner's morgue on the island. They are getting anxious to know what your plans are. Do you have a preference for the funeral home? Had Mr. Frias made any prior arrangements?"

Catalina looked at the detective with her mouth sagging open, her eyes squinting.

He turned to me. "Does she speak English?"

I nodded. "Oh yeah."

When he turned back to face Catalina, she said very softly, "That's it? The police are not going to do anything more than that? You call my husband's death an accident? You wash your hands and you think that makes you clean?"

"I don't understand what you're talking about, Ms. Frias."

"Detective, my husband's death was not an accident."

Frias held up his hand like a traffic cop. "Whoa, ma'am, there is absolutely no evidence to suggest—"

"What do you mean, no evidence? Sir, Nestor was a windsurfing national champion in the Dominican Republic. He has windsurfed in much stronger wind than what we saw here in Key West on Sunday."

"Well, he might have been a champion, ma'am, but even champions—"

"No, you did not know my Nestor."

The detective looked at me as if asking me to help him with this woman. I shrugged. "I'm staying out of this," I said. "I just told her what I saw."

Lassiter turned to Catalina and it was obvious that he saw her, really saw her, for the first time. He saw the determined chin held high, the rigid posture, the full lips, and something in his face softened. That was when I realized that Catalina had something of the same effect on men that B.J. had on women.

She reached for the folder on the table. "Do you have the pictures? Seychelle said the Coast Guard took pictures."

Lassiter slapped his hand on the folder and drew it closer to him. "No. Bad idea. I don't think you want to look at these pictures. Not in your condition and all."

"Detective, I want to show you your evidence. Then you can check to see if the wound on his head fits with the mast on the sailboard."

"Begging your pardon, Ms. Frias, but I think you've been watching too many of those TV cop shows. You are understandably upset. Your husband was a very young man. But this accident was a tragedy, and I don't think you need to make more of it than it was."

"Show me the photos." Her voice was quiet, but firm, her eyes locked on his face.

Again the man turned to me with those sad brown eyes that made me feel sorry for him. He didn't want to cause Catalina any more pain. He didn't want to show her the photos. He was probably afraid of causing her to have a miscarriage or something, and he wanted me to help.

"Detective Lassiter. Catalina Frias is a very strong and determined woman. I don't want to be here all afternoon, and I know she won't leave until she sees those photos. I think you ought to just show them to her."

Slowly, he opened the folder and extracted two eight-by-ten color glossies. He slid them across the table.

Catalina stopped breathing. For a minute it felt as though we had all been frozen right along with her as we waited to see what her reaction was going to be. Far off in another room I could hear the sound of men's voices. Someone was telling a story, and the others were laughing each time he told another line. I couldn't make out the words—only that it seemed very odd that they were laughing while we were afraid to breathe.

I reached across the table and took Cat's hand. Her skin felt cold. I squeezed her fingers and felt reassured when she squeezed back.

The first photo showed Nestor lying facedown, his head half immersed in a pool of water on the windsurfer sail. His body, in the colorful neoprene wet suit, was lit by the flash, but the water looked inky black around his head. I'd been there, I'd seen this scene in real life, but it looked even more cold and cruel in the photo. The uphaul line that windsurfers use to pick the sail up out of the water was clearly wrapped once around his wrist.

In the next photo, two Coast Guardsmen in dark blue jumpsuits and orange life vests were lifting him out of the water onto a platform at the stern of their vessel. One of the men was reaching down to disentangle the line from the hook on his harness. In this one, Nestor's face was visible in profile, his head hanging down, chin on his chest, the large swollen bruise reflecting the light from the flash. I gritted my teeth and turned away. I didn't know how she was doing it, how she could sit there staring at the photo for so long.

At last, she exhaled a long clear smooth breath. There was no hitch in her breathing, no sniffling. That was when I knew that Catalina Frias was probably the strongest woman I had ever met. I felt certain then that she was going to get through this and take care of her kid and be okay. She was going to be one hell of a great mother.

She pointed to the uphaul line in the first photo. "Detective. It is true, what you said. Very good sportsmen have died in this sport. But they do not get tangled with their harnesses and uphauls. You see this?" She pointed to the line wrapped around his wrist. "And this?" she said, pointing to the second photo. "His body had been arranged on that board."

"I don't see how you can draw that conclusion, ma'am."

Maybe Lassiter was having a hard time seeing it, but now that I could examine the photos, I was starting to think that Catalina might have a point.

IX

WHEN we left the police station, I told Catalina that I would do whatever I could to help her out with funeral expenses. We had spent another half an hour in there with Lassiter while he had told her that she needed to make arrangements to have Nestor's body moved out of the hospital morgue. She explained to him that she didn't have the money for his funeral; she would need time to try to get it. She asked them to hold the body for a few more days to give her a chance to raise the funds.

"Seychelle, if I bury him, they will never have another chance to find evidence on his body."

I told her that there was nothing more we could do that day and hailed a cab. I asked the driver to take her back to Robbie's on Stock Island, and I paid for the trip in advance. "Just get some rest. I think they're going to put the boat back in the water this evening, and I'll be out there first thing in the morning." I didn't tell her it would be to meet the new captain Berger had already hired.

The afternoon was sunny but cool, so I decided to walk back to the marina and enjoy some of the back streets of Key West. The walk also gave me the opportunity to think about the events of the last couple of days and try to sort out what I believed and what I didn't.

Could Catalina be right? Was it possible that Nestor's

death wasn't an accident? The problem I had with that scenario was motive. Who could possibly want Nestor dead? Even if Ted Berger had tried to sink his own boat and then learned that Nestor was going to rat him out, was that enough to drive a man to kill?

I had been working my way slowly toward the Historic Seaport, zigging and zagging on streets lined with houses that dated back to the nineteenth century. Many of them had been renovated—a few turned into elaborate private homes—but more often than not they'd become small inns or bed-and-breakfast guest houses. I paused in front of a three-story Victorian house on William Street and admired the ornate gingerbread fretwork along the balcony and balustrades. I imagined the sea captains and their families who had once called this street home. They had made their living as wreckers, fishing for sponge and turtles when there were no wrecks to work. I'd heard that at the height of the wrecking business in Key West, as many as two or three wrecks a week went up on the reefs off this coast. The wrecking fleet grew ever larger as more and more entrepreneurs came to Florida seeking their fortunes. That was what led to the construction of these mansions and what had led this town to prosper so.

Once the lights were constructed on the reefs and the railroad to the West was completed, though, there wasn't as much shipping from New Orleans around Florida to the northeast, and fewer ships wrecked on the reefs. There were many tales and legends about the Key West wreckers taking matters into their own hands and paying off captains to cause wrecks. There was even an old John Wayne movie I'd seen about it once—*Reap the Wild Wind*. Most people found it was easier to believe in conspiracies, to imagine that someone had deliberately caused a captain to wreck his ship, than to accept a plain accident.

I decided that when I returned home, I would have to talk to my grandmother to see what she remembered from these times. A native Floridian, she was born only a few years after the end of the nineteenth century and had heard many stories that she had yet to share with me. As a child, she may even have met some wrecking skippers at the Stranahans' store on the banks of Fort Lauderdale's New River.

I was almost back to the marina when I paused to look in the window of the Key West Marine Hardware store on Caroline Street. The door opened and out walked Ben Baker. The sight of his sun-streaked hair with those Costa Del Mar sunglasses perched on top of his head made me smile. For some reason I didn't quite understand yet, seeing him fired up something inside me. He was deep in conversation with a very dark-skinned black man who wore shoulder-length dreadlocks. Ben was shaking his head and telling the man he didn't think he could help him when he looked up and saw me.

"Seychelle, good to see you again."

"Ben," I said, nodding in his direction. It was weird for me to feel so tongue-tied. Not that I'm all that talk-ative, but he was an old childhood friend; we had once spent hours together. Why was he making me feel all aflutter now? It was as though some alien—and a damn good-looking one—had taken over the body of the kid I once knew as Ben. That was the only way I could de-scribe how I felt. And I wanted him to feel some of what I was feeling, and I wasn't sure that was happening.

"Sorry to hear about your friend," he said.

"Yeah, it's been pretty bad. I've just spent the morning with his wife. She's about eight months' pregnant."

"Man. As if it wasn't bad enough just knowing the guy died. He left a wife and kid, too? Well, look, if there's anything I can do," he said, grasping my shoulder and giving me a friendly little shake, "you just let me know."

"Sure."

The other man put his hand to his mouth and gave a little cough, a very deliberate cough.

Ben turned to him with a half smile. "Okay," he said. "I get the hint." His hand still resting on my shoulder, he turned back to face me. "I guess my friend here wants me to make some introductions. Seychelle, this is Quentin Hazell, formerly of the island of Dominica and now here in Key West bugging me for a job."

Quentin put out his hand and we shook. He wasn't quite as tall as me, about five foot nine, but clearly he was in great shape. His shoulder-length dreadlocks were neat, the hair nearly black at his crown and bleached to a light brown, almost blond color where they brushed his broad shoulders. He was wearing a faded shirt that said RUDY'S, JOST VAN DYKE, BVI tucked into plaid Bermuda shorts, and though the shirt was a couple of sizes too big for him, the forearms that protruded from the sleeves were knotted with muscles beneath the black, ashy skin and the hand that grasped mine was rough with calluses.

"Hey, Quentin."

"It's a pleasure to meet you, miss." When he smiled his cheeks formed two smooth half globes and his dark eyes sparkled with humor. I wouldn't have called him handsome, but he had a face that made you want to get to know him better. There are some people you feel comfortable with the instant you meet them, and Quentin was one.

"You sure you want to work for this guy? The last time I saw him race—granted, that was more than fifteen years ago—the boat he was sailing sank under him." I laughed. "Isn't that right, Glub?"

Quentin began to laugh, but the laugh died in his throat when he turned to Ben.

Ben pulled his hand back and looked at me through narrowed eyes. "Very funny, Sullivan," he said deadpan.

For a minute, I was afraid I had hurt his feelings by teasing him with the old nickname.

But Ben couldn't keep his face straight any longer and as the corners of his mouth started to turn up, he said, "Gotcha."

"Geez, man. That's not fair," I said, but what I was thinking was that I couldn't ever remember a case of Ben teasing me before. A sense of humor had never been his strong point.

He turned to Quentin. "Sorry, man, no jobs today. Like I told you, I've got a mate on the boat and that's all I need. But I will keep my ears open, and I'll let you know if I hear of anything. Talk to you later."

He turned his back on the dreadlocked man. I could see the mild surprise on Quentin's face, but then he shrugged it off as though he was used to being dismissed. He turned to go.

"It was nice meeting you, Quentin," I called out.

He turned and tilted his head back, giving me an appraising look. "Likewise," he said, smiling and drawing the word out. Then he turned and walked off down Caroline Street. I watched him go with regret and thought how odd it was that I felt more comfortable with him than with the man I'd known since I was a kid.

"You got time to come down, see the boat, have a glass of wine?" Ben asked. "I haven't got a sunset charter booked today, so I'm free." He held out his hands as though offering himself to me.

"You're tempting me, Baker. I would love to see your boat." Both statements were true and probably in ways Ben never dreamed of. I wondered if part of my nervousness around him was due to the fact that I was supposedly in a permanent relationship with B.J.—at least as close to permanent as I could make it. B.J. wanted to talk marriage and kids, and I just wasn't sure I'd ever be comfortable with all that. And now here was a good-looking, slightly scruffy sailor who could make my heart beat faster just by looking at me.

"Hey, it's not often I have an evening free. You should take advantage."

His schooner was spectacular, and I did want to see what he'd done with her. "Okay, you've convinced me. I shouldn't stay long, though. I've got to get back to my boat."

"Come on," he said, slinging an arm over my shoulder and starting to steer me toward Schooner Wharf. "I'll show you what I've done to turn her into a nice charter boat."

I tried to make my voice sound calm and businesslike— just the opposite of what I felt. "You know, lots of people think chartering sounds great, but the part about being a slave to a schedule like that would wear thin for me. That's one thing I like about my business. Every day's different."

As we walked toward the docks, Ben told me about his business, about how he'd found the boat and brought her to Key West. "Chartering is such a different lifestyle than being in the service. This might sound weird to you, but I kind of liked the regimentation of the service, the discipline." He laughed. "Frankly, I'm not the most disciplined person—I really have to work at it out here. I like my home to be orderly, and in the service when someone is coming to inspect your quarters, you *have* to clean up."

"I guess I can understand that, but it would never work for me. I don't do well taking orders."

"I remember," he said. "When we were kids, you were always the captain."

"And things haven't changed. Here I am, thirty years old, still the captain." I looked up at his face, acutely aware of that mouth, those lips spread wide over impossibly white teeth. We had arrived alongside the dark-hulled schooner, and he pointed to a center-console runabout tied up off the bow of the big boat. The name on the stern was *rapid,* and I remembered him telling me he owned a fishing boat as well. I nodded, acknowledging the boat. With a gallant sweep of his arm, he motioned for me to step aboard the schooner.

"Surely, you have a boyfriend," he said as I walked past him, his mouth so close I felt his breath on my hair.

I snorted a laugh. "I have a friend. He's male. But he's certainly not a boy. I hate the terms *girlfriend* and *boyfriend.* We're adults, for Pete's sake. It's a shame that we don't have better words for it."

He motioned for me to sit on the white cockpit cushion. "I agree with you, completely."

"And what about you, Ben? Any women in your life?"

"Well, look around you. I meet a girl, invite her back here. Sure, the boat looks beautiful out on the water, but have you seen the size of the bunks or the head on a boat built in 1922? I mean, I cook on a diesel stove in the tropics. And then when they figure out that I spend all my time working on her, well, most last about a week and then it's *adios.* Some people say boats should be referred to as females, and if so, I guess *Hawkeye* here is the only woman in my life."

He bent to unlock the brass padlock on the companionway hatch, and I admired the view. I found it difficult to believe that single women weren't throwing themselves at him. Here he was, handsome, funny, charming, the owner of an awesome boat, and so distinctly male. I thought about B.J. back home taking his midwife classes. I was trying to understand that. Granted, it fit in some weird kind of way with his other interests in New Age stuff that he was into and I wasn't. I appreciated that B.J. was this great sensitive guy and all, but sometimes, with midwifery and such, I wasn't sure I wanted a man who was *that* sensitive. At the moment, I found this guy who preferred to talk boats, who had bottom paint under his nails, salt-stained Top-Siders, and jeans that fit snugly on a very nice ass, to be a welcome change.

"So do I get the tour?" I asked Ben.

He took me below first and showed me around the guest cabins, main salon, head, and nav station. I'd been aboard lots of classic boats and had never seen one so meticulously maintained. Ben had told me that he had trouble with discipline, but I didn't believe a word of it. I made all the appropriate oooing and aaahing sounds as he showed me around the warm oak-and-mahogany interior. The main salon had an elegant feel with velvet upholstery, dark wood, and stained-glass cabinets; in the cabins, the bunks were made up with country quilts, and there were ceramic sinks in oak vanities. I was almost afraid to touch the woodwork—the varnish had attained such a perfect glasslike finish, it would be a shame to mar it with fingerprints. The boat even smelled fresh and clean, which was nigh on impossible in an old vessel like this.

"How do you do it?" I asked him. "This looks like it's been kept in a museum—not like a working charter boat. Like hell you have problems with discipline."

He reached out to adjust the curtain over a porthole. "I'm really glad you like her. I thought about you when I was boat shopping. I'd always ask myself if Seychelle would approve of this boat or that. I had to find the perfect boat, and I guess from my childhood on I always saw you as an expert on boats."

What he was telling me made me feel a tad strange, but I guessed it made sense. Around the child Ben, I had always been kind of bossy. I told him what to do and he did it. It made perfect sense at the time, but now, looking back, remembering everything that I had seen happening at his house, I was more than a little ashamed of how I had behaved.

Ben had taken a bottle of wine from a cabinet in the galley and opened it. Reaching for two glasses in a stained-glass cabinet, he polished them with a clean paper towel, then motioned up the companionway ladder. "Shall we sit topside?"

The golden light was slanting through the masts and rigging of the boats on the far side of the harbor, casting long shadows across the water. The sun had lost its warmth, and I gave a little shiver when I sat down on the now cold vinyl of the cockpit seat.

"It's chilly out. Would you like a jacket?" Ben asked.

"No, I'm fine."

"It's too cold for you. I insist." He headed down the companionway steps and emerged a few minutes later with a soft fleece jacket that he draped around my shoulders.

"Thanks," I said as he settled back down on the seat next to me. "You know, I love watching the sunset here. I can understand why they make such a big deal of it over on Mallory Pier. I'd really like to paint this someday."

"Your mother used to paint, didn't she?"

"Yeah. That's one of the best memories I have of her—when she used to teach me to paint. She wanted me to grow up to be a painter. I've been working at it whenever I can."

"Really? Here's to a new side of Seychelle Sullivan."

We clinked glasses. "Hey, back when we were kids, Ben, we all thought you'd grow up to be a marine scientist—and now look at you. I never would have guessed that you'd grow up to become a handsome, self-assured charter boat captain."

"Yeah, especially the *handsome* part, right?"

I felt the heat rush into my cheeks. "No, that's not what I meant. It's that most charter boat captains are only about their good looks. Too many of them get hired for their photos instead of their resumés. I can accuse you of being handsome, but nobody can ever accuse you of being stupid."

"It's okay, Sey. I know what you meant."

It sounded odd hearing the shortened version of my name coming from his lips. When we were kids, he'd always insisted on using my whole name, even when the rubber bands on his braces gave him a slight lisp. It was as though he never dared try for that kind of familiarity.

"Ben, what I was trying to say in my inept fashion is that while I know I'll always love boats, I've started not liking what I do. The towing and salvage business is changing, and I guess I'm changing, too." I took a long sip. The fruity, smoky taste of the red wine was starting to warm me from the inside out. "Sometimes, I dream of doing it full-time."

"Doing what?"

"Painting. You know. Being an artist instead of just being a tugboat driver."

"Oh," he said, and then he drank and contemplated the dropping sun. "Is that how you see yourself? As *just* a tugboat driver?"

I shrugged. "Well, yeah."

He sniffed out his disagreement. "Right. That's how you think people see you when their boat is sinking and they're afraid they're going to die and then you show up?"

Whether it was the wine or his eyes or the way the new look of him made me feel confused, I didn't know, but I became acutely aware of the way our legs touched on the cockpit seat. Ben *got me;* he had since we were kids. He understood what drove me to go out there and save people. He knew how much it pained me to try to save someone and to fail. We were adults now, and I wondered what it would be like to explore this new body of his.

"Ben, I don't do much of that lifesaving work anymore. Those days are few and far between. Most of the time, I'm towing some rich asshole's boat up the river and he's hating me because he thinks I'm ripping him off. Or else I go out and take on a rescue, and it ends up in court."

"Sounds like you're talking about something in particular."

"Yeah, there's this guy. He's suing me. Melvin Burke. I can't even say the guy's name without getting really pissed off."

"Do you want to talk about it?"

"I don't know." I looked around me at the shining stainless steel and the gleaming white paint. This was a boat being cared for by a perfectionist. He would never risk this vessel, or someone's life. It was too bad there weren't more people like him. "I don't normally answer mayday calls," I began. "I restrict my work to the towing jobs that have been prearranged, moving large yachts up the New River and towing boats between yards." I meant to tell him the short version, but between the wine and the warmth that was growing between us, once I started, I couldn't stop.

The call came on an afternoon when I was steaming along offshore returning from towing a lovely Hinckley up to Lake Worth. It was a Sunday, and the traffic on the intracoastal had been brutal, so at Hillsboro Inlet I slipped out through the breakwaters with the idea that offshore, I could put her on autopilot and get something done on the trip home.

It had been bumpier out there than I thought, though. The forecast had been for light and variable to ten knots out of the north, but these winter northers can surprise you, and this one did. It was blowing a solid fifteen to twenty knots, with seas building to six feet and higher out in the Gulf Stream.

And that's where the new little twenty-four-foot Grady-White was that called for help on the radio—out in the Gulf Stream. Their engine had quit while they were trolling, and I was only a couple of miles away. I figured it would be simple enough to tow them on into Everglades, especially since I was going that way anyway.

When I arrived on the scene, I saw it was a dad and his preteen daughter. She was a tiny girl with thin blond hair and too much makeup for one so young. He was one of those guys built like a bulldog, probably wrestled in college but hadn't worked out in years. His shaved head showed a tan line round the back where he usually wore a hat. He'd undoubtedly lost it in this wind. They were both wearing life jackets and looked scared. The swell was throwing them around pretty good, and their boat was taking on water. For the time being, the bilge pump was keeping ahead of it. They took my line and soon we were under way for Port Everglades.

It happened so quickly I still can't quite believe it. I was in the wheelhouse, and it seemed like I'd just checked on them minutes before when I heard *Gorda*'s engine bog down as though a huge load had just been put on her. I stepped outside, looked aft—and their boat was gone, sunk, underwater in a matter of minutes. I throttled back, threw her into neutral, and headed aft to pick up survivors. We'd been traveling at about four and a half knots, but pulling that waterlogged vessel had done a damn good job of bringing *Gorda* to a stop. That twenty-four-footer was hanging just below the surface, held there by some air pocket in her hull but ready to sink straight down if she burped up that bubble.

The dad's white head was easy to spot. He was splashing around, flailing his arms and hollering at me to get his daughter, but I couldn't see the girl anywhere. Then I saw the shadow of orange just beneath the surface. I kicked off my boat shoes, grabbed a polyprope line I keep tied aft for just this purpose, and dove overboard.

A plastic buckle on the girl's life jacket was jammed in the tubing that supported the bimini top. She was trying to swim downward to take the pressure off it, but the life jacket's flotation was keeping the webbing taut. Her arms and legs were thrashing about dangerously. Panic.

I pulled my rigging knife out of my pocket. Trying to keep my head above the chop, I took a deep breath, then dove.

She wasn't moving by the time I reached her. She'd run out of air. I sawed through the webbing, and she shot to the surface with the aid of the life preserver. I kicked my bare feet to follow. When my head broke through, I gasped for air. The seawater temperature was barely seventy degrees in winter, and I wasn't used to the cold. It was harder to fill my lungs with air. I grabbed her life jacket with one hand and began pulling us back to the tug, breathing hard, trying to hold on to her and the bright yellow line at the same time.

The girl's father was already aboard, and he lifted his daughter onto the aft deck like she weighed nothing. As I pulled my body out of the water, I could see that the weight of the waterlogged vessel was dragging my boat down in the stern. Whatever air pocket had been giving her neutral buoyancy was leaking out fast. At this rate, I could lose both boats.

I ran to the deckhouse and grabbed the small hatchet I kept there—again, for just this purpose—dashed back aft, and with one high swing cut the hawser that was binding the Grady-White to *Gorda*. The little fishing boat disappeared into the blue depths. When I turned to look at the girl lying on her back in the orange life jacket, her lips looked just as blue. She wasn't breathing.

It happened the same way it had always happened to me. I'd been a lifeguard for many years on Fort Lauderdale Beach, but it still happened every time I saw a drowning victim. The face of the victim blurred and transformed into the face of my mother. I felt that same gut-wrenching dread that I'd felt that day when I had stared at my dead mother's face as a lifeguard tried to blow air into her, and at that moment, though even a keen observer might not have noticed it, I knew that I hesitated. I'd been eleven years old when my mother drowned, and there had been nothing I could do to save her. Though I'd schooled myself and trained since then, become a lifeguard and an EMT, I still always had that moment when I felt helpless all over again. When I felt it was all my fault and everyone would know that this person had died because of me.

I dropped to my knees, peeled the girl out of her life jacket, cleared her airway with my fingers, and began artificial respiration, staring into half-open eyes rimmed with running black mascara. After the fourth breath, she spewed up seawater and started coughing. I got her out of the wet clothes and into dry blankets on the bunk in the wheelhouse. I called for an ambulance on the radio as I raced *Gorda* into Port Everglades, and though they kept her in the hospital overnight to make sure she didn't have pneumonia, the girl came through just fine.

"So what did her father do to thank me for saving his daughter's life?" I said after swallowing the last sip of wine in my glass. "He filed a lawsuit against me for over a million bucks for negligence. He claimed it was my fault that his boat sank and his daughter almost died, and I should pay not only for the loss of the vessel, but also for his mental anguish."

"Wow. That's quite a story."

"Sorry to go on and on like that."

"It's okay." He smiled. "I'm used to it."

"I guess I used to do almost all the talking when we were kids, too."

"Yeah, you did."

I laughed. "There was no hesitation there. I'm sorry about the way it was back then. I wasn't always a very good friend to you."

He turned away, face pointing across the harbor, but I was certain his eyes weren't seeing the assorted yachts and fishing boats.

"It's sure a beautiful boat you've got here, Ben Baker."

He faced me, his eyes searching my face as though trying to tell whether I was serious or teasing him one more time. "I'd like to take you sailing on her someday."

"I'd like that, too."

"There's a spot, not far from here. It's my getaway spot. A little anchorage out off Boca Grande Key on the way to the Marquesas. It's deep protected water. Most of the anchorages around here aren't. The old wreckers used to anchor out there. It's nothing but you and the frigate birds and egrets and herons. I imagine what it was like back when my ancestor, the first Benjamin Baker, anchored his schooner out there. It's the kind of place I used to dream about when I was a kid."

He didn't say anything more for the longest time. We finished off the bottle of wine in silence.

"Hey, are you hungry?" he asked as though waking out of a trance. "I was just thinking of heading up to the Schooner Wharf Bar to get me something to eat. Want to join me?"

"I don't know—"

"Aw, come on. Have dinner with me." He took my glass, reached through the hatch, and set both wineglasses and the bottle inside the companionway. Then, standing, he reached a hand out to mine. "For old times' sake."

WE were seated at a table toward the rear of the open-air bar, close to the small stage where the live music would be tuning up a little later. It was still too early for the inevitable Jimmy Buffett cover singer. The Schooner Wharf Bar was built on the site of an old shrimp factory; half of the establishment was located in part of the old factory building, while the other half was made up of an assortment of tables and umbrellas out on the sandy island soil. Twinkling lights, fishing nets, flags, T-shirts, and other assorted flotsam hung from the rafters and pillars that supported the roof on the side of the old wooden building.

We had ordered and were waiting for our clam chowder to arrive when I noticed Neville Pinder slide onto a stool at the bar. He was still wearing shorts, but he had put on a jacket and a baseball cap. His longish blond hair stuck out like tufts of grass around his ears.

"See that guy at the bar?" I said. "The big guy with the baseball cap?"

"Yeah."

"Do you know him?"

"I know who he is. Nearly everybody who lives in Key West does. Neville Pinder. He owns Ocean Towing. But

if you mean, are we friends? No. I don't remember ever
having talked to the man."

"Do you know much about him?"

"Just that he has a reputation for being a jerk."

"So I've heard."

I was watching Pinder at the bar. His voice carried
across the open courtyard as he joked around with the
charter captains and made himself the center of everyone's attention.

"If I do wind up getting out of this business, it will be
because of guys just like him."

"I can't imagine anything ever making you want to
sell *Gorda*. That boat's been in your family as long as I
can remember."

"That's true. In lots of ways, she represents all I have
left of Red." I tilted up the plastic cup that had held my
draft beer and pretended to examine the bottom. There
it was, that stealth emotion that had a way of sneaking
up my throat and making me cry when crying was the
last thing I wanted to do.

"You were lucky. He was a good dad."

Something in his voice made me look up at Ben's face.
I could see in the set of his chin that he was fighting his
own unexpected emotion.

"Ben, you just said Pinder was a jerk, but he had nothing on your dad. If they gave prizes for being the biggest
asshole on earth, your dad would win."

He made a noise with his mouth closed, and it exited
through his nose. It sounded like a vain attempt at a
chuckle. "My dad," he said, looking away, refusing to
meet my eyes. "Good old Junior Baker. Owner of Baker
Ford. Big man in Fort Lauderdale."

That was part of what was making me feel so awkward around Ben. I realized that now. I hadn't wanted
to acknowledge the memory, but at that moment I saw

again in my mind's eye that night Ben's father had come to my house and taken his terrified son home. "I still remember, Ben. There's a lot in my life I wish I had done differently. That night is one."

When he turned to look at me, it was as though we'd stepped into a time machine. I wanted to say, *There you are. That's the boy I knew.* It was in his eyes. That darkness, the loneliness that was so much a part of the young Ben I knew. He'd done a good job of burying it, but it wasn't gone.

"Do you?" he asked. Then without waiting for me to answer, he put his hand on mine and gave me the saddest smile. "But we don't really get do-overs in life, do we?"

I was looking for the words to answer him when another voice interrupted us.

"Hey, Ben, check this out." The voice came from behind us, and Ben turned to greet a young man wearing shorts, Polo shirt, and rain jacket—the charter crewman's uniform.

"I've got pictures my girlfriend took at the Wreckers' Race yesterday. There're some good ones of *Hawkeye.*"

"Let's see."

The kid slid into one of the empty white plastic chairs, nodding at me. Ben said, "Seychelle, this is Jack. He crews on the *Western Union.*"

Jack spread out the photos on the table and pointed to the various shots of the schooners under way, heeled over, white water foaming at the bow. "It was awesome weather, wasn't it? Most of the time when we race these big old boats, it's a drifting match."

"Yeah," Ben said, "it takes a lot of wind to move our kind of tonnage."

There were also several photos of the fleet anchored out off Sand Key Light, dinghies circling in the water, some pulled up onto the sand beach. My eyes scanned across the photos looking for Nestor. I wondered if he had made it out to the lighthouse as he'd told the kid at the rental shack he'd intended. I'd checked almost all the photos without seeing any sign of him when I stopped and went back to a photo I'd already examined. It wasn't Nestor or a windsurfer that caught my eye. It was a white boat with a center console that was pulled up on the sand. A yacht tender. Written on the side was T/T POWER PLAY.

I closed my eyes for a moment and replayed the scene in my head. There was no doubt about it. Ted Berger had told me he'd spent all afternoon fishing Bluefish Channel. That was in the opposite direction—nowhere near Sand Key. The question I now wanted answered was this: Why did he lie?

X

WHEN I got to the boatyard the next morning, I was feeling just a little bit wobbly. Wine wasn't my drink of choice, and I'd had too much of it the night before. Ben kept pouring and I kept drinking. Stupid. I was sort of hoping that we would get back around to talking about personal history again, but he steered the conversation toward the safe topic of boats. Something about the man fascinated me, but I knew we would never be able to move forward until we cleared the air about the stuff that had happened long ago.

When I'd gotten out to my boat around eight o'clock, Abaco was thrilled to see me after nearly twelve hours alone. I had taken her ashore in the dark, and as she romped around in the trees snuffling out night creatures in the underbrush, I walked the shoreline feeling a monster headache coming on, and wondering what had been going on in my friend's home as he was growing up.

The *Power Play* was back in the water that morning, tied to the dock at Robbie's Marina, and my headache hadn't subsided yet. In the clear dry air after a cold front, anything white bounces that Florida sunlight right back into your eyes like lasers. The big slab sides of the yacht were making my teeth hurt.

"Hi, Seychelle." The perky voice came from behind me, and my headache threatened to turn to nausea. I turned away from the brilliant yacht to find Debbie crossing the dirt yard waving at me. Her slender arms were tanned a nutmeg brown, and her short, shiny hair bounced as she arrived beside me and took my arm. "You don't look too good. Are you feeling okay?"

I was only months on the far side of thirty and this little twenty-something was making me feel ancient. I shook my arm free of her grasp. "I'm fine. It's just that *Gorda* isn't really meant as a live-aboard boat. She's a little river tug. My digs aren't nearly as luxurious as yours."

She giggled. "*Digs.* I never heard anybody say that before. Well, come on. Our new skipper, Jeremy, is up in the yard office with Mr. Berger. They want you to join them up there. That's why they sent me out here."

"Okay. I got that. I'm going."

She fell in step beside me. "This new guy, Jeremy, he's like really cute. Wait till you see him."

"Oh, I already have."

"Really? How? I thought he just got here."

"Debbie, I've met lots of Jeremys. Trust me."

"That's weird, 'cause I've never met anybody named Jeremy before."

The yard office was in a makeshift metal building, new quarters after the last hurricane season had driven them out of the old place, Debbie told me. She led me into the lobby and back into a private office, where two upholstered office chairs held Berger and a gentleman I assumed was the yard manager. A metal folding chair scraped back when Jeremy stood and extended his hand to me. His blond hair was perfectly coiffed, the epaulets on his white shirt starched and pressed, and the palm of his hand as baby-smooth as his hairless chin.

Berger pointed to the other metal chair. "Take a seat."

The yard manager introduced himself as Bob, and I took my spot next to the other hired hand. I looked at

Berger's profile as he continued the story he had been telling Bob when I walked in. It was something about the women on his female roller hockey team. He obviously felt no compunction about calling the women broads and bitches in my presence, especially to an appreciative audience like Jeremy who laughed too loudly at his jokes. But just because Berger was an ignorant Neanderthal, did it follow that he could commit murder?

Bob was a heavyset older man, and judging from the pictures on the shelf behind his desk, he was also the father of daughters. Berger's language was making him squirm. As soon as he could interject, he changed the subject to what had brought us there. He explained what work had been done to the boat, and what still needed to be finished up before we could depart. The three of them began to discuss the trip north as though I weren't even there. In a pinch, the yacht could probably run on one engine with her makeshift rudders, but they anticipated a very slow speed for her—and they talked as if they were expecting us to run straight up the coast without stopping.

"Can I interrupt a minute here? Gentlemen, I just came down the coast and there are about a million lobster pots in Hawk's Channel between here and Miami this time of year. There's no way we're running at night."

Berger started to complain that he needed to get the boat up to Fort Lauderdale as soon as possible.

"You either do this my way, or you do it without me. If I'm the one running your towboat, we'll stop the first night off Marathon, the second night off Rodriguez Key, and then we'll run straight back, getting into Lauderdale late on the third night. While south of John Lloyd and the park waters, we only run during daylight hours. Once we're clear of the pots, we head straight home. If it kicks up and gets nasty, weather-wise, we may have to dodge into Government Cut and go up the intracoastal between Miami and Lauderdale. You know how it is this time of year with these fronts. They come sliding down from the north as regular as fleas on a dog. If we're lucky, the weather will hold, and if we get away Thursday morning, we'll get in—" I paused and tried to see the calendar in my head. "—late Saturday night."

Berger tried to argue with me, and Jeremy—as a good company man—stuck right behind the boss, but in the end I told them that it was a take-it-or-leave-it kind of deal. Especially now that I'd met Pinder, I knew more or less what Berger's choices were, and I was confident he would give in. He did.

Once we had established that we would be leaving on Thursday morning, I stood to excuse myself from the group.

"Wait a minute," Berger said. "Have you read the paper this morning?"

"No."

"Your girlfriend has been talking to the press." He held up the front page of the *Key West Citizen*. The headline read SUSPICIOUS CIRCUMSTANCES SURROUND WINDSURFER DEATH.

"How do you know it was Catalina?"

"She's quoted three times in the story, that's how. She's insinuating that Nestor's death was no accident."

"You've got to understand, she's just lost her husband."

"Bullshit. I don't mind giving her a ride up to Lauderdale, but not if she's making defamatory remarks about me to the press. Shut her up or she's gone. You understand?"

"Yeah," I said. "I hear you."

I was tempted to slam the door on my way out of the office. What was Cat thinking? She must have called that reporter yesterday after I'd sent her home in the cab. My first impulse was to be angry with her, but then I had to back off and realize that if it had been B.J., and I believed someone had killed him, I would be doing exactly the same thing. Maybe the question I should have been asking myself is why I didn't feel the need to do this for Nestor.

I took off to find Catalina. She now had only a short time in which to take care of business in Key West, and she'd want to know we were leaving day after tomorrow. I'd do my best to avoid the topic of the newspaper. As I approached the dock, I saw her sitting at a table on the *Power Play*'s afterdeck, her head bowed over a book, a pen in her hand. It looked as if she was writing in some kind of journal.

I walked up to the edge of the sea wall and called out, "Permission to come aboard?"

She glanced up, appearing momentarily dazed, like she was trying to remember where she was. "Seychelle?"

"I'm over here," I called out as I stepped through the gate in the bulwark and made my way aft. When I reached the deck, she closed the book and rested her pen on the table. "How are you feeling today?"

She placed a hand on her belly and slid it around in smooth circles. "She is resting now, but she was awake all night. It felt like she was dancing in there. I could not sleep, either, but it was not all her fault. Part of me is afraid to sleep. I am afraid I will have dreams and in my dreams Nestor will be alive. Then, when I awake, I will have to lose him all over again."

"I can understand that," I said, but I was thinking that every time I asked her how she was, she answered me in part with how the baby was. I wondered if my mother had felt so connected to me when I shared her womb. If so, was it just her illness that had changed her so, that had led her to leave me all alone on the beach that day?

"What were you writing?" I asked.

"Just my thoughts about what might have happened. Who might have done this to my husband. That woman at the newspaper asked me to."

"Jesus, Catalina. Berger's seen the article. He's threatening to throw you off this boat."

"I don't need him. I'll get my things and go." She put her hands on the arms of her chair, ready to push her body to a stand.

"No. I don't want you to do that. I understand that you want to find whoever you think did this, but I'm still not sure—I just want to get you home safe to Fort Lauderdale."

I considered telling her then about the photo I had seen of Berger out at Sand Key Light and how he had lied to me about being there. I was afraid for her health and safety, though. I didn't know what she was likely to try. At the moment, I just wanted to get her back to Fort Lauderdale and through this pregnancy.

"Speaking of that, Cat, I was up in the office talking to Mr. Berger and the new captain he hired."

"A new captain already?"

"Yeah, he's really anxious to get the boat back up to Fort Lauderdale so he can get it repaired. They want to leave Thursday morning."

"So soon? But I have to take care of my husband."

"I know. That's why I came to tell you. But really, there's nothing that you need to be here for. You can talk to the Key West authorities by phone."

"I cannot just go off and leave him here."

"What do you say we go into town and find out just what it would cost to have his body shipped up to Fort Lauderdale? I'm assuming that's what you want to do? . . . You don't want to try to send him back to the DR, do you?"

"No, his family there is all dead. I would like to make a life for my baby in Florida."

Before I could respond, the doors to the salon opened and Jeremy stepped out, followed by Drew, who seemed to be giving him the tour. As they approached the table where Catalina sat with her back to them, I could see Drew's lips move as he whispered something to his new boss.

"Catalina," Drew said aloud, "I'd like to introduce you to Jeremy Andersen. He's the new captain of the *Power Play*."

Jeremy held out his hand to her. "I'm sorry about your husband."

Cat stood. "You will want your cabin. I will get my things."

"Okay, that would be very nice of you," he said.

"Hang on," I said as I stepped forward and slipped my hand inside Jeremy's arm. I led him, practically dragging him, into the salon. "We'll be right back," I said over my shoulder.

Once inside, I slid the door closed. "Look, here's the situation. That woman out there is a friend of mine, and she has suffered a terrible loss. You'd have to be a total asshole to kick her out of her quarters, and I'm counting on the fact that you aren't. There are plenty of cabins on this boat, and you can bunk somewhere else until we get to Lauderdale. Once we're there, she'll be off the boat and out of your hair."

"But—"

"No. Stop. There are no buts here. I'd take her with me aboard my boat but there isn't room. Do you understand what it's doing to her to see her husband replaced after one day?"

Without another word to me, he slid open the door and asked Drew to head up to the bridge deck with him. I had a feeling that Jeremy and I were not going to be the best of friends.

"You should not have done that," Cat said.

"Come on," I said. "Let's go take care of your business. I'm ready to get out of this town and head home."

I'D used a pay phone at the yard to call Lassiter on his cell, and he agreed to meet us at eleven. The receptionist ushered us back to the detective's desk. He stood up, all smiles and happy to see us.

"Ms. Frias, I've got good news for you. You don't have to worry about the funeral costs. It's all been taken care of," he said as Cat and I settled into chairs opposite his desk.

"What?" she said. "I do not understand."

"Your husband's employer, Mr. Berger, he called me yesterday to ask about the case, and when I mentioned to him that you were having difficulty finding the money to pay for funeral expenses, he said he'd take care of it. In fact, the funeral home went by the hospital and took the body this morning."

"This morning?" Catalina repeated. She swiveled her head from me to the detective, as though one of us would be sure to explain.

"Detective," I said, "this is the first we've heard of this. I just met with Mr. Berger this morning and he didn't mention it. Can you tell me the name of the funeral home they took the body to?"

"I'll find out," he said, pushing back his chair.

"Seychelle, what does this mean?" Cat asked me when he had left the room.

"I don't know. Maybe Berger was just trying to be a Good Samaritan. Maybe he decided to do you a favor."

"But I am Nestor's wife. They should not release the body to another."

"Yeah, well, this is Key West. They're pretty laid-back here sometimes about the rules and regs. They are also perpetually out of money. My guess is that they were worried that they were going to get stuck with the funeral costs, so they figured that if anybody stepped forward to pay, they'd be happy to oblige with the paperwork."

Detective Lassiter came back into the room with a slip of paper that he handed to me. "They took him to the Dean Lopez Funeral Home over on Simonton. I wrote the address down for you there."

"Thanks." I looked at Catalina and raised my eyebrows as though asking if we were done here.

Cat leaned forward as if she was about to stand, then sank back in the seat again. "Detective Lassiter, I know you do not believe that Nestor was murdered because you say there is no evidence. Yet, did you look at the body?"

"Ma'am, that's not my job. That's the medical examiner's job. But yes, he did an autopsy, and his conclusion was your husband died after being thrown into the mast, which knocked him unconscious and caused him to drown."

"Did you speak to a windsurfing expert? Show him those photos?"

"I can't continue to investigate the case if it has been ruled an accidental death. It doesn't matter what you say to the papers or what you think. I have to go by the law."

I reached out and laid my hand on Cat's arm. "Come on. Let's go over to the funeral home. Maybe we'll be able to get Berger to pay to send the body up to Fort Lauderdale."

Catalina stood slowly as though she were moving

through a very thick liquid. When she got to the door, she turned back to Lassiter. "I can see you are a good man, Detective. You want to do what is right. Ask someone who knows this sport of windsurfing, please. Just ask."

AS soon as Catalina identified herself as the wife of Nestor Frias and asked to see her husband's body, the young man in the dark suit who met us in the entry at the funeral home excused himself. He motioned for us to sit down in the reception area and disappeared down a long dark hall.

I really don't get why so many people feel that everything associated with death always has to be so dark and somber. The funeral home lobby was decorated in dark woods and heavy velvet fabrics. The thick carpet hushed our footfalls, and fresh flowers filled the air with their sickly sweet smell. When Red, my father, had died a few years ago, my brothers and I had gone to the Neptune Society in Fort Lauderdale, and we were thankful for their bright, airy rooms and many paintings of ships and the sea. The man who helped us had not worn a dark suit or talked in whispered tones. We'd had a rather raucous memorial party for Red's old buddies and family friends, and then my brothers and I had taken his ashes out to sea. I liked it that way better.

It was an older man who stepped out, introduced himself as Mr. Gomez, and invited us to join him in his office. He started in with all the usual about how sorry he was for her loss, and he really did sound like a close friend of the family. The man was good. He'd probably sat behind that desk and said those same words hundreds of times, but he managed to make you feel as if he meant them.

"When Mr. Berger contacted us this morning, I'm afraid he failed to mention that Mr. Frias had a wife here in town."

"I don't live here," Cat said.

"I see. Well, Mr. Berger told us that the young man in his employ had died and that he was taking care of his affairs on behalf of the family. Had we known the family was here in town, we would have contacted you to find out how many copies of the death certificate you require. As it is, we only ordered what we needed to proceed. We were very lucky that the paperwork was processed at such a speed. Oftentimes here in Key West, well, you know things tend to run on Island Time. The county government rarely works this fast, but I guess it has been a slow week and they needed something to do over there. At any rate, now that I have you here, perhaps you would be interested in looking at a decorative urn?"

Catalina turned and looked at me as though she expected me to translate.

"Mr. Gomez, what do you mean? Are you saying Mr. Berger left directions to have Nestor's body cremated?"

"Oh yes, indeed. And as I was saying, the county government is usually not so swift at getting a death certificate to us, but you were very fortunate this time."

"But Mrs. Frias doesn't want her husband's body cremated. She would like to have the—"

Mr. Gomez inhaled sharply and cocked his head to gaze at Catalina. There was something about him that reminded me of a raptor—a hawk or osprey. "Ladies, there was no reason to delay, and Mr. Berger had said his vessel was departing for Fort Lauderdale in the morning. Mr. Frias's body was cremated earlier this afternoon shortly after it arrived."

XI

I HAD so much work to get done before our departure, I decided to hail a cab on the street outside the Dean Lopez Funeral Home. Catalina hadn't said a word to me as we'd walked out of the dark parlor, and the silence had stretched out long and awkward. It felt as though she were accusing me of being happy about this state of affairs—because I didn't believe that someone had murdered Nestor and now there wouldn't be any evidence. But there wasn't anything that could be done about it at that point, and it didn't seem to be Gomez's fault. Granted, I did find it curious that Ted Berger seemed to have greased the wheels to get rid of the body, but it was possible he had his reasons. He wanted to get his boat back up north as soon as possible; in a certain light, what he had done could even be seen as a kindness.

I finally spotted a taxi and raised my arm. The driver pulled over on the opposite side of Simonton Street and waited at the curb. When Cat stepped off, I said, "Wait." I followed her and put my arms around her, drawing her as close as her belly would allow. Then I held her at arm's length and said, "When we get back to Lauderdale, we're going to have a wake for Nestor, okay? The hell with funerals and cremation and all that. We're going to throw a party to celebrate his life, okay?"

She broke away from me, her cheeks wet with tears, and started to flee across the street. The waiting cab had been partially blocking traffic, and a large SUV with tinted windows that had been waiting in the line of cars suddenly accelerated to pass the line of traffic. Catalina was stepping right into his path.

"Cat! Look out!" I screamed and ran into the street, grabbed her by the waist, and pulled her toward my side of the pavement. My feet got tangled with hers and I felt us falling backward as the wind of the SUV's passing blew dust and gravel into my face. I took much of the fall on my elbows and tailbone, because I refused to move my arms from Cat's body. Her weight falling on top of my abdomen knocked the wind out of me.

"Hey!" the cabbie yelled. "You all right?"

I couldn't breathe, much less speak. My hands were holding the sides of her enormous belly, and I felt the life within her. I yanked back my arms as though I'd touched a too-private part of her. Cat rolled off me and stayed on her hands and knees panting, the whites of her eyes visible through the dark hair around her face. I curled onto my side, dazed and struggling for air. I could tell we were in the shade of a sudden crowd of people, but they were just looking at us, not saying anything.

Then I heard a couple of nearby whoops from a police siren. Within seconds there were two cops there, taking each of us by the arm, lifting and escorting us over to their car. It all happened so fast.

"What happened?" the female officer who was holding my arm asked me. "We were just around the corner when someone called it in."

I lifted my arms and saw the pavement rash down both sides. The blood was dripping down my wrists, into my palms. "My friend was crossing the street." I pointed with a bloodied hand. "This black SUV, big thing, came from that direction and nearly ran her down. Is she okay? Is the baby okay?"

"We've got paramedics coming."

"Cat," I said, squirming loose from the officer and stepping over to her side. "Are you hurt?" She was leaning against the back fender of the police car, her eyes closed, the male officer standing at her side.

She shook her head and then opened her eyes. "I fell on top of you." Her eyes dropped to my arms. "Seychelle, you are bleeding."

"Just some road rash. Nothing big."

"Miss, please step over here so I can take down some information," the female cop said. I told her what I knew, which was damn little. I still couldn't believe the guy hadn't even stopped. If I hadn't pulled Catalina back, he would have hit her. No question about it. It was as though he was trying to do it. I thought about the newspaper story that had run that morning, and I wondered if I should mention it to the police. Could it have been someone trying to run her down? They'd probably laugh at me, think I was being paranoid. This was Key West, after all, and drunk drivers were practically the norm. And I had to remember that as far as the cops were concerned, Nestor's death had been an accident.

When the paramedics arrived, they insisted on cleaning up my arms and wrapping me with white gauze and bandages. They checked Cat and listened to the baby's heartbeat, pronouncing both of them fit. While we'd been sitting with the medics, the cops had worked the crowd, and they returned to tell us that no one could either name the exact make and model or remember the license plate of the big vehicle. They concluded that it was a near accident and that we had been lucky. The female officer offered to drive Cat back to the boatyard on Stock Island, and I thanked her profusely.

My first stop on my walk back to my boat was just around the corner at a phone booth outside Fausto's market. I needed to give B.J. a call to let him know what was going on. We didn't have the kind of relationship where we were joined at the hip. In fact, I wasn't even sure that *relationship* was the right word. But I knew that he thought about me and wanted to know I was safe. Heck, it was only polite to give him a call now and again, and after what had just happened, I really wanted to hear his voice. It wasn't as if he could call me. I didn't realize how much I longed to talk to him until I heard the recording of his answering machine start. I wanted to tell him everything that had happened these past couple of days, to hear his calm voice, his intelligent, even-tempered take on everything. The man kept me grounded, and I was really surprised to realize how much I missed him. I left a short message telling him about Nestor. I added that the loose plan was for us to arrive back on Saturday evening, but that he shouldn't be concerned if we failed to show up. Plans have a way of changing on board boats, and I didn't want him to worry.

When I hung up, I stepped back and glanced down Fleming in the direction of Ocean Towing. Pinder was standing on the street arguing with a man I didn't recognize. They were too far off for me to hear what they were saying, but their body language made it clear that Pinder was dressing the other down. After pointing his finger in the man's face, Neville turned, yanked open the door to his office, and disappeared inside. The other man strode off down Fleming and turned the corner at the far end of the block. I wondered briefly what it had been about, but I figured it was just Pinder's management style. He had to do something to merit his island-wide reputation as a jerk.

I don't have much of a galley on *Gorda,* but I didn't

want to feel dependent on the *Power Play* on the trip north, so I headed into the grocery store first to buy the fresh stuff, got some ice for my on-deck cooler, and made my trip out to the boat with a loaded dinghy by four in the afternoon. My dog yelped with joy when I pulled up and did her best to get in my way as I heaved the bags onto the deck. Abaco is a social dog, and these long days alone on the boat were boring for her. She kept running aft and staring longingly at the dinghy as I put my food away, but when I started the tug's engine, she ran into the deckhouse and mouthed my hand—her way of saying, *Thank you for moving this boat someplace more interesting.*

I had decided to head for the fuel dock at the Key West Bight Marina to take on diesel and water. After that I would motor around to Robbie's Marina, where I could tie up next to the *Power Play* so that we could work out our lines and take care of all the tow details during the day tomorrow. As I pulled alongside the fuel dock, a familiar figure came out of the office to take my lines.

"Hey, Quentin," I said, tossing him a spring line. "Thanks for the help."

He nodded shyly then tied the spring off while I went back into the wheelhouse to give her a squirt in reverse to stop the boat's slight forward motion. By the time I got back outside, Quentin had secured the bow and stern lines and was readying the diesel pump to hand to me.

"Are you hurt?" he asked, nodding at my bandaged arms.

"No, I just fell and scraped the skin off my elbows." I grabbed a rag from inside the wheelhouse. "It's nothing."

"Dat's good."

"It's nice to be around somebody who knows boats,"

I said, taking the pump from him and dragging the hose on deck toward the deck fill.

As I watched the numbers flipping over on the pump, he approached me with the water hose. I pointed to the freshwater deck fill and he climbed aboard, opened it up, and inserted the hose. Watching him, I thought about Jeremy, Drew, and Debbie—my crew for the tow north.

"So you're working here now, Quentin?" I asked.

"No, miss, I just help out here because it is a good way to meet the captains and the harbormaster can always use the help."

"Sounds like pretty good thinking to me."

He shrugged. "I thought so, too, but no job yet. I think these charter boat captains aren't interested in a fella who looks like me."

"You might be right. Maybe Key West isn't the place for you. Did you ever think about going up to Fort Lauderdale? There are lots more yachts. Maybe you'd do better finding a permanent spot on a boat up there?"

"I'll go where I need to go if it means there is work."

I wasn't aware of having made the decision, but next thing I knew I heard myself speaking. "Quentin, I'm leaving Thursday morning to tow a ninety-four-foot yacht up to Fort Lauderdale. If you're interested, I'd like to hire you to work as my deckhand."

"I am very interested," he said, nodding briskly, making his dreads bounce.

"Okay, can you collect your gear and meet me out at Robbie's Marina on Stock Island in an hour?"

The smile lit up his whole face. "You bet, skipper."

As it turned out there was no slip available at Robbie's, so I rafted up alongside the *Power Play*. The crew brought out some enormous fenders to protect the yacht's paint job and tied off my lines while Jeremy watched from the bridge deck in silence.

Once *Gorda* was secure, I jumped aboard *Power Play*. When I opened the sliding door to the aft salon, Jeremy was standing inside, blocking my path.

"Can I help you?" he asked.

"I just came to check on Catalina. I want to make sure she's all right."

"She's fine. She's resting."

"Look, kid, are we going to have to have a pissing contest every day of this trip? Just let me go talk to her."

At that moment, Ted Berger emerged from the companionway that led to Catalina's cabin. With both his hands he was smoothing the white hair at his temples. "What's going on out here?" he asked.

"I'm here to see Catalina. This asshole is trying to stop me."

"I told him not to let anyone disturb her. She's resting. She was very upset when she returned to the boat this afternoon. It seems something happened in town."

Jeremy was grinning and I wondered for a moment if his could have been the face behind the tinted glass in that monster SUV, then dismissed the idea. I was really getting paranoid. Berger had just met this guy; I doubted he could convince him to attempt murder for him within twenty-four hours.

I held up my gauze-covered elbows. "It happened to the both of us. Some asshole almost ran her over, and I pulled her out of the way."

The concern in Berger's face appeared genuine. "Are you all right?"

"Yes, but I just wanted to talk to Catalina, to see if there was anything else she remembered about the vehicle."

"Sure. Come on," Berger said.

Jeremy stepped aside, and Berger led me to the closed cabin door. He knocked softly, and Cat came to open the door herself. She frowned when she saw Berger and looked as though she was about to let loose with some harsh words when she saw me.

"Hey," she said. "You're back."

"Yeah, can I come in?"

"Sure." Without looking him in the eye, Cat thanked Berger and closed the door in his face.

We sat on the edge of her bunk, quiet at first. Finally, I broke the silence. "Is everything okay over here, Cat?"

"Yes, it's fine."

"When I tried to come aboard, it seemed as though Jeremy had been assigned to run interference to let Ted Berger have some time alone with you."

"No," she said. "It was not that." She twisted the hem of her blouse in her fingers. Then she looked up at me. "Seychelle, tomorrow we will go back to that place and get Nestor's ashes and then we will leave Ted Berger and this island for good, yes?"

ABACO and I met Quentin at the boatyard gate. His gear amounted to a single duffel, but he had changed into a long-sleeved, collared white shirt that he wore buttoned to the neck. With a different pair of plaid shorts and orange flip-flops, the man exuded a certain dignity. I liked the look of him, and I knew that on this trip north I was going to need a strong ally. My dog jumped up and put her paws on his shirt; rather than scold her, he kneeled and scratched her ears while she looked adoringly into his eyes. Any doubts I had harbored about hiring a man I barely knew disappeared at that moment. I knew no better judge of character than Abaco.

WEDNESDAY passed in a flurry of preparations. I barely saw Catalina. The only words we exchanged came when

I gave her my handheld VHF and made her promise to call me if anything or anyone bothered her on the trip home. We set up a schedule for radio checks on channel seventy-two.

The weather held and we made good time Thursday on the trip north to Marathon, a fact I was thankful for due to our late departure from Robbie's. Berger had shown up just before we were supposed to leave, and he got into some kind of disagreement with the yard over the final bill. With *Gorda* towing *Power Play*, we weren't going to be traveling any faster than five or six knots, and we had almost forty miles to cover. When we got under way at ten o'clock, I was fuming.

The anchorage outside the entrance to Marathon's Boot Key Harbor offered little protection from southeast winds, but as the daylight faded out of the sky, the winds dropped to a near calm. I always get a little nervous when the weather cooperates to that extent. I wonder what kind of havoc is ahead. We approached the anchorage just south of the harbor entrance and cast off *Power Play* to drop and set her hook first. Quentin stowed the towline aft while I circled, and then he went forward to drop our anchor. I positioned us alongside the motor yacht and signaled him to let the chain fly as I backed down. Quentin's teeth glowed in the light from the big yacht when he turned to give me the thumbs-up, the anchor was set, but the smile faded from his face when I shut down the engine and we heard a panicked voice from the VHF radio.

"Mayday, mayday! This is the sailing yacht *Rendezvous*!"

XII

FOR the next several minutes it seemed like everybody in Marathon harbor was attempting to answer the guy. They all tried to talk at once, and the result was garbled static and squealing from the radio. Quentin and I stood in the wheelhouse listening to the occasional bits of intelligible talk, and within less than five minutes a boat came roaring out the Marathon entrance channel. He passed close under the stern of the *Power Play,* and we could make out the bright yellow-green of an Ocean Towing boat. Near as I could tell, we didn't even know where the guy was yet, but the Ocean Towing craft swung around the point and turned northeast. The Coast Guard finally came on the air and told everybody to be quiet.

"Sailing vessel *Rendezvous,* what is your location?"

"Hard aground close by Coffin's Patch."

"What is your vessel's description?"

"*Rendezvous* is an eighty-four-foot ketch drawing nine feet."

Quentin turned to look at me. We'd been checking the chart all afternoon, and I figured we were both thinking the same thing. How the hell had he done that? He'd gone aground at dusk, but there was a light out there off Coffin's Patch. No skipper in his right mind would take a boat drawing nine feet across that patch.

* * *

WE listened to the *Rendezvous* rescue play out on the radio as we prepared our meal. We had considered inflating the dinghy to dine on board the big yacht, but we opted instead for soup heated on the single gimbaled burner in *Gorda*'s makeshift galley and pointed the dog toward her Astroturf. The tide was dropping, and the big sailboat was hard aground. The Ocean Towing boat got to her and started to rig lines to pull her free, but they decided not to try right away because of the damage they might inflict on the marine environment dragging the yacht across the coral. The morning high tide around dawn would not be nearly as high as the tide that had put her aground. Looking at the numbers on our tide chart, Quentin and I thought they'd likely not get her off until the next evening.

A friend of the *Rendezvous* captain hailed him on the radio to offer his assistance, but the tired voice of the stranded captain replied that there wasn't much more that could be done at the moment.

"I don't know what happened. It was some kind of glitch with the instruments. We were going around Coffin's Patch, man."

The friend replied, "Bad luck, buddy. Let me know if there's anything I can do. I'll stand by this frequency."

The radio went quiet.

"There's too much bad luck going 'round these days," Quentin said as he sliced some cheese to go with our crackers.

"Is it bad luck or just stupidity?"

"It's both to count too much on GPS." He pointed to his eyes. "I count only on these."

"I guess GPS is amazingly accurate—but it's only as good as the charts, and some of the islands are several hundred yards out of their charted positions. My only

GPS is just that old handheld one because I usually don't go where I'd need it."

"When I come up from down-island, boat I was on almost wrecked by following GPS. Down in the Dry Tortugas. Fella on watch was staring at the chart plotter when I showed him we were headed for the breakers."

"There seems to be a lot of that going around."

Later in the evening, once the dishes were done and the decks had been sluiced down with fresh seawater, we sat in my folding captain's chairs on the aft deck and watched the stars in a companionable silence. *Gorda* was not designed for long overnight trips; she had only the one berth at the aft end of the wheelhouse. When my dad took on crewmen, they generally had to bunk down out on deck or on the floor inside the wheelhouse. I hadn't made many changes to the boat since I'd inherited her, and Quentin had said he didn't mind sleeping on deck.

Abaco got up and nudged her nose at Quentin's hand until he reached out and began to stroke her silky head. From time to time the radio broke the silence as fishermen or live-aboards hailed one another and then switched to another frequency on what is essentially the boaters' big party line. The *Power Play* was anchored about a hundred yards off our beam, and with her big generator that ran all night and day, she was lit up like a parade float. We could see her crew sitting around the table under the bright lights on her afterdeck. Catalina was not in sight. I watched as Jeremy stood and headed into the salon. Through the windows, I saw him continue forward toward the bridge. I wondered if I had been too hasty to judge him. A serious captain would take some time this evening to look over tomorrow's course, noting the dangers and possible trouble spots for the following day's run. Just because he was a pretty face and a suck-up to the boss, it didn't follow necessarily that he had to be incompetent.

"I like your boat," Quentin said. His voice startled me. We'd been quiet for so long. "Someday I would like to earn enough money to buy myself a small boat for such a business in Dominica."

"Really? Is there that much yacht traffic down there?"

"Yes, my island is located between two French islands. We have our own fishing boats, and there are many charter boats. They like to sail from Guadeloupe to Martinique, and my home is in between. Where I live in Portsmouth, I could find plenty of business towing boats between the islands with the better boatyards and going on rescues."

"Well, Quentin, I tell you, I've loved being in this business for most of the years since I took it over from my dad. But this year, I'm starting to have my doubts."

"And why do you say this?"

"Lots of reasons. Insurance rates are skyrocketing, and that's making some people do crazy things—like wrecking their boats intentionally."

"This is not something new."

I nodded. "You're right. People have been doing that for a long time, but this year, it seems to be worse. And it's impacting me more than ever before."

"Are you talking about Mr. Berger?"

"Well, you do put it right out there, don't you? Yeah, I don't know anything for sure, but I have a feeling that Ted Berger is tired of boat ownership. That's another reason we aren't running at night on this trip and taking things slow. No screwups."

There was no sign of rain, but the night was going to be cold. I had a down sleeping bag I loaned to Quentin, and with his air mattress he said good night and headed out for the foredeck. I checked my watch. It was nine thirty. I reached for the VHF mike, switched channels, and pressed the key.

"This is the tug *Gorda* calling for a radio check."

Catalina's voice came through immediately. "*Gorda,* this is the *Power Play.* I read you five by five."

Good girl, I thought. Just as I'd taught her. That meant everything was fine on her front, anyway.

I bedded down on the bunk in the wheelhouse with Abaco at my feet, and though I was plenty warm and comfortable, I found I could not sleep. My mind kept churning numbers of time and tide and depth and draft, and none of it added up.

THE next couple of days were fairly boring—which, in my business, is always a very good thing. It's when it gets exciting that I have to worry. The anchorage off Rodriguez Key was calm on Friday, and we heard no more excitement on the radio. Catalina and I checked in regularly, and her voice sounded stronger the farther we got from Key West. Saturday, we made better time than I'd anticipated and found ourselves entering the breakwaters at Port Everglades just before eight o'clock that evening, much earlier than I had planned. I towed the *Power Play* straight upriver to the yard at the New River Marina. They were expecting us and had cleared an outside dock, which made dropping off the big yacht simple. I said my good-byes to the crew and to Quentin, then helped Cat and her gear get aboard the tug. It was roughly nine thirty when Catalina, Abaco, and I pulled up to my dock at the Larsens' place on the New River.

Light was spilling out through the open front door of my converted boathouse/cottage, and Hawaiian music was playing from some source out in the dark yard. Barbecue smoke and colored lights floated over the grounds of the Larsens' estate. The main house was a towering structure that had suffered dozens of remodels and additions since its first incarnation in the 1930s, and now it could only be called something like neo-Colonial Moorish-Asian, thanks to the columns and towers with red barrel roof tiles and the Larsens' latest addition of a blue-roofed pagoda. Most people would have simply added a gazebo if they wanted a little shade, but not here. The Larsens absolutely loved the place, though they rarely were able to spend time down here, assuring me of a residence and a steady job watching the place for them.

Through the years, this Rio Vista neighborhood had grown rather sedate as the homes' values skyrocketed and the population aged and grew more moneyed. I wasn't sure how thrilled the neighbors would be at hearing the ukulele of Iz Kamakawiwo'ole wafting across the water at this time of night. Over the roar of my big Caterpillar engine, I also heard the laughter of kids from out in the yard, and on the periphery of the light I caught flashes of movement. B.J. stepped out of the shadows looking better than a cold beer on a hot day, and it took all my willpower to pay attention to docking *Gorda* before jumping onto the dock and throwing my arms around him.

XIII

THE next one to appear out of the darkness was Zale, the teenage son of my childhood friend Molly, with whom I had recently reconciled after many years of silence. Those tumultuous days last year after Zale's father, Nick Pontus, had been murdered had also rocked my family with the revelation that Nick had not been Zale's biological father, that Molly's son was actually my nephew. Every time I saw him, he looked more and more like my brother Pit. This night his light hair was tousled and he was breathing hard, squinting at me through his wire-rimmed glasses. No sooner had he stopped running, though, than two blond dervishes launched themselves at him and knocked him to the grass. It was Jeannie's twin boys, and as the three of them rolled on the ground making roaring monster noises, Abaco leaped the gap between the boat and the dock and began barking at the scuffling kids. I saw Jeannie resting a hip against the door frame to my cottage; Zale's mom, Molly, was now standing over the wrestlers pointing her finger at them.

I handed B.J. the last stern line and turned to see Catalina staring at all the people and commotion with her mouth open.

"Catalina, welcome to my world," I said, and went into the wheelhouse to shut down the engine.

I was clicking off switches on the instrument panel,

shutting off running lights and instruments, when I felt his hands slide around my waist and the warmth of his body wrapped around my back.

"Welcome home," he said, his voice barely a whisper blowing warm air in my ear.

My shoulders quivered as a shiver danced up my spine. I pressed my behind into his pelvis and arched my back as his tongue flicked at my ear. I tried to hide my ear with my shoulder and said, "Hey, I just got here. No fair." But then I ducked that shoulder down, spun around in his arms, and kissed him for so long I thought I might just fall into a trance standing there, our tongues entwined, and stay that way until morning.

I pushed him away finally and looked into his dark eyes. "So what's going on? It looks like a party around here."

"Not a party. We're just celebrating the sailor home from the sea."

"When I went upriver, I didn't see anything going on here."

"We were inside. You can hear that engine of yours for miles, you know. We wanted to surprise you."

Jeannie called out, "Would you guys stop necking in there? B.J. wouldn't let us eat till you got here."

I stepped out of the wheelhouse and looked over at Jeannie walking down the brick path, her usual flowered muumuu billowing around her ample figure. I looked at my watch, then back at her. "Yeah, like I believe that. You and your kids haven't eaten at this hour?"

"Well, he wouldn't let us have seconds or dessert."

"You guys will come up with any excuse for a get-together."

"Listen, it's Saturday night and your yummy fella here invites us over for a barbecue—hell, you think I'm turning that down?"

I slid my arm around B.J.'s waist. "Yummy is right."

Catalina had retreated to the afterdeck and was leaning against the bulwark, one hand resting atop her bulging belly, looking away from the gathering in the yard at the far side of the river. I headed back there and took her arm. B.J. was right behind me.

"Catalina, I know this might seem strange to you." With my free arm I swung an arc to indicate the laughing people, the lights, and the music. "With what has happened to you." I paused, trying to get the words right. "With the loss we've all suffered, it must seem strange to you that we are playing music and laughing. But this is how we deal. Most of these folks here knew Nestor, and we knew him well enough to know he felt like us. He was one of us. We don't cry and wear black when one of us dies. We get together and celebrate life. Nestor was a gift and he brought us you. Now you're one of us, too." I turned and wrapped my arms around her and we stood there like that for several seconds. When we broke apart, I turned to B.J.

"You remember my friend B.J.?"

"Yes," she said with a half smile. "You are studying childbirth."

He nodded at her swollen belly. "And you look like you're nearly there."

She looked down at her blouse. "I just get bigger and I still have a month to go."

"A big baby's usually a healthy baby," B.J. said.

"Speaking of which, this lady is eating for two. Let's go get her some food before it's all gone."

"Right," B.J. said. "You're only concerned about making sure our mommy gets enough food."

I made a cross over my heart and raised my hand. "I swear."

He rolled his eyes. "Follow me," he said to Catalina as he helped her off the boat and began to introduce her around.

The night was unusually mild for January—the temperature had barely dipped down into the sixties. I saw her sitting in a rattan chair someone had dragged out from the Larsens' porch. Her white hair was pinned up off the neck of her blouse, and her thin knees made sharp points against the black fabric of her skirt. And there were the same dirty sneakers she'd been wearing that first time I noticed her walking the streets a year ago.

"Hi, Grams," I said, leaning down to give her a kiss on the cheek. "How did you get here? I hope you didn't walk."

I'd discovered the existence of Faith Wheeler, my grandmother, only a year earlier, finally putting an end to a family feud that had kept us apart all my life. I was slowly getting to know the eccentric old woman who had spent most of her ninety-plus years walking the streets of this town, attending commission meetings and shaming the politicians into moments of restrained greed.

"B.J. picked me up and fed me a very nice dinner. Welcome back, dear."

"Thanks."

"You go on. Enjoy yourself. I'm happy watching the children play. Didn't really get to watch my grandchildren do this foolishness. And now there's a great-grandchild."

We watched Zale run across the yard chasing one of the twins. The younger boy giggled as Zale let him get away.

"Let me know if you need anything."

She nodded.

Molly was wearing some outfit that looked like black Chinese silk pajamas with embroidered red dragons. Her long black hair fell in a thick braid on her back, and with her part-Seminole features, she almost looked like a little Chinese doll. She gave me a quick hug and turned her attention to Catalina. She put her arms around her and held her in a long hug. She was whispering in her ear, and I could see Cat nodding. Molly had never met Cat, but they shared one terrible thing in common—both knew what it was to lose their children's fathers, to be left alone to raise a child.

"Come on over here and sit down," Molly said at last. "Your legs must be killing you." She guided the younger woman to a wooden picnic table at the edge of the Larsens' big yard.

It was great having Molly back in my life after thirteen long years of silence. We'd shared our childhood like sisters; now it was as though we hadn't lost that decade in between. I'd discovered I had room in my life for two women "best friends," and it felt great to be home and have all my family there.

"So, Molly, what's with the fancy getup?" I asked. "You look gorgeous and here I am in salty jeans and a sweatshirt."

"B.J. didn't tell you? We both passed our first courses in midwifery science. That's what we're celebrating."

"Oh really?" I looked to catch B.J.'s eye, but he was nowhere in sight. I settled on the table bench opposite Catalina, and Jeannie joined me.

"I never would have made it without his help," Molly continued as she dug around in a cooler. "All those hours we spent studying together really made the difference. I took all my anatomy and bio classes about five years ago, back when I was still married to Nick and I thought I wanted to be a nurse. I really just wanted an excuse to get out of the house. Anyway, I hardly remember any of it. B.J.'s been great."

While she talked, Molly was setting food and cutlery in front of Cat and me. Her compact body moved with startling efficiency. Without asking, she brought me a beer and a box of apple juice for Catalina.

"So are you giving up on your painting?" I asked her.

"No, not at all. That's just on hold for a while. Assisting home births is not exactly full-time work. I can do both."

When we were teenagers, we'd made an odd pair, the two friends who looked like opposites. Molly with her Indian blood and long dark hair had developed early, and the boys were drooling over her from the sixth grade on. I was tall and lanky, and what curves I had were well hidden under my oversize T-shirts and jeans. But our tastes and interests had always been similar, and she had gone on to become the artist my mother always wanted me to be. Now both our lives were taking another turn and for the first time, I really didn't—or didn't want to— understand this direction she was taking.

"Seychelle, I know you don't think it sounds like a very serious school, but the Birthwise School of Traditional Midwifery has really difficult classes. It's a tough program. We'll be lucky to complete it in a year and a half."

"Well, look. Just don't talk about it, okay? I don't want to think about birth canals and fluids and forceps before I eat. We've been cranking since daybreak to get in tonight and I'm beat."

Jeannie's boys Adair and Adam appeared and leaned against the end of the picnic table. "What does *forceps* mean?" one of them asked—which one I couldn't say, because I could never tell them apart.

"Never mind," Jeannie said. "Auntie Seychelle just gets cranky when she hasn't eaten. Go inside and wash your hands if you want dessert."

"I'm not cranky," I said, and in that split second difference between the time I said it and the time I heard myself say it, I heard just how cranky I sounded.

All the adults burst out laughing.

* * *

WE ate green salad, baked beans, and B.J.'s grilled skewers of dolphinfish, scallops, grape tomatoes, and squash while the others dug into a huge pan of boysenberry cobbler that Molly had brought over and kept warm in my oven. I reckoned that was about the first workout that oven had seen in a year or more. Zale sat next to me just long enough to help himself to a huge plate of cobbler and to tell me that he had received a postcard from my brother, his newfound dad. He pulled the wrinkled piece of cardboard from his back pocket.

"The photo on the postcard is awesome," Zale said. "He's on a delivery, he says, sailing one of the Volvo race boats back from the Med via the Canaries. He should be back here to visit in a few weeks." The card was from Tenerife, he said, with a photo of green mountains but, he added, no canaries.

I'd yet to hear Zale refer to my brother as his dad. He seemed to think of him more as a cool uncle—and that was all right with Pit, too. Nobody was putting pressure on the wayward windsurfer and itinerant sailing crew member to change his ways. Still, I'd seen more of Pit in the last year than I had in the previous three.

"Did you show the postcard to Grams? I'm sure she'd like to see it, too."

B.J. slid onto the seat when Zale left, and Abaco put her head on the space where our thighs touched. He reached down to scratch her head, then slid his hand over and petted my leg right along with the dog. I cleared my throat. "I see you missed my dog almost as much as me."

"I'm happy to be of service to the females in the Sullivan household," he said. His hand abandoned Abaco and slid to the inside of my thigh.

Abaco whined softly and looked up at him with the eyes of a jealous woman. I reached for her ear and scratched her. "It's okay, girl," I said. "There's enough of him to go around. I think." I gave her a rough rub on her neck and then noticed something. "Hey, where's her collar?"

"I took it off inside while you were talking to your grandmother and Molly. Your dog was so happy to be home, she'd decided to roll in something foul out in the yard. I had to clean her up a bit. She reeked." His hand moved up my thigh, and I was determined not to show any reaction.

"Aw. You gave my dog a sponge bath. You are a handy guy to have around."

"I aim to please," he said and his hand took more precise aim, causing me to collapse into a coughing fit from inhaling a piece of fish.

Molly then monopolized B.J. and Catalina with talk about the baby while we ate. It seemed to me that all pregnant people ever talk about is babies, and I was sick of it. I did my best to tune them out once we all sat back full and tired, and the kids took off for one last round of capture the flag: the twins against Zale and Abaco. I was contemplating joining them when I remembered something from the Key West trip.

"Hey, Molly, guess who I ran into in Key West?"

"Ah, don't make me guess. Tell me."

"Here's a hint. His nickname in high school was Glub."

"Not Ben?"

"Yup. And you would never recognize him."

"What do you mean?"

"No glasses, no braces, and not an ounce of fat on his hot body."

"You're joking."

"I'm not. I swear. It was his voice and his eyes in this strange but very hot body. He's captain of a schooner that does day charters down there. It was so weird how we just ran into each other on the dock."

"Life is full of odd coincidences like that. He always had a thing for you, you know."

"Ben?"

"Yeah. Big time."

I turned to see if B.J. was listening. He had his back to me as he talked to Cat.

"Well, if I'd known back then that he'd turn out like this, I might have been a little more interested myself."

Molly laughed. "I can't imagine Ben Baker as a hot bod! I always thought he'd wind up a nerdy scientist."

"Oh, and that reminds me, I also saw Arlen Sparks down there. Have you heard about his wife?"

It turned out that Molly did know and had been taking food over to help out, but most of the neighbors now felt that what they needed most of all was live-in help. I told Molly about Arlen losing his job and his benefits; that was something she didn't know.

"He still gets up and leaves each day as though he's going to work." Molly said. "I wonder where he goes? He shouldn't be leaving her alone."

The subject that had been hanging over the meal, quiet and unspoken, was the death of Catalina's husband. We were all thinking about it, but my friends didn't know Cat well enough yet and they weren't the kind of people who mumbled empty platitudes. I needn't have worried, though: Cat brought it up herself. When the conversation lagged, she turned to me and said, "I thank you for making me so welcome here at your home and among your friends. You are like a big family. Nestor would have liked this. He always wanted a big family."

Molly draped her arm over Catalina's shoulders and told her again that she would not be raising her child alone—that we would all be there like a great crowd of doting aunties and uncles. Then Jeannie chimed in with her offers to help in any way, and B.J. reached over and took Cat's hand.

It's always the sympathy that gets to you. Catalina's face started to crumple and her eyes shone with tears. "Seychelle, I don't want to be a burden on you. I have the room at the crew house and the rent is paid through January. If I can ask one more favor, can you take me there tonight?"

"No way. Not tonight. We're both too tired. You stay here with me tonight, get some sleep. I'll take you over there tomorrow."

"These two days on the boat, I have been wondering about the future for me and my baby. I don't even know if I will be allowed to stay in this country now that I am no longer the wife of an American."

"Jeannie here might be able to help you." I stood up and pulled Jeannie to her feet from the redwood deck chair she'd been sitting in. I dragged her closer to Cat. "I'll leave you two alone while I go inside to help B.J. with the dishes."

B.J. looked startled for a minute, then jumped up and joined me in collecting armfuls of dirty plates and heading for the kitchen. Once we were safely inside, I dumped the dishes on the counter and collapsed on the couch. B.J. began running water in the sink.

"You don't really have to do those now. I just needed to escape before I invited her to move in with me."

"Yes, that would have been terrible."

I sat up and looked at him. He was standing at the sink, his back to me, running the hot water, his shoulder-length black hair held back in a ponytail with a leather thong. He was wearing a long-sleeved white T-shirt and khaki cargo pants. The pants fit nice and snug on his butt. The sight made me think about Ben Baker, and I wondered what in the world I'd been thinking when I'd contemplated bedding Ben. I enjoyed the sight for several more seconds before I said, "B.J. Moana, are you making fun of me?"

He turned and smiled at me without showing any teeth, his lush lips pressed together tight. "You are perceptive." He went back to his soapy water.

"You of all people know that I can't stand to have someone living with me."

"Indeed," he said into the sink without even turning around.

"And being around someone who's pregnant and always talking about babies is just a little more than I can take."

"Clearly."

"She doesn't know if they're even going to allow her to stay in the United States at this point. But the worst thing of all is that she wants me to help her by looking into Nestor's accident and at this point, frankly, I don't want to get involved. I haven't got the time. I mean, I might be about to lose my own career here. I have my own lawsuit to worry about."

"That's right."

"Dammit, B.J., I hate it when you agree with me all the time."

"I know."

I rolled my eyes at his backside. "So what do you want me to do?"

At that moment Jeannie came strolling through the open front door, and she caught my last question. "Man, how do you do it? She's cranky as all get-out to the rest of us, won't even offer aid to a poor pregnant widow, and you, she's asking you what in the world she can do for you."

"Jeannie, that's not fair," I said. "She's staying here with me tonight. And I've been with her through all this in Key West. But for Pete's sake, where does it end?"

"Why don't you ask her?"

I couldn't say anything to that. I knew that it wouldn't ever end for Catalina. Losing a loved one to an unnatural death is something from which you don't ever quite recover. Both my parents were now dead. Red, my father, died from complications from melanoma, and though he hadn't yet made it to that average life span the insurance guys now have on their actuarial tables, he had died from something brought on by nature. My mother, however, died at the hand of a human being, even if that hand was her own. It wasn't some omnipotent natural force that had reached out for her. She chose to walk out into the sea that day, and I had blown my chance to stop her. That kind of thing never ends.

"What I didn't say in my phone message to B.J. is that she's convinced somebody killed Nestor and tried to make it look like an accident."

"Why?" Jeannie asked.

"Nestor thought that the initial wreck of the *Power Play* was suspicious. He was running on instruments, and according to him the instruments malfunctioned. He thought somebody had monkeyed with them. He claimed Ted Berger was having financial difficulties, which could have been improved with a little insurance money. Nestor had been talking about trying to get someone to come look at the boat to prove the instruments had been tampered with, and it's possible Berger overheard him."

B.J. walked over, drying his hands on a dish towel, and sat next to me on the couch. "That's not much in the way of evidence. It's normal for her to want to lash out, to blame someone besides her husband."

"There's more. Catalina knows more about windsurfing than I do, and she claims that the placement of the body was suspicious. She says if he had been thrown into the mast and knocked unconscious, he wouldn't have ended up lying on top of the sail with some of the rigging lines actually wrapped around one wrist. She says it reeked of a setup. She wanted the cops to look more closely at the head wound but before we could convince them to run those tests, Berger paid to have the body cremated."

"How could he do that?" Jeannie asked.

"Well, Cat told the cops she couldn't afford to deal with the body right away. Next thing she knew, Berger had stepped in saying he would take care of it as a kindness to the widow of his former employee. They took him up on it. I guess the city of Key West thought they were going to get stuck with the tab for burying him in a pauper's grave and they grabbed at Berger's offer."

"She should sue them."

"It won't give her another chance to get at the evidence. It's gone. Nestor's ashes are out in *Gorda*'s wheelhouse."

"Poor kid," Jeannie said.

"Yeah, I know. But don't say that to her. She's one brave woman. You should have seen her chewing out those Key West cops and those poor folks at that funeral home. She's in her last month with that baby and she is determined to snoop around and find out what happened to her husband. Then she went and talked to this reporter and was quoted in the paper saying that there were suspicious circumstances surrounding her husband's death. The next day a truck almost ran her down on the streets of Key West." I lifted the long sleeves of my T-shirt to show the scabs on my arms. "If I hadn't pulled her clear, she and her baby would have been roadkill. She's going to get both of them killed if we don't stop her."

"We?" She shook her head. "So how do you intend to do that?"

"I guess I've got to give her what she's been asking for since the day he was killed. I've got to promise her I'll ask around for her."

B.J. kissed me on the cheek. "What took you so long?"

XIV

THE next morning Catalina was still under the covers of my hide-a-bed when I came stumbling out of the bedroom in the size XXL T-shirt I wore as a nightgown. I'd reluctantly sent B.J. off to drive Grams home the night before, knowing that Catalina didn't need anything else to make her feel awkward and alone. My cottage was just too small to afford any kind of privacy when I had visitors. I opened the front door to let Abaco out then filled my teakettle, set it on the burner, opened the refrigerator, and stared at the mostly empty interior. Unless I could figure out a way to make breakfast out of soy sauce and sweet pickle relish, we'd better figure on eating out. I closed the door and started rummaging for some coffee for me and herb tea for the pregnant lady. The coffee I had, the tea B.J. had left for mornings he woke up here.

With a steaming mug in each hand, I sat on the edge of the bed. "Good morning."

She pulled the covers off her head, saw the tea, and struggled to roll up into a sitting position. "Thank you," she said when I handed her the mug.

"You know, you could just about use that belly of yours as a TV tray."

Her lips turned up in one corner.

"You sleep okay?"

She took a quick sip of the hot fluid and nodded.

"Now I know you're lying. I've slept on this damn thing before, or tried to. There's some kind of bar running right down the middle, and the mattress is only a couple of inches thick."

"It was okay. The bed would not have mattered. I cannot turn off my mind."

"Yeah, I know what you mean."

"It was not an accident, Seychelle. I do not know how I will do it, but I will find the proof that my husband was killed."

"Catalina, you aren't one person anymore. Look at you. You can't go running around chasing after supposed killers."

She put down her mug and heaved her body upright. She crossed barefoot to the window and looked out at the sun-filled yard. She was wearing one of my night T-shirts, the cotton fabric stretched tight around her belly. Her navel made a small bump like the stem on a fat tomato. "I used to look out at the world and see *esperanza,* hope. I do not want to raise my child in a world where a man is killed and no one cares."

"That's not true. I care."

"You care that he is dead, but you do not even believe that he was killed."

I nodded. "True, I can't go that far, not yet." Cat opened her mouth to disagree and I held up my hand. "*But* I agree with you that something is wrong. I'm afraid, though, that it might be something even bigger than Ted Berger."

"I think you are wrong," she said, crossing her arms over her breasts.

"Geez, Cat. I didn't think I'd ever meet anybody who was just as stubborn and hardheaded as me. I was wrong. I thought you'd be happy about me volunteering to help you. Listen. I'll take a look at Berger, but you've got to promise me that you won't do anything on your own. I want you to stay home, rest, and keep that kid healthy."

She came over to where I was sitting on the bed and took my hand in both of hers. "Thank you. Really. I appreciate your help and your hospitality. Tonight, though, I will not bother you anymore. I will go back to the crew house."

"You keep acting like that's a solution for you, Catalina, but the last day of the month is only two days off. I've been thinking about where you might go, and I've got an idea. This just might work out for you and for an old friend of mine. You're a nurse, right?"

I pulled my 1972 Jeep onto the swale in front of the Sparkses' house on my old street. An old boyfriend had nicknamed my ride Lightnin', in reference to her speed, or lack of it, but even though she was working on her second hundred thousand miles on her second engine, she started when I turned the key; that was all I asked of my vehicle. I'd owned her for almost ten years, since my days as a lifeguard on Fort Lauderdale Beach, and some owner before me had stuck a plastic Jesus statue on the dash that had watched over me all these years. Since my relationship with religion was something along the lines of *Don't ask, don't tell,* I wasn't going to credit J. C. with keeping my car running, but I wasn't about to remove him, either.

Ever since I'd reconnected with Molly last year, I'd been spending more time in Shady Banks, my old neighborhood, but I hadn't noticed before how run-down the Sparkses' yard looked. Gardening had been her thing and their house was usually the showpiece of the block, but now weeds grew in the flower beds and the bushes were ragged with long tendrils of new growth.

Catalina and I had gone to Lester's Diner for breakfast, then I'd dropped her off at the crew house with a promise to come back and bring her up to date on my plans. After that, I'd stopped at a bakery for a cake. It was now approaching eleven o'clock, and I assumed this was an hour I could go calling on a Sunday morning.

I would not have thought Arlen could look worse than he had in Key West, but when he opened the door the bags under his eyes were the size of walnuts and his hair hung long on one side of his head—he hadn't even bothered to comb it over. His pants and shirt looked so wrinkled, he might have slept in them. "Hi," I said. "I just thought I'd stop by to see how your wife is doing. Is there any chance she's feeling like a visitor?"

"Come in," he said, stepping back and ushering me into their living room.

"I brought a cake for Mrs. Sparks. I remember how she always used to bake for us, and well, I don't bake, but I can buy."

He stood in the middle of the living room staring at my bakery box. His face was blank. It was like he was trying to process what it was.

"Mr. Sparks? Your wife. May I go see her?"

His eyes slid up to my face, but he didn't say anything.

"Your wife? Mrs. Sparks?"

He still didn't say a word. He just turned and walked down the hall that was off to the right of the front door. He stopped outside an open door and waved me in.

She was sitting up in one of those hospital beds that you can rent and bring into your home. People didn't usually do that unless their loved ones were not expected to get out of those beds. She looked tiny, like a little paper doll in a big white envelope. Her eyes were closed, and thin black wires trailed out of her ears. At first, I thought they might be some kind of medical paraphernalia, but then Arlen went to the bed and touched her shoulder and her eyes popped open. She reached up and pulled the ear buds out of her ears.

"Oh my goodness. Seychelle!" She fumbled in the covers on the bed and lifted up a small box. It was a cassette player. She pushed a button on the machine and it made a loud clack in the otherwise quiet room. Her voice had been little more than a whisper.

"Hi, Mrs. Sparks. I brought you a cake." Next to her bed was a long narrow table on wheels just like they have in hospitals; I set the box on the end. "It's angel food, just like you used to bake for us."

It was the strangest thing I thought of when I got closer to her. Under her eyes were hollows the same size as the bags under her husband's eyes, and I wondered if they could fit together when they kissed. It was a stupid thing to think, because it was pretty obvious there hadn't been much kissing in this house for a while. She wore a red scarf on her head, and the bright color made her skin look the color of dried putty.

"Thank you, dear."

"What were you listening to?"

"I can't read much anymore. My eyes tire too quickly. I listen to books now on audio."

I smiled at her. "Should have known you wouldn't be in here watching the soaps."

"No, I'm listening to *Treasure Island*. I've always loved that story."

"It's good to know some things don't change, Mrs. Sparks."

"You don't think I've changed?" she asked, the surprise evident in her voice.

"Sure, you look different. I expected that. But you still act the same and, as usual, that's what puts a smile on other people's faces."

"I'm going to take that as a compliment."

"Good, because I meant it as one. You know, I'm sorry I haven't been by before now, but I didn't know you were sick."

"Well, now, why would you? You haven't lived here in years."

"But I should have been checking up on you. I'm sorry."

"Dear, we old folks expect the young ones to grow up and move away." Her eyes closed, and she sighed. "There's nothing wrong with that."

"But I only moved a few miles away and I feel bad. I mean, you were like a mom sometimes when I didn't have one, and I should have been like a daughter when you needed one."

It occurred to me then how capricious nature was—bestowing motherhood on those like the women in my family who make lousy mothers, and denying children to a woman like Sarah Sparks.

She shook her head and opened her eyes. It seemed to require a great deal of effort. "Seychelle, you were always so hard on yourself. You didn't owe me anything. You children gave me more pleasure—"

She didn't finish the sentence. Her breathing was slow and regular. She was asleep. I straightened the covers and set the cassette recorder on her table. "Likewise, Mrs. Sparks," I whispered.

I found Arlen in the kitchen fixing himself a roast beef sandwich. He asked me if I wanted one, and then without asking he poured us both glasses of a dark Cabernet. He put the bottle on the table, too.

"She's got this morphine pump," he said. "When it kicks in it knocks her right out. She'll just drop off in midsentence. The cancer's in her liver now."

"It must be really hard taking care of her. You look exhausted."

"I should have taken them to court." He reached for the wine bottle and refilled his glass.

"Who?"

"Motowave. It's all their fault."

"What do you mean?"

"When they canned me, I got depressed and there I was moping around, feeling sorry for myself. I didn't pay any attention to the fact that my wife was sick again. We didn't get her to the doctors quick enough because she was trying to take care of me."

"That doesn't sound like the best logic."

"She wouldn't be like this if it wasn't for them. The bastards—" It sounded like he'd been about to say something more about Motowave, but when he spoke again, the anger was gone and his voice was flat. "I can't stand just sitting here watching her die."

He drank off the rest of his second glass and reached for the bottle again. He hadn't touched his sandwich yet.

"Arlen, why don't you eat your sandwich? I want to tell you about an idea I have."

He took a bite and chewed with his mouth half open. "Okay. What is it?"

"I have a friend who is a nurse and she needs a place to stay. You have a three-bedroom house and you really could use some live-in help for your wife. You'd really like this woman, and I know your wife would love her."

By the time I left, I had settled Arlen into his recliner to sleep off his lunch and Catalina had a place to stay.

I stopped by Sailorman on my way to Jeannie's, to see if they had a manual for my little Nissan outboard. When

I walked into the store, I ran into Tia from Offshore Marine Towing standing in line at the register.

"Hey, Seychelle. I've been trying to get hold of you. You haven't been answering your phone or the radio."

"I've been out of town. Just brought the *Power Play* up from Key West."

She shook her head. "I heard about Nestor. That was awful. I didn't know you were down there."

"Yeah." There wasn't anything else to say about it. Certainly not anything that I wanted spread around as gossip.

"The reason I was trying to reach you is that there is something happening tomorrow I wanted you to know about."

"What?"

"The Marine Industries Association is sponsoring a symposium on maritime salvage laws over at the International Game Fish Association headquarters. Starts at three. Think you can make it?"

"Tia," I said drawing her name out into a long whine, "that sounds like something for the big corporate boys. I'm just a small business. I fall asleep when I go to business meetings."

"Sey, this is for everybody. You've seen it. You know how our business has been growing. Not everybody who's been jumping in lately knows the business like you do."

"What you mean is, it's a symposium on piracy."

The woman who was ringing up Tia's purchase at the register laughed out loud. Tia frowned at her and then continued. "I didn't say that. It's just that some operators in our business seem to be having trouble lately with the difference between what constitutes a tow and what's salvage. We thought we'd bring in a maritime attorney, a representative from the Coast Guard, and then get all the towboat companies together and maybe we'll be able to police our own industry."

"That does sound interesting."

"So I can count on you, then? You'll be there?"

"I guess. But don't expect me to get up and talk. I'm just coming to listen."

XV

I CUPPED my hands on either side of my face and pressed against Jeannie's front screen door, trying to see into the dark recesses of her apartment.

"Hello! Anybody home?"

I knew better than to try to open the door. Jeannie had an alarm system on all her doors and windows, and I'd set it off more than once by just strolling into her place. I was standing on the landing at the top of the outside staircase hollering when I heard a dog barking behind me, and I turned to see Jeannie being pulled down the street by an enthusiastic and overweight beagle. She let go of his leash, and he beat her to the top of the stairs. As she climbed, she explained between breaths, "The boys talked me into dog-sitting this weekend while the folks who live downstairs are off on a cruise."

She arrived on the landing and stopped to catch her breath. The dog was whining and scratching at the screen door. "You can let him in," she said. "The alarm's not armed."

"Why aren't the boys walking the dog?" I asked as we made our way into her kitchen.

"It's a Sunday afternoon and the two of them vanished right after lunch. They're probably over at their friend Jason's house. The excitement of having a dog pales when a friend invites you over to play with the latest video game. So what brings you over here this afternoon?" She motioned for me to sit at the kitchen table. It was piled high with folders and stacks of papers. A laptop computer and printer were set up on the far side, and Jeannie sat in the rolling office chair located on that side of the table.

Lawyers are often characterized as money-grubbing scumbags; Jeannie was anything but. I admired the way she worked, doing just enough to keep their standard of living comfortable but never so much that she couldn't be home when her boys needed her. Jeannie always valued quality over quantity, and she sailed through life doing the things that made her happy. Housework was not one of those things.

"I didn't want to bring up our *Seas the Day* friend at the barbecue last night, but I do want to know what the status is."

"Not a whole lot has changed. Except for the fact that we now have a court date. It's this coming Thursday."

"Jeannie, I couldn't sleep last night thinking about this. I mean, what if that girl had drowned? Maybe there was something else I should have done when I agreed to tow him in. I shouldn't have let them stay on their boat. I was towing, bottom line is, it was my fault."

"Girl, watch your mouth. Don't ever let me hear you say that again. Your fault, my ass—and that, my dear, is making a big statement."

"Jesus, Jeannie," I said, but she did know how to make me laugh.

"This Burke character has a history that goes way back. I'll bet if you had asked him to get aboard *Gorda*, he would have refused. He needed to be aboard his little boat to open a valve and let her sink."

"I don't know. It's possible he didn't do anything. It

was really rough out there. I should have known better than to leave them on the boat. I was in charge."

"Seychelle, in the last two years the man has been in five automobile accidents and he's sued companies three times for product liability. Then there's the McDonald's case that's still pending. Seems he has a cousin who's an attorney and they're in cahoots. Doesn't cost him anything to bring these suits and with you, he thinks he's hit the jackpot."

"But I told you to talk to him. To tell him I don't have that kind of money."

"Seychelle, you talk as though you think this is a rational man. This man almost let his daughter drown so he could get some money out of you."

"Okay. You've got a point. But I need to know what's going on. What's the deal? Am I in danger of losing this lawsuit? Like I said, I couldn't sleep last night. All I kept thinking about is what could have happened out there, and then what could happen now if I lose and I owe this guy millions of dollars."

"That's what you have insurance for. Even if you were to lose, and it's not likely, you'd come out of it okay."

"I don't think so. Not if I got branded negligent. It would kill my business. Nobody'd hire me after that."

"Listen, we're not going to let it happen. In the next few days, we need to put together a case that proves this guy is a scam artist. Right now, he's claiming that he can't go back to work because he's suffering from post-traumatic stress disorder."

"You're joking."

"Nope. I told you the man is no brain surgeon."

"I wish I'd never answered his goddamn distress call. I should have known better."

"Honey, everyone who knows you knows that you can't walk away from someone in trouble. You might try to talk tough, you might say you're going to look the other way, but it's just not in your makeup."

"Maybe not forever, though. I really am tired of this. I keep saying it and nobody seems to be listening. *Gorda* and I are not married. Let's get through this lawsuit, and then I'm going to make a decision."

"Okay. I'll get the proof that he has shown a pattern of making fraudulent claims like the one against Mc-Donald's. You need to take a look at his police statement here"—she picked up a photocopied document and set it on the table in front of me—"and find the places where he has lied. You need to find people who will swear that his boat didn't have all that expensive gear on it, that he lied when he took out his boat insurance." She dropped a sheet of notebook paper on top of his statement. "This is where he lives." She reached into a file cabinet next to her chair, drew out a small camera, and set it on top of the pile. "Finally, this is a digital camera. If you could get me some photos of our dirtbag friend doing something that proves he is not disabled from post-traumatic stress, it would go a long ways toward convincing him that he wants to drop the lawsuit."

"Okay, I can do that. It's going to make me feel better doing something." I put the camera and folded papers into my shoulder bag. "In the meantime, I thought you'd like to know that I found a place for Catalina to stay for a while. Remember last night when Molly and I were talking about the people named Sparks who live on our old street? I went over there this morning, and the wife needs a live-in nurse. Catalina's a nurse, but she's not licensed to practice here, so she can't go out and look for a job. They get a nurse and Cat gets a place to live and a job. Pretty good, eh?"

"Yeah. Now what's the real story about Nestor? What happened down there?"

I started at the beginning and filled Jeannie in on the whole story, from the wreck of the *Power Play* to everything that had happened afterward. "This morning, I promised Catalina I would talk to Ted Berger for her, but I swear I don't know what to say to the man."

"Why don't you start by asking him when he's going to pay you for the job you just did for him?"

"Hey, that's good. Then I suppose I can segue right into, *By the way, did you kill Nestor Frias?*"

"It's not like this is the first time you've tried to get someone to talk to you. Just get a feel for the man. You know that he lied to you about where he was that afternoon. Try to get him to talk about that."

"I know. It's just that it seems to me that the incident with the *Power Play* is really only part of a bigger picture. I've never known so many high-priced yachts to go aground and need salvage as we've seen in the past few months. And it seems I'm not the only one who has noticed." I told Jeannie about my conversation with Tia at Sailorman. "You know those old stories about the days of the wreckers, back in the nineteenth century? I can't help but wonder, is it possible someone is causing these wrecks today?"

"Now, that's an interesting concept, Seychelle. But it doesn't rule out Berger's involvement. This could all be some kind of insurance scam."

I looked at my watch and was surprised to see it was already nearly three o'clock. "Look, Jeannie, I've got to go. I promised Catalina I would get back to her today, and now I need to get her over to the Sparkses' place."

"Okay, but before you go, there's one more thing. About your insurance. I tried, honey, but you are not going to find any better rates out there. You're going to have to live with this increase. With the hurricane seasons we've been having lately and the current stats on the number of boats that are getting into accidents, you're not going to find anything cheaper. I'm afraid that's just the cost of doing business these days."

"And maybe it's one more reason for me to get out of this business one day real soon."

IT took less than an hour to load Catalina's possessions into my Jeep. There was her suitcase, Nestor's duffel, and an old-fashioned trunk that contained books and photo albums as well as Cat's wedding dress. One of the young guys staying at the house helped me hoist her gear into the back of the vehicle. As we climbed into the front seats, I asked her if she had other things at her family home back in the Dominican Republic, and she shook her head. She told me that her parents were both dead, that she and Nestor had had that in common.

"And now my child will have no grandparents and only one parent."

I didn't know how to respond to that. I knew life wasn't easy for single mothers. Jeannie was sacrificing any hope of a ladder-climbing professional life to stay home and be with her boys. Another friend of mine, Celeste, had been willing to risk her life for her daughter, Solange. Mothering was a talent. There had been a time once when I had contemplated it. Long before I met B.J., back when I was younger and I made a mistake. Before I'd realized it was a talent that didn't run in my family.

"Cat, remember when you said that my friends and I are like a big family?"

"Yes, I remember."

"As far as I'm concerned, you and your baby are now part of that family."

* * *

WHEN we turned down my old street, I saw B.J.'s black El Camino truck parked in front of Molly's house. I beeped my horn and when Molly came to the door, I told her that I was taking Catalina to the Sparkses' house; she should get B.J. to come haul her stuff inside. The Sparkses' house was only two doors down from Molly's, and by the time I had opened Catalina's door and she had swung her legs out into the air, B.J. was there to offer her an arm and help her out of the high vehicle.

Arlen answered the door and while he showed B.J. where to put Catalina's things, Molly and I took her in to introduce her to Sarah Sparks. I could see immediately that I had been right. They meshed from the moment Sarah took her hand and expressed her profound sorrow over Nestor's death. She didn't talk in euphemisms; she meant what she said. After a little while, Molly and I just backed out of the room. Catalina had found a home.

I drove Lightnin' half a block up the street and parked in front of Molly's. When I stepped through her screen door, the living room looked like it had been decorated with photos taken from a gynecologist's examining room. Fetuses in various stages of development were on display, along with photos of instruments that must have come straight out of a torture chamber. B.J. was sitting cross-legged on the floor, leaning back against the couch, tapping the keys of a silver laptop computer that was set up on the coffee table. His face shone bright with excitement. I focused on him and tried to shut out any recognition of the pictures that littered the room.

B.J. would always be a student, no matter what his age. He already had a couple of degrees in classical studies or some damn thing, he had a black belt in aikido, and his last interest had been computers. He'd gotten this MacBook about six months ago and gone crazy talking about digital this and Internet that. While I did own an old laptop, I only used it for keeping the books for my business—like a slightly fancier adding machine.

"Hey," he said without looking up. "We've just started a new online course called Antepartum: Embryology and Fetology. Molly's got wireless so I can download all the photos we need right here."

Molly's long black hair was piled on top of her head and held in place with an enormous plastic clip that made her look a little like she had devil horns. She sat on the couch, and I couldn't help but notice that her left leg was touching B.J.'s body from knee to ankle. She held up a color photo of a fetus. "See?"

The sight of the photo struck at me like a hot iron in my gut. Closing my eyes, I fought down the memory and the nausea. "Geez," I said. I held my hand out in front of me. "Stop right there. I can't take it. You know that. If you want me, I'll be in the kitchen." I walked straight through the living room.

I found my nephew standing in front of the refrigerator staring at the contents. I pointed a finger over my shoulder in the direction of the living room. "Is it always like that around here?"

"Pretty much," he said without moving from his spot in front of the door.

"Doesn't it gross you out? I just can't understand what they think they're doing. Do you get it?" I asked, looking over his shoulder, hoping to find something to snack on. He didn't answer my question. We stood side by side staring at the little plastic tubs of sprouts and hummus, packages of some very dense-looking, dark bread, and

Baggies filled with an assortment of fruits and vegetables. "This is pitiful. Zale, you are seriously junk-food-deprived."

"You've got that right."

"Maybe we should freak out your mom and order a meat lover's pizza."

"Naw, I think they're doing some stir-fry thing tonight. It's not too bad."

They this, they that. I'd thought I was past being jealous of Molly in a lover's sense. But now she and B.J. had entered into this buddy phase. They were always studying together, cooking together, hanging out together. Was I being naïve to think it meant nothing?

"Zale, I just don't know about you. You actually eat their cooking? All this healthy food just might stunt your growth."

He looked over his shoulder at me and screwed up one side of his face into an ugly grimace. "I just want to be a real boy," he said in a goofy falsetto, then he grabbed two apples out of the crisper bin, tossed me one, and strolled out of the kitchen, his long legs taking him around the corner in an instant. I tried to reach him to pinch his ear, but he was too quick for me.

In the year since I'd first met Zale, he had grown nearly three inches in height. Now, as a fourteen-year-old, his voice was starting to change and he seemed to be all arms and legs, but he had a confidence and a sense of humor that made him seem much more mature than other teens his age. Pit and Zale had both shown a love of sailing early on, but for Pit it had started with surfing and then windsurfing. For Zale, it was competitive dinghy sailing, and he took it all much more seriously than my brother ever had. Qualifying for the Laser National Championship series up in North Carolina might have had something to do with that, too.

I took my apple and went out to Molly's screened-in back porch. A flock of wild parrots was circling overhead, screeching and squawking, sounding like a chorus of squeaky hinges. A gray squirrel was playing hide-and-seek with me, peering first around one side of the trunk of the huge oak tree, then disappearing and popping up on the other side a few seconds later. The late-afternoon sunlight was casting a golden aura over the scene, making Molly's backyard look like a magical place from a fairy tale.

When we'd first moved to this neighborhood here in Shady Banks, my family and Molly's used to enjoy summer-evening cookouts in this backyard. It was mostly families that consisted of parents and children who lived in the modest sixty-year-old cinder-block houses on the street. Molly's family sometimes included her Gramma Josie, but in the Sullivan household, we'd been told all our grandparents were dead.

I'd learned recently that it had been my grandmother Faith who had worked behind the scenes to find the waterfront house my family lived in and make sure it was available at a price my parents could afford. My mother, Annie, never knew. She wouldn't have accepted help from her mother. They'd argued when she'd married Red and never spoken again, and of course once my mother died it was too late for Grams to apologize to Red. So we three kids grew up thinking our grandparents were all dead—until last year.

I was slowly getting to know Faith Wheeler. Even now, after almost a year, I was still working on getting comfortable with the way my family had grown. My brother Pit was trying to transition from friendly uncle to father, while I was spending one night a week eating dinner at my grandmother's house. And I was learning about the family's long line of mothers who had pretty much struck out in the mothering department. There wasn't a reason in the world to think I'd be any different.

I liked the extended family I had now—Grams, Zale, my brothers, Molly, Jeannie, B.J. And I didn't have to give birth to have this family.

I heard footfalls behind me and then felt fingertips slide over my shoulders, his firm belly pressed against the back of my head. He kneaded the muscles on either side of my neck, and though I know it should have made me feel more relaxed, given my current circumstances, it made every little nerve ending in my body start screaming for sex. It was as though every place where his body touched mine, pure heat flowed from him. He bent down and kissed my ear, and I bolted out of the chair.

"Jesus, B.J., unless you think it's a good idea to tear our clothes off right here, you'd better slow down and—" When I turned around he was laughing.

"You are funny, Sullivan."

"I hate it when you laugh at me."

"I know. Do you want to talk about what's bothering you?" He was leaning against one of the frames that supported the screened-in porch. I noticed the light dusting of black hairs on his forearms, the clean white half-moons on his fingernails, the promise of strength in the breadth of his chest. At that moment, talking wasn't really what I wanted to do with the man. I wanted to be the one sitting on the couch with him, snuggling, not Molly.

"No."

"Why not? You don't think I'll understand?"

"No, that's not it. You always understand. You understand too much sometimes. Let me keep some secrets."

"Okay. No secret talk, just business. Remember when

you asked me a couple of weeks ago to help you with a tow this week?"

"Yeah. Wednesday, I need a deckhand for that sailboat."

"This new class Molly and I are starting. We're supposed to go to a meeting Wednesday morning. I'll still go if you need me, but it would be better for me if you could find somebody else."

"Don't worry about it. I'll find somebody. Go to your birthing babies thing."

"Thanks." He turned to go inside.

"B.J.," I called out, and he turned back to face me from the doorway. "I don't really understand what's going on with you and Molly. What's this midwife thing really all about?"

"She asked me to take these classes with her and I said yes."

"But why?"

He sighed and looked out into the backyard. "For me, it's about karma. Every spiritual view has in its moral code something similar to the First Commandment or Buddha's First Precept—'I undertake to abstain from killing living beings.' There was a time when I was in my teens, back in LA, when I didn't live by that code. I had some bad friends back then and I hurt some people. Some of my actions generated a boatload of bad karma. If by helping Molly and by learning to ease life into this world I can generate a bit of good karma, then that's the right path for me." He turned to me and smiled. "This isn't making much sense to you, is it?"

"I'm trying to understand. In all the time we've been together, I never knew that you had a stage when you were a bad kid. How bad is bad?" I looked at the size of him, how he filled the doorway to the kitchen. "You didn't kill anybody, did you?" I said it half jokingly, but he didn't smile.

"No, but I learned how. I trained and I did hurt people. The guys I hung out with were all Asians, and we were into martial arts. I guess, in a way, we were a gang. We didn't have a name, but we could do more damage with our hands than some guys did with knives. I don't like to think about those days. I continue to practice aikido for the spiritual quality of the art, not the martial side. I do my woodworking on boats and now I'm doing this with a friend—studying to deliver babies. Because she asked me to. Because she needs me."

"And you don't think I need you?"

He laughed. "You need me for something else. Not for babies. Not now. But here, now, I have a chance to be a part of this giving of life and I'm enjoying it."

I wanted to understand him, but I knew that this was about more than karma. "Do you really want a baby of your own that much?"

He paused before he spoke, and his eyes answered my question. "Yes, I do."

"And it's okay with you that I really don't?"

"Yeah," he said. He turned around and then called back over his shoulder, "For now it is," as he walked back through the kitchen to join Molly in the living room.

IT was dark when I pulled into the drive at the Larsens' place, and when I turned off the engine, I just sat for a while in the front seat of the Jeep. I could hear Abaco whining on the other side of the gate. She recognized the roar of Lightnin's engine and she didn't understand why I wasn't moving. I didn't, either.

The night could have ended differently, more like I had originally planned. I could have had B.J. follow me home to share my bed. But I wanted to be his first choice, not the person whose needs could be met after Molly's. I had pushed him away all evening, and with B.J. being who he was, he didn't miss the signals. He didn't say anything except good night when I decided to go.

I slammed my open palms on the steering wheel. "Dammit."

Catalina and her swollen belly, Molly and her midwifery, B.J. and his baby dreams. I was surrounded by reminders. Childbirth might be normal and natural to 99 percent of the population, but not to me. I couldn't handle it. Motherhood. Ha! Some people were born with certain genetic defects. I was born maternity-impaired. You only had to look at my history.

Abaco danced her wiggling doggyjoy dance down the walkway in front of me as I made my way back to my cottage. It wasn't until I opened the front door and turned on the light switch that I became aware of an impression that I'd been feeling all the way down the walkway. Something was wrong.

At first, I couldn't put my finger on it. I stood frozen in the doorway looking around the cottage trying to see what was out of place. Abaco sat down in the center of the room, cocked her head, and looked at me as though asking me what was up.

"I don't know, girl. There's something—" I stepped over to her and reached down to scratch her ear. I understood when I felt the leather under my fingers.

Abaco was wearing her collar.

Had B.J. come over while I was gone all day? Surely he would have said something at Molly's if he had. I walked out into the kitchen and looked around. The two mugs were upside down in the dish drainer. I hadn't washed them. Had Catalina done it this morning before we left? I couldn't remember. I crossed into my bedroom, flicked on the wall switch to turn on the bedside lamp, and Molly's stir-fry almost paid me another visit. I distinctly remembered leaving my covers in an unruly mound, but now the spread on my bed was pulled so smooth you could bounce a quarter on it.

XVI

THE offices of Berger Communications were located in the 110 Tower across from the courthouse in downtown Fort Lauderdale. Parking was always impossible around there, so Monday morning I was standing on the seawall lowering my Boston Whaler into the river when Perry Greene came by in his towboat *Little Bitt* pulling what looked like a forty-five-foot cruising sailboat.

"Morning, beautiful," he shouted over the roar of his engine. As usual his boat had black soot streaks down the sides and a heap of old lines and fenders and crap piled in the aft cockpit. It was getting to the point that Perry and I were almost the only one-boat owner-operators in the South Florida corporate world of towing and salvage. I wasn't thrilled to have anything in common with the fellow who, at that moment, stood up from the helmsman's seat and bent over to check on the clearance on the starboard side of his tow, flashing me with the sight of a good two inches of butt crack in the process.

The Whaler splashed into the water. I was reaching out to tie off the lines when I noticed that Perry had stepped away from the helm and turned his back on the forward progress of his vessel. He pointed first at himself, then at me, and then he started thrusting his hips forward and back, his hands balled up in fists, his tongue lolling out the corner of his mouth in what I assumed was his imitation of ecstasy.

I pursed my lips, attempted to raise one eyebrow, and pointed upriver. I laughed out loud when Perry turned around and saw that *Little Bitt* was lined up for a head-on collision with the *Carrie B.*, a 112-foot replica of a paddle wheeler bringing her first load of sightseers downriver. He nearly gave himself a hernia trying to get back to the helm to steer his boat out of the way of the *Carrie B.*'s broad bow, her laughing captain blowing the whistle as he passed.

Behind me Abaco whined, asking if she could go along on this river ride. "Not today, girl. I'll take you down to the beach for a swim later, okay?" She gave me a look that told me I'd been neglecting her.

The outboard started up at the first turn of the key, and I kept the boat speed slow to enjoy the beautiful winter morning—and to prevent any danger of catching up to Perry. I wondered if he had heard about the symposium that afternoon over at the fishing museum. Perry was more of a fringe player in the towing and salvage business, but he'd been around quite a few years now, and he had his customers who were loyal to his cut-rate prices.

I stifled a yawn and shook my head to try to clear the sleep from my brain. I hadn't slept well. With all I'd been through the last couple of years, I had installed new locks on the front door of the cottage as well as an inside chain. After checking all the windows and closing all the blinds, though, I still lay staring at the ceiling and listening much of the night. A stranger had been in my house, and that idea had shattered my ability to relax.

I tied the Whaler up to the seawall now in front of the Downtowner, my favorite riverfront restaurant and bar, and ran a lock and cable through a cleat. With the Broward

County Jail not more than a hundred yards away, the location tended to attract some interesting individuals, and I supported the concept of keeping honest people honest—and keeping the dishonest people the hell away.

The offices of Berger Communications occupied the entire ninth floor, so when I exited the elevator, I approached a receptionist seated at a low desk behind an enormous flower arrangement of orchids and bromeliads.

"May I help you?" she asked in a voice that suggested she could have had a career recording voice-overs for Disney.

"I'm here to see Ted Berger."

"Do you have an appointment?"

"No, but I'm sure if you tell him I'm here, he'll see me."

While the look on her face said she'd bet a month's salary against it, she said, "And your name is?"

She wrote it down on a lined notepad on her desk. "If you'll just take a seat. Mr. Berger is on the phone right now, but I will let him know you're here as soon as he's available."

I strolled over to the seating area intending to settle onto the couch, but stopped for a bit to look at the pictures on the wall behind the furniture. Ted himself was featured in every single photo. Many of them were team shots of women hockey players gathered around Ted, and in each one he wore a different garish, loud Hawaiian shirt.

"Your boss sure does seem to like photos of himself."

"Mr. Berger *is* Berger Communications."

"I see. So it's just marketing, not egomania?"

She laughed. "Well, maybe it's just a little of both."

She picked up the phone and spoke quietly into the handset. A few minutes later, the door behind her opened and Ted Berger came out wearing a shirt with blinding orange flowers, a color that surely had never appeared in nature.

"Come on into my office. I've only got a couple of minutes." He ushered me through the door into a huge modern office with windows that looked out across the treetops to the ocean beyond. His desk had three different computers, one laptop and two with large flat-screen monitors. He pointed to one of the chairs opposite his, and I sat on the buttery leather. "I want to thank you for getting the *Power Play* up here right on schedule. I wish the folks at the boatyard could move as fast. They're telling me a month, minimum."

"The yards here get pretty backed up at this time of year. I just thought I'd stop by and present you with this invoice." I reached into my shoulder bag and withdrew the envelope I had prepared that morning. I placed it on the blotter under one of the monitors. "I realize I could have just left it with your secretary out there, but I've had something on my mind and I wanted to ask you about it."

"What is it?"

"That afternoon down in Key West when you stopped by in your boat and asked me to help you in the search—" I paused, not exactly sure how to go about asking my question.

"Yeah, what about it?" He sat up straighter and ran a hand through his white hair.

Great. Now he was acting guilty. I figured it would be easy enough to ask him about the photos because I didn't really believe he killed Nestor. But here he was tapping a pen on his desk, clearing his throat, and acting like he wished I'd get the hell out of his office.

He stuck out his arm and looked at his watch. "As I told you, I don't have much time. What is it you wanted to speak to me about?"

"I have a friend. He has a charter schooner in Key West. He and I went out to dinner, and a friend brought over some photos from the Wreckers' Race. I was very surprised to see your yacht tender pulled up on the beach in a couple of the shots because you told me—"

"Ah, yes. That I had been out fishing Bluefish Channel."

"Right. And see, if you had been out at Sand Key during the race, even considering the speed you'd make with that big outboard, I just don't see how you could have been fishing out there barely half an hour after the race was over. And since Nestor's death was peculiar with him being a windsurfing champ and all, I just wanted to ask why you lied." There. I'd said it. I supposed there was the remotest chance that he did kill Nestor, but I felt certain he wouldn't hurt me there in his office with the secretary on the other side of the door.

"Have you ever been married, Seychelle?"

"What? No. But I don't see what that has to do with it."

"I'm married. We met when I was in college— actually, it was a community college. I couldn't afford the tuition at any better school. We've both changed a great deal since that time and, at this point, we really don't like each other very much. We stay together because neither of us wants to give a whole lot of money to the lawyers."

"I still don't see what this has to do with the Wreckers' Race."

"I met up with an old friend in the bar at the Pier House on Saturday night. She's from Copenhagen and after the pleasant evening we spent together, she invited me out to her boat Sunday afternoon. We went on a little excursion out to Sand Key, then retreated back to her boat in the anchorage when all the people from the Wreckers' Race flooded ashore. Logically, I know that you aren't likely to tell my wife about this, but lying has become a habit. One of the few things my wife and I still have in common."

"I didn't mean to pry."

"How can you say that? Of course you meant to pry. You had the gall to walk in here and ask me where I was that afternoon."

"What I meant was—"

"I know what you meant. You think there's something fishy about Nestor's death. You and that wife of his just can't face up to the fact that the guy was a screwup. I see it in her eyes when she looks at me. She thinks I had something to do with it. Would you tell her I was with a lady friend, that I can prove it, and she needs to move on? It was a tragic accident, but the guy just hit his head and drowned. There's no one to blame."

At that moment I wanted to be just about anywhere on earth but there. I stood. "I'm really sorry that I wasted your time."

"You're damn right. Not to mention your own."

I was standing on the seawall staring down at my Whaler trying to decide what rock I could go crawl under when I heard someone call my name. This time I recognized the voice.

"Ben. What are you doing up here?"

He walked over and gave me a hug, and we both hung on a little longer than just friends should. He was wearing a tropical print shirt made of a smooth fabric that felt incredibly sensuous as I slid my hands up his back and over the muscles in his shoulders.

"Hey, lady, it's good to see you again. We got to stop meeting like this," he said with a laugh.

I thought about Molly and B.J. snuggled up together studying.

I held my hands out in a gesture of surrender. "I don't

know, Ben. It works for me. What are you doing up here?"

He pointed to one of the outdoor tables in front of the Downtowner. "I'm having lunch with my grandfather. I drove up this morning for his birthday. Come on over. I'll introduce you."

The man sitting at the table we approached had a head that reminded me of one of those dried-apple dolls. It looked as though his nose, in the drying-out process, had curled right down over his bristly white mustache. He was wearing faded navy Dickies work pants, a long-sleeved shirt, and those heavy tan lace-up work boots.

"Gramps, this is Seychelle." The old man stood and stuck out his hand. His grip was firm and dry, but I could feel the loose skin sliding over the bones in his hand. His fingernails were black with dirt. "Gramps here is also Benjamin Baker, but everybody calls him Old Ben."

"I'm pleased to meetcha," he said. "Seems I saw you a time or two over at Junior's house when Ben here was just a kid." His eyes had the bloodshot and watery look of a serious drinker.

"You probably did," I said, glancing at Ben. "We spent lots of time together back in those days."

" 'Course Junior sold that house now. He bought some gaddamn mansion out west. Out in what used to be Everglades when I first come here back in '46. Why don't you sit down and join us? We was just fixin' to have some lunch."

"I don't want to impose," I said, when really, I felt awkward with the conversation about Ben's parents.

"What that you say?" The old man pointed to his ear.

I tried forcing the volume up. It felt like I was shouting. "I said I don't want to impose. Ben said it's your birthday."

"Shit. Much as I love my grandson here, I'd be a whole

lot happier spending my birthday looking at a pretty woman. Besides, I think my grandson's got a thing for you, miss."

"Gramps!" Ben said. He turned to me and rolled his eyes. "Just ignore him."

I sat on the edge of the chair Ben had pulled out for me. "I can only stay for a few minutes. I've got to go to this symposium thing this afternoon."

"What would you like to drink, young lady?" The old man waved at a waitress, but she was already bringing me a cold Corona with a lime wedged in the neck. Old Ben nudged me with a bony elbow. "They know your drink in a bar, you must be a drinker." He pointed to his own empty highball glass and twirled his finger. The waitress nodded. I noticed the younger Ben was only drinking water.

"What's this about a symposium?" he asked.

When I started to speak, Old Ben cupped a hand behind his right ear.

"I just heard about it yesterday. A bunch of the towboat operators are getting together at the IGFA—the International Game Fish Association—this afternoon to talk about the business. I don't know that it will do any good, but I'm willing to go."

"I was in the towing business," Old Ben said.

"Seychelle's in the *boat* towing business, Gramps."

"I know that, son, but it's not all that different."

Ben turned to me. "Gramps here owns Hubcap Heaven—you know, that place out on 441?"

"I know that place. I've driven by there hundreds of times. I'm pretty sure Red used to do business out there."

"Well, honey, that's me," the old man said, smiling his thanks at the waitress when she brought him another drink. "I bought that land when I first got out of the service. Now rich folks like his daddy"—he used his thumb to point at Ben—"Junior, think it's an eyesore, they want to close me down. But honey, I got over twenty-five thousand new and used hubcaps, rims, and wheel covers of all kinds on three-quarters of an acre. I got me a lift and a wrecker truck and I'm open twenty-four hours a day, rain or shine, three hundred sixty-five days a year. Junior can take his fancy dealership and shove it up his ass."

"Gramps! Sorry, Seychelle. He and my dad have been arguing like this for years. Dad's ashamed of the fact that he was raised in a trailer in a junkyard."

"It ain't no junkyard!" The old man reached into the breast pocket of his shirt and pulled out a pack of unfiltered Camels. He struck a match on the side of the box, and his cheeks hollowed out as he sucked deeply on the cigarette. After he blew a stream of smoke at the ceiling fan, he said, "Junior wouldn't even let Ben here come visit my place when he was a kid. He hated Hubcap Heaven ever since his momma died." The old man lifted his drink and swung it around as he continued to speak, gesturing to make his point. "He was seven years old when he started working at the corner store so's he wouldn't have to come home from school. He saved his money and bought himself clothes. Damnest thing I ever seen—this third grader wearing a blazer and tie to school in Florida. Didn't even have air-conditioning back in the '50s. Hell, I got more in common with Ben here than I ever did with his old man." He drained his glass.

"Gramps, I don't think Seychelle wants to hear all our family history." Ben reached over and brushed a cigarette ash off his grandfather's sleeve.

"Leave me alone," Old Ben said, waving his cigarette at Ben. "Stop your fussing at me."

"Gentlemen, I have enjoyed this, but I really do have to go." I pushed back the chair and stood.

"You can't go," Ben said. "I was going to buy you lunch."

I turned to him, laughing, assuming his words had been meant as a joke, but the look on his face was serious. I thought of the times Maddy had teased him and he had just stood, his head bowed, and taken it, never speaking up in his own defense for fear of the beating that might follow. This was a different Ben. This man was strong and commanding, reaching out to take what he wanted. There was something very sexy about that—about being desired like that. B.J. always let me go when I said I wanted to go. He never argued, never asked me to stay.

"Ben," I said, reaching for his hand and giving it a squeeze. "I'm sorry. I'd love to stay with you and your grandfather, but like I told you, I have someplace to go this afternoon and I have some business to attend to before I go. How 'bout a rain check and you can buy me lunch next time. Okay?"

Old Ben winked at me as I got up and headed toward the seawall. Young Ben didn't say a word.

XVII

AFTER I'd cranked the dinghy up in the davits, I unlocked the door to my cottage and collapsed on the couch. Abaco climbed up next to me, put her head in my lap, and then looked at me with her big brown eyes. She was telling me she remembered my promise to take her swimming, I was sure of it. Before I could go anywhere, I needed to call Catalina, but I didn't know what I would tell her. She'd had enough things go wrong in her life. I didn't want to be one more disappointment to her.

I was reaching for the portable phone on the coffee table when from the corner of my eye I saw movement. My front door started to swing inward slowly, and my pulse jumped into overdrive. "Hey, anybody home?" B.J. poked his head around the door. Abaco leaped to the ground and ran to him, jumping up on him and making her talking noises.

"You scared me," I said.

"Really? Why? I've come in that door—the one you never latch—a hundred times before."

"I'm just a little jumpy, that's all. There's some strange stuff going on, and I just came back from seeing Ted Berger. I'm convinced now he had nothing to do with Nestor's death."

"That should be good news, I think."

"Yeah, I guess. Really, it just leaves me more confused. The more I'm convinced there's something going on, the less certain I am of what. So what brings you to my door? I thought you and Molly were joined at the hip these days."

"Could the lady be jealous?"

"Who? Me? Just because you're spending long hours cheek-to-cheek with my voluptuous best friend? Should I be?"

"You're right, she is a beautiful woman, and we are spending lots of time together."

"And?"

"And that's why I'm here."

"Speaking of which—you didn't stop by my cottage here anytime yesterday and let yourself into the place, did you?"

He shook his head. "I wouldn't do that. The only time I come into your home is when you're out of town and I'm looking after Abaco." He smiled. "Or when we're preparing a welcome home barbecue."

"That's what I thought. Somebody's playing head games with me. Things were moved—changed in here when I got home last night."

"You sure? Maybe Catalina did it before you two left."

"No, some of it was subtle, like washing the dishes that I had left in the sink. But I think somebody put the dog's collar back on her—and I don't think Abaco would let just anybody do that."

"She's not the greatest watchdog. But it's true she wouldn't likely let a stranger in here without putting up a big fuss."

"I thought that Catalina might have done it, but B.J., somebody made my bed—better than I've ever made it. And Catalina never went near my room."

"Let me get this straight. You had someone break into your cottage and commit random acts of housekeeping."

"Yeah. Weird, huh?"

"I'll say. Think you can get them to come back on a regular basis?"

"Hey, this is serious. Somehow, it creeps me out more than if they'd torn the place apart. I barely slept a wink last night."

"Perhaps that was the intent."

"If so, it worked. When somebody trashes your place, you figure they're done. This was like somebody telling me they can come and go as they please here."

"Why you?"

"That's the question. I've been thinking about it. I don't see how this could be related to the Nestor situation—especially now that Berger is out of the picture. The only other person I can think of who might want to freak me out is this Melvin Burke guy."

"He's the one who's suing you?"

"Right. I'm not sure what he thinks he could gain by it, though. Maybe he was in here looking for something to use against me in the lawsuit. Or maybe he just wants to force me to settle. I've got to admit, the thought of being able to make this all go away is very appealing."

"To do that, you would have to admit fault. Is that something you want to do?"

"I just don't know. I feel like I don't know anything anymore. Maybe I was wrong to leave them on the boat when I was towing them in. What makes me think that I know enough to make the right decisions when I'm dealing with people's lives? That child nearly died. B.J., I don't think I can do this anymore. I'm not sure I should. Maybe I'm not any better than any of the other

Johnny-come-lately salvers who don't know what the hell they're doing."

He sat next to me on the couch, put his arms around me, and pulled me to him. His fingers slipped my hair behind my ear, then slid around to the base of my skull and began kneading at the knot in the muscle there.

"All the doubts in the world aren't going to change who you are," he said. "There isn't always a right decision, a right thing to do. You just do the best you can—and I'd take your best over almost anyone else's."

I wanted to believe him. My cheek pressed against the hard muscles of his chest, and I could smell his soap, the clean laundered smell of his T-shirt, the earthy scent of his skin. I wanted to be my best for him, and I ached with a hollowness I wanted him to fill. His hands slid up and down my back gently massaging the muscles. All thoughts of Molly evaporated as my mind focused only on his touch. I leaned my head back and admired the smooth brown skin of his neck. I opened my mouth and began at his neckline with tiny nibbling kisses, letting my tongue linger on his skin, enjoying the slightly salty taste of him. Then I arched my back and worked my way around to his ear, and I heard his breath quicken when I took his earlobe in my teeth.

"I've missed you," I whispered, breathing hot air into his ear.

He pulled away for just an instant, then swept the hair up off my neck and began kissing that tender skin and lightly tracing his fingers around my collar, from right to left, finally settling in the center where he grasped the button between his fingers and in the next instant it was undone. He lowered his hand to the next button on my shirt.

"Hey, you're pretty good at that," I said. Button number three fell open and he was still doing it with only one hand. His fingertips brushed across the tops of my breasts, then slid between them. "I think you've had some practice."

He didn't answer me.

IT was ten till three when I dashed out the front door, apologizing to Abaco for still not taking her for a swim and realizing I would have to see Catalina that evening, after the symposium. I was trying to button my jeans, tuck in my shirt, and buckle my belt while navigating the path out to my Jeep. B.J. had disappeared when I'd jumped into the shower after suddenly sitting up in bed and shouting, "Oh shit!" I'd seen the time on the digital clock on my nightstand. We'd been naked, our limbs tangled beneath the sheet, and I'd been so relaxed and just on the verge of falling into some deep much-needed sleep when I remembered the meeting set for three.

I threw my shoulder bag onto the passenger's seat and leaped into the vehicle. At that hour on a Monday afternoon, the streets were already starting to clog with the after-work traffic. I was going to be at least half an hour late. Taking the shower had made the time worse, but better to be really late than to walk in a little late smelling of sex. There were some things about working in a man's world that were a given.

I shook my head when I turned Lightnin' into the lot at the IGFA. It was downright amazing the sorts of things men could turn into a pissing contest. The parking lot looked like somebody was holding tryouts for a monster-truck extravaganza. Ocean Towing's bright green diesel truck was the most ridiculous. It looked like it had overdosed on steroids. Even a man the height of Neville Pinder would need a ladder to climb up into that vehicle, with tires taller than most school-age children. The damn thing bristled with antennas and spotlights, mini cranes and winches. Offshore Marine had an extended-cab white Ford F-350 with the BOAT/US logo painted on the side; Sea Tow had both a yellow truck with a winch on the back and a yellow SUV. Nearly all the vehicles in the lot were trucks or large SUVs. In that crowd, my poor little Jeep looked like a toy—one that had been left in the sandbox and rusted, too.

When I slipped into the back of the meeting room, I saw a long table on a stage, and more people than I expected sitting at round tables scattered throughout the room. I slid into an empty chair between Perry Greene and Captain Cassidy, who worked with Perry sometimes. The guy up front was droning on about the elements that had to be present for a tow to change into a salvage operation. A name placard in front of him identified him as a representative of the Marine Industries Association of South Florida. I figured he had to be a desk jockey. I'd never seen him on the water.

I leaned over and whispered to Cassidy, "What did I miss?"

"We're getting Salvage 101 up there. This is a waste of time."

"Why did you come?"

"Because we all know there's a problem but nobody here's really talking about it."

The panelists continued to talk, but I tuned them out and looked around the room. I guessed there were about fifty people, and I knew, or at least recognized, most of them. There were quite a few captains from Sea Tow. They generally owned their own boats and bought into a franchise agreement with that company. Neville Pinder was present with a large entourage of local Ocean Towing captains wearing neon green shirts, OCEAN TOWING stitched over their pockets. In his case, Pinder owned all the gear—including the monster truck out front—and the boat drivers worked for him. Compared with the other captains, they were a scruffy-looking group with shirttails untucked, baseball caps worn backward, and tufts of hair sprouting from under their caps. The slouching postures of the Ocean Towing group seemed to signal a contempt for the proceedings. I saw Tia sitting at the Offshore Marine table. Their group looked shipshape in white shirts and blue shorts, the typical captain's uniform. I even saw a group from the Water Taxis and Dania Harbor Tugs. All the players were sitting there in that room.

So, I thought, if it's true that somebody's up to no good in the salvage business, odds are that someone is sitting in this room.

After another fifteen minutes of presentation from a maritime attorney, the Coast Guard officer, with a placard in front of him that read LIEUTENANT A. J. GUNNAR, asked the audience if they had any questions for the panel. Several hands shot up. The first fellow started in on a long story about a particular case where an inexperienced salvage crew caused even more damage to the stricken vessel, which eventually sank. For an instant, I feared he was going to tell the whole gathering the story about me and Melvin Burke and *Seas the Day*.

As the questioner continued, Perry groaned. Finally, the moderator interrupted the man and asked him to ask a question. Turned out he was a boat owner who had been towed off the beach by Perry and before he could get pumps on her, she sank. The Coast Guard guy cut him off saying that they were not there to comment on individual cases. The next question was about whether a tow could become a salvage operation if the owner never signed a form.

Cassidy was right. Nobody was talking about the real

problems in our business. I raised my hand. After a couple of minutes, Lieutenant Gunnar called on me.

"I don't know about you guys, but I'm sick and tired of hearing salvage called piracy. And the folks doing the name-calling have good reasons sometimes. Something stinks in this business these days. Some of you in here are telling customers that your work is salvage when it really should be a tow. You're ripping people off. People out there are getting afraid to take a line from us. And now there's a new wrinkle. I know that it's just like in prison—everyone who puts his boat on the beach cries innocent. Says it wasn't his fault. But lately, some of those cries have been ringing true. I know one guy who said it—Nestor Frias—and most of you knew him, too. And now he's dead. Instead of sitting around here politely discussing maritime law, somebody needs to figure out who and what is going on." I turned around to make sure my chair was still lined up behind me and saw a face at the back of the room. Quentin was sitting in a chair against the back wall. He smiled and lifted a hand. I nodded at him, then sat down and faced front again.

The crowd stayed quiet for several seconds. Then the noise level rose as dozens of conversations broke out at the tables all around the room. Lieutenant Gunnar started shouting, "Could I have your attention, please?" but he'd lost them. This group had sat still just about as long as they could stand it. Chairs scraped as people got up. The formal part of this meeting was over.

Along one wall there was a long table with brochures and information, as well as plates of cookies, bags of chips, soda, and a coffeepot, and most of the captains in the room got up and headed for the free food. A lady took the microphone from the Coastie, thanked everyone for attending, and insisted that everybody sign the attendance sheet on the table by the coffeepot.

I was watching some very thick-looking coffee trickle into my Styrofoam cup when Neville Pinder appeared at my side.

"I see you and Mr. Berger's boat made it home okay."

I blew on the liquid in my cup and watched him over the Styrofoam rim. He was helping himself to a cup, but the corners of his mouth turned up and his eyes kept glancing to the side. He knew I was watching him, and he was enjoying it.

"We had a nice trip—except for Thursday night off Marathon. Heard the calls on the VHF—some poor guy put his boat on the stones. A big sailboat, *Rendezvous*. Your guys sure were quick to get out there."

"Oh yeah, my guys are good," he said, and when he turned to face me, I noticed for the first time that the pale green of his eyes appeared nearly as unnatural as the neon shade of his shirt. "They floated him free the next day. Almost no damage to the boat."

The coffee wasn't as bad as it looked. I took another sip. "I guess that means you'll be able to buy another new boat pretty soon. Or maybe another truck like that monster out front."

He smiled. "You know, I just might do that."

"So, I was wondering, how is it that you showed up on the scene about a year ago and suddenly you're the biggest thing in salvage in this town?"

"I tell you what it is. You're old school, Sullivan. The times have passed you by. You're like an old dog, not good for much but eatin' and shittin'. Time to let go of the little piece of this business you still got." He held his thumb and forefinger up about two inches apart—and I couldn't take my eyes off the scarred stubs that had once been his fingers.

Tia walked up and said, "Seychelle, I haven't met your friend."

The way he smiled at her, it was clear he thought of himself as the rock star of the towing business. He didn't realize Tia was no groupie.

I introduced her to Pinder and took the opportunity to slip away. I wanted to put distance between the big Bahamian and myself. And I wanted to catch more of the gossip in the room. Captain Cassidy was standing with a group of guys who worked with him. When I walked up, they all started congratulating me for speaking up.

"After what I've been through this week, I'm tired of being polite and talking around things."

"Yeah, we all heard about Nestor," Cassidy said. "Is it true you found him?"

I didn't want to have to talk about that again, but in fact, Nestor was really the reason I was there. I just nodded, then said, "I don't get it. Who called this get-together and what did they think they were going to accomplish?"

"It was the Marine Industries Association. I guess they've been hearing the complaints. It seems there was one really blatant case of taking advantage of a poor schmuck who didn't know any better. Like typical boat people, the guys who did it had to brag about it."

"Are you naming names?"

"Let me just say the amount of money they made could make you *green* with envy." The two other captains laughed at Cassidy, but what he said didn't surprise me.

"Just that truck out front must have cost him over fifty grand," I said. "I wondered where he was getting the money."

Cassidy squinted as he watched Pinder having an animated discussion with Tia. "Lots of us have been wondering about our friend Neville. From what I hear, he started with one crappy little boat in Key West and suddenly, a year later, he's got new boats in every major port from Key West to Stuart. He's also picking up the lion's share of the emergency calls. He's had an amazing run of luck—his boats have been first on hand to more than half the wrecks in the last six months."

I thought of Nestor. Maybe he was right about the *what,* just wrong about the *who.* "You sure it's luck?"

"What else could it be?"

"I don't know—but I intend to find out."

Cassidy shrugged and patted me on the shoulder. "Keep me posted."

I saw Quentin standing alone and hurried over to him. "How's it going?"

"Good to see you, skipper. I'm doing okay. Jeremy let me stay on *Power Play*—I'm doing some brightwork for him, but I'm looking to be on a boat that will move. Took the bus here hoping to find a job."

"I saw you talking to one of the green shirt guys."

"Yes, that is Brian. I have an interview with his boss tomorrow."

"Be careful. I don't like that bunch."

"Brian's okay. He has an interesting story about a boat he just pulled off the reef here in Fort Lauderdale."

Perry Greene joined us then and interrupted me before I could find out more. "Hey, you guys headed to the Downtowner? I heard Neville Pinder's buying drinks."

"You're kidding," I said.

"Yeah, I am," Perry said, and he threw back his head and let loose with his high-pitched cackle. "Everybody is heading over there, though." He rubbed up against my arm. "How about you, sweet cheeks?"

"Perry, did you see that lagoon outside the door of this place? You rub that body of yours up against me one more time and I'll reach into your drawers, rip off your privates, and feed them to the gators in the pond out there."

Perry grinned so wide I could see his receding gums. "I love it when you talk dirty, girlfriend." And then he took off at a run before I could catch him.

XVIII

I'D barely reached my Jeep before fat raindrops began to splat against the windshield. When I parked in the lot behind the Downtowner, I pulled an old rain poncho out from under the backseat and ran from the parking lot to the covered walkway that faced the river. The temperature had dropped into the low sixties again, and only the die-hard smokers were sitting, huddled together, at the outside bar.

Stepping inside, my ears were assaulted by the volume of the music, conversation, and general revelry, and the warmth came not only from all the bodies packed into that small space but also from the sense of homecoming I felt. The place was a throwback to another era. No marketing firm had decorated the interior, and the menu didn't have pictures of plastic food. The main bar was built of wood and fitted together as though by shipwrights, while the windows at the bartender's back opened via shutters onto an outside bar and the view of the river beyond. Small brass plaques affixed to the bar marked the stools of the regular customers, and each strange item hanging from the walls had its own story. There was the name board off a wartime hospital ship, the life ring from a former judge's yacht, and the outboard once confiscated by the Fort Lauderdale police when a mayor's son had been caught joyriding. Black-

and-white photos hanging on the walls showed a Fort Lauderdale from the early days when the river out front was a supply highway for the town and the docks off-loaded vegetables from the farms around Lake Okee-chobee. To most of the people in the bar tonight, the river was still the main artery keeping their careers alive.

A group of the towboat captains had pushed three ta-bles together and had been joined by some of the regu-lars like Captain Kaos and Wally. I considered joining them but instead I made my way left to the side bar and asked Pete for a Corona. When he set the bottle in front of me, he leaned over the ice bin and said, "That sucks about Nestor. How's his wife doing?"

"How do you expect her to be doing?" After I said it and saw the hurt look on his face, I felt bad. "Sorry, Pete. I'm just frustrated. Something's not right and I can't even figure out what it is."

"You want to talk about it?"

"No, I'd just get myself more confused. I came tonight to talk to some people and see if I couldn't make some of these things gel, but when I walked in here just now I realized I don't really feel like talking to anybody." I took a long drink; even the cold beer didn't taste partic-ularly good. "You know, Pete, I think I need to get out of this business. It's just not fun anymore."

"You think this job's fun?" He waved his hand to in-clude the whole bar.

"Pete, you like to bitch, but I can see it. You love what you do."

"Well . . ." He pulled the towel off his shoulder and wiped his hands. "Some days are better than others."

"You are a part of this place, you know."

"And things wouldn't be the same on the river with-out *Gorda*."

"That's true, but it doesn't have to be me running the boat."

"Are you serious? You're thinking about selling?"

The direct question stopped me for a minute. This was the end result of what I'd been talking about, but I hadn't really thought it through to that point. "Yeah, Pete, I guess I am. Thinking about it, anyway."

Pete shook his head and headed down the bar to get the orders from two couples who looked like they were in the wrong bar. The men wore dark suits, and the women's dresses sparkled with sequins. My guess was the guys had talked the ladies into some adventurous slumming before walking across the bridge and going to the theater—when, in fact, it was a way for the guys to score free parking.

The door at the end of the bar opened and a gust of cold air blew in around Neville Pinder and two other Ocean Towing captains. Pinder was in the middle of a story. Despite the bar's noise, his voice rose above the interior volume. "And then she said, 'I've never seen anything that size in my fuckin' life.' " The two guys in the matching green shirts roared their approval. "Gimme three Kaliks," Pinder shouted over the tops of the heads of the folks at the bar. The bartender on that side jumped to bring him the three Bahamian beers, and all the heads that had turned to watch his entrance, returned to their former conversations.

What's wrong with this world, I asked myself as I sipped my beer. Everybody was looking for the deal, the scam, the few quick bucks. It was one thing to pretend you were eating at a restaurant in order to score free parking; it was something totally different to kill a man to preserve your cushy deal. And yet that was what Catalina insisted someone had done, and the only one making lots of money that I could see at this point was Neville Pinder.

I watched him at the bar, where he had now brought several other patrons into his group and was regaling them all with stories told at a volume that was, like the rest of him, big and rude.

"Hi, skipper, you're watching my fellow islander." Quentin had come up behind me and settled on the empty stool. I couldn't figure out how I hadn't seen him come in, and I noticed that he sure did get around well without a car.

"Hey, Quentin. That guy's got nothing in common with you. Can I buy you a beer?"

"No beer, thank you. But I would like an orange juice."

"Sure," I said, lifting my hand to signal to Pete. When he made it to our end of the bar, I introduced him to Quentin.

"Pete, this is the guy who crewed for me coming up from Key West. He's from down-island, Dominica." The two men shook hands. "He's a hell of a good crewman and he's looking for work around here. Keep your ear to the ground for me, okay?"

"Will do," Pete said. He gave me a little mock salute, then poured Quentin his juice.

I tapped my bottle to Quentin's glass. "Here's to us both finding work we love."

After he drank, Quentin said, "I saw you watching him." He inclined his head toward Pinder.

"Yeah, it seems to be the Neville Pinder Show."

"I was starting to tell you that story I heard from Brian this afternoon, about the boat accident that caused that meeting today."

"Oh yeah, what did he say?"

"Brian works for Ocean Towing in Hillsboro and he got a call to go out and pull off a seventy-five-foot motor yacht that had grounded just south of the harbor entrance."

"Sure, if people try to cut the corner going into Hillsboro from the south, they'll be aground in a heartbeat."

"Yeah, that must be the place. Brian said the weather wasn't bad and it was a soft bottom. He got a phone call on his cell from Ocean Towing. His towboat was already offshore on another job. He said it took about an hour to tow the boat off, but his boss filed it as a salvage operation."

"You're kidding."

He shook his head, and his dreads swung around his face. "The owner paid the salvage claim, then filed with his insurance company."

"I'll bet they went through the roof when they found it had just been a soft grounding with no damage."

"Apparently so."

"What's the name of the boat?"

"*NautiBoy*—it's spelled—"

"Yeah, I got it. I've seen that one a few times. Do you know where the boat is now?"

"He said it's docked at a small marina just inside Hillsboro."

"I think I might go over there tomorrow and talk to the captain. See if he noticed anything peculiar about his instruments like Nestor did."

"You have an idea about these groundings?"

"An idea, yeah, but I don't really know if it's even scientifically possible."

"What are you thinking?"

"I don't know much about electronics, but the thing is, most of these boats that have gone aground have been relying on their GPS for navigation. It's possible that there's a certain unit that's malfunctioning in all these boats. But I'm wondering about something else—if such a thing is possible. I'm thinking about how much money a salver could make if he could make a boat's nav systems go haywire when he wanted them to."

"That is a very interesting question."

"Isn't it?"

"You have been very good to me. If there is anything more I can do for you, I would like to help."

"Just keep your ears open and let me know if you hear anything that doesn't sound quite right. You've got an interview with Pinder tomorrow, right?"

"Yes."

"Well, start there. I don't mean for you to specifically ask any questions, just listen. And be careful. I'd especially like to know if there was any connection to Ocean Towing before these boats wrecked. If anyone from Ocean Towing went on board for any reason."

He smiled and raised his glass to me. "I can do that."

"I have one more favor to ask, too."

"What is that?"

"I liked working with you, Quentin. Wednesday morning I'm supposed to tow a forty-three-foot sailboat for an out-of-state owner. Boat's name is *Wild Matilda*. I'm just taking it upriver for the annual haul-out. My usual crew guy can't make it. He's taking a class. Do you think you could give me a hand?"

"No problem."

I told him where and when to meet me. Quentin then finished off the last of his drink and said good night. Watching him head for the door, I caught Neville Pinder staring at me from the other side of the room. When our eyes met, he nodded at me, and then turned back to the thirty-something woman with eye-popping cleavage who had cozied up to him at the bar. She sat on a stool, her brown legs crossed and her elbows resting on the bar behind her. He leaned in and whispered something in her ear, and when she laughed, her whole torso bounced.

Did he have it in him to kill? Being a jerk and a loud-mouth doesn't necessarily mean you have what it takes to bash a man's skull in. And why? Why did Nestor have to die? I thought about my conversation with Neville in Key West and remembered his words about Nestor disrespecting him. Would that have been enough? I didn't think so. No, this was about the money. It was about the *Power Play* and all the other yachts with competent captains that had grounded recently. It was about a three-hundred-dollar tow becoming a half-million-dollar salvage job.

I was trying to decide whether or not I wanted to eat when I saw Ben walk in. I waved when he looked my way, and he joined me at the bar.

"Did you see Quentin out there?" I asked him.

"No, was he here?"

"Yeah, he just left. He was at the symposium, too."

"Really?"

"Yeah, he's got some job leads. So first lunch, now dinner. Have you spent the whole day around here?"

"No, I had to run some errands this afternoon, but I decided to come back here—in the hope I might find you here. Have you eaten?"

"No, but I was thinking of heading home."

He put his hand on the back of my neck, and I was certain my face flushed as I thought of B.J.'s hands and where they had been a few hours earlier. "Stay," Ben said. "Have another drink with me. I'll buy you dinner. I'm heading back to Key West in the morning." The way he smiled, I was certain Ben thought he had been responsible for the sudden rise in my body temperature—and in a way, he was right. Not for the first time, I wondered what was wrong with me. Why was it that I couldn't just settle down with B.J., get married, and feel the same things I assumed other women felt? Why was it that I could be so crazy about B.J. and yet still be attracted to other men?

I hiked my bag up onto my shoulder and said, "I really ought to go."

Pete walked by on the other side of the bar, and Ben pointed to my beer bottle and shouted, "We'll have another couple of these." Pete nodded, delivered the two drinks in his hands, and before I knew it I had another bottle of beer in front of me.

"Ben, I'm going to make this fast. All of a sudden, I just don't feel like being here anymore."

"What's wrong?"

"Him," I said, indicating Pinder and knowing that it was really only half the truth. I felt I needed to leave before I got myself in trouble.

"Why? What did he do?"

"Quentin just told me the story behind the meeting we had this afternoon. There was some yacht, *NautiBoy,* and Ocean Towing took a simple tow where there was no peril to anybody involved—just a little grounding on a sandbar—and made it a salvage claim. It seems to me that Neville Pinder represents everything I'm coming to dislike about this business."

"Tell me about it."

I shook my head, watching Pinder. "Look at him. You know what he makes me think of?"

"No."

"The wreckers. You know? The old Key West wreckers."

"Like my great-great-grandpa."

"Sort of. Not necessarily him—your relative, I mean—but guys like him. There were so many of them for a while there. Guys who didn't know what else to do with their lives were flooding into Key West from all over the country after the Civil War, come to make their fortunes. Sound familiar?"

"You mean like the salvage business here today?"

"Yup. You ever hear about what happened down there when the government started putting up the lights on the reefs and the number of ships started declining, when they put the transcontinental railroad through, and ships began to have engines?"

He smiled as though he knew the story well, but he rested his chin in his palm and focused all his attention on me. "Tell me."

"It was the pressure of the marketplace. All of a sudden, there were too many wreckers and not enough ships wrecking on the reefs. There's no real proof that it happened, but the legends say that some enterprising individuals came up with a plan to *make* wrecks—which back then meant paying off the captains or messing with the lights. What I keep asking myself is what would a modern-day wrecker do to—"

A glass crashed to the floor and a woman's voice rose above the noise of the crowd. "You goddamn son of a bitch. Buying me one drink does not give you the right to put your filthy fucking hands there."

The woman who had been laughing with Pinder was now screaming and making a scene. The way she slurred her words made it clear she'd had too much to drink. Pinder was just smiling at her, making no attempt to apologize. One of the waitresses ushered the screamer out the door, and Pinder moved down to join the other captains at the far end of the bar.

"Ben, that's it. I'm out of here. Have a good trip back to Key West."

He wrapped his hand around my wrist. "Please, Seychelle, stay. We have so much to talk about."

I looked at his hand then lifted my eyes to his face. I didn't like myself much in that moment. I was really tempted to push B.J. out of my mind and stay. Stay all night. And if I didn't? Then once again, I hadn't been playing fair with Ben. In a way, I'd been using him when I felt that B.J. was ignoring me. "Ben, no. I just want to go home."

He released my arm. "Okay. I'll walk you to your car." He reached for his wallet and threw some bills on the bar. Then with his hand on the small of my back, he steered me toward the door. Once outside, he draped his arm around my shoulders. We walked to the parking lot in silence. At my Jeep, he slid his fingers under my chin and pressed his lips against mine.

I pushed away, startled. "Ben, no. I'm involved with somebody else."

"You said you didn't really call him your boyfriend. I was under the impression it was a sort of open relationship."

For just a moment, I wondered if that was what B.J. thought, too, when he was studying cheek-to-cheek with Molly.

"No, Ben, I'd have to say we're pretty monogamous."

I looked at him as he stepped back away from the Jeep. He didn't take those eyes off me. I knew then that Molly had been right about Ben and me. About how he'd felt back when we were kids. There was more to this than just tonight.

XIX

THE last thing I needed at that point was a balky vehicle. Through the plastic side window, I saw him standing in the yellow-orange glow of the street lamp, his hands buried deep in his pockets. Under my breath I whispered to the statue on the dash, "Jesus, don't fail me now," not really expecting anyone to be listening, but covering all my bases just the same. I turned the key one more time and finally Lightnin's engine roared to life. Dark smoke pouring from my exhaust pipe, I pulled out of the parking lot spewing water and gravel out of the puddles that had accumulated with the late rain.

I felt the tension ease out of my body the more distance I put between the Downtowner and myself. At Andrews and Sixth, I caught the red and my Jeep sputtered into stillness.

Shit.

The red light reflected on the slick wet pavement, turning the entire intersection crimson. I glanced up at the rearview mirror. Mine was the only vehicle within sight. What was I expecting? That he would come charging after me? Not his style. He was better than that. I just hated myself for causing Ben Baker any more pain than he had already experienced in his life. He hadn't had it easy as a kid—not by a long shot—and here I was putting him through more crap.

I turned the key again, and the engine ground but would not catch. The light changed the pavement to a sea of green and I turned the key again. On my third try, just as the light turned yellow, the engine caught. I roared on through as the light turned red.

I had one more stop this evening, and since it was getting late, I drove over the Davie Bridge a little faster than I should have on the rain-slicked streets. When I tried to brake at the bottom of the incline, my brakes felt soft and mushy. Old Lightnin', my trusty Jeep, must be feeling her thirty years of age tonight, I thought as I stomped on the pedal to make the turn into Shady Banks. I noticed in the rearview mirror that the car behind me, the only one I'd seen on the road since leaving the Downtowner, did not turn into Shady Banks, and I relaxed a little more.

Luckily, lights were still on when I pulled up in front of the Sparkses' house. I knocked on the door lightly, hoping not to wake Sarah, but trying to raise someone inside. After a couple of minutes, Catalina opened the door.

"Thank God," she whispered as she opened the door wider to let me in. She threw her arms around my neck.

I peeled her arms off me. "What's wrong?"

She held her finger to her lips and made a shushing noise.

She showed me down the hall into her small bedroom and closed the door behind us. "Mrs. Sparks is sleeping."

"Where's Arlen?"

"I do not know. He left after we returned from the market and I have not seen him since." She motioned for me to sit on the small twin bed. "He was here," she said.

"Who?"

"The man who killed my husband."

"What?"

"Look. There." She pointed to the box we'd retrieved from the Dean Lopez Funeral Home. The white cardboard box that contained Nestor's ashes. It was resting on top of the dresser; hanging off the front was a Saint Christopher's medal on a silver chain.

"What am I supposed to see?"

"The medal. When I left to go shopping with Mr. Sparks, it was not there. I have not seen that medal since the day I kissed my husband good-bye. I come home today and it is there, just as you see. Someone was here, in this room."

"No, Cat, that's crazy," I said, but I was picturing the tightly made bed in my own bedroom. "There's got to be another explanation."

"It was not Mr. Sparks—he was with me. Nor she—she cannot walk. And it was no ghost. It was flesh and blood."

"Catalina, what the hell is going on?"

"I tried to telephone you but I got no answer. I think he is warning me. Telling me to be quiet."

"Cat, I'm sorry. I thought you'd be safe here." I hadn't noticed before how much she had changed in the past week. Her face looked less rounded, more gaunt, and her big brown eyes had hollows beneath them. "Are you okay?"

"I am fine, Seychelle. I will not leave this house. I like her very much. And she needs me. I will not be frightened away."

"One thing at a time. What about your doctor? When do you go next?"

"I canceled the appointment. I have a little money we saved to get an apartment, but it will not be enough to pay the hospital. We thought we would have insurance for the baby through Nestor's job."

"You have to see the doctor. You've been through tremendous stress."

"But I am very healthy."

"You're a nurse. You know what can happen." I also knew—too well. "Don't worry about the money. The baby and you come first. We'll figure out a way to pay."

She opened her mouth as though to argue again, but then closed it. After several seconds she said, "You are right. Thank you. I will do this for her." She rubbed her hand over the top of her belly. Then she reached out to me. "Give me your hand."

I reached out. If I had known what she intended to do, I never would have done it, never would have let her take my hand. I would have changed the subject, rushed to the bathroom, done just about anything to avoid it.

She placed my hand palm-down on the side of her belly. "There. Can you feel it?"

Something small and sharp pushed into the center of my palm.

"I think it is her elbow," Cat said.

It pushed again, this time at the base of my fingers. The muscles of my throat tightened and my eyes blurred. I saw the tiny arms, hands, fingers. The closed eyelids, the petite mouth. The bluish gray skin. It was so long ago, but once loose, the memory was bright with detail. I pulled back my hand as though her belly was charged with electric current and I'd just been shocked.

"It is frightening, yes? I feel the same. It is a real person inside me."

It took me a few seconds to calm my breathing, to shake off the mental pictures. "I'm certain you'll be a great mother," I said and I thought, *unlike me*.

"Thank you. It will not be easy to do this alone. I never imagined I would not have my husband for help."

For a moment, neither of us spoke. I worked at pushing back the unwelcome images. I had come here for a reason.

"Catalina, there is something else. I went to see Ted Berger today."

A twitch pulled at her mouth. "What did you learn?"

"I don't think he had anything to do with it, Cat. It's not him."

She stood and walked the short distance across the room and stared at the white box on the dresser. "But I have to be certain."

"I'm not saying I don't believe that something or someone killed Nestor. I just don't think Berger had anything to do with it." I went ahead and told her all of it, from the photos that the young man had shown to Ben and me to Berger's story about his Danish lady friend. She paced the room as I talked.

"And you believed him," she said, settling into the small wicker chair next to the bed.

"Cat, it's too easy to disprove. I don't think he would have made the whole story up."

"With him, anything is possible. There is something I have never told anyone. But perhaps you will understand if I explain. When Nestor first went to interview, I went with him. Mr. Berger had invited us both to lunch in his offices. We sat at a conference table and a gentleman served us. At the end of the meal, when he agreed to hire Nestor, he sent my husband to another floor for papers. While Nestor was gone and I was still in Mr. Berger's office, he touched me."

"What do you mean?" I asked the question even though I was pretty sure I knew.

She picked up a scarf off the arm of the chair and began twisting the fabric as she spoke. "He said things to me. Said I was the reason he was hiring Nestor—because I was so beautiful. Then he came over and tried to kiss me. He put his hand under my blouse and touched my breast." Her face screwed up in a grimace of disgust. "His hand squeezed my arm so hard it left a bruise. I was struggling, pushing him away, when he heard Nestor coming and stepped back. My husband walked in looking so happy to have the job of his dreams, and I could not say anything. I felt dirty and ashamed." She looked up from the mangled scarf and tears streaked down her face. "Every time he comes near me, he touches me, and it makes me feel so filthy. If *I* was the reason—do you see? I have to know."

I remembered that morning in the restaurant in Key West. Berger had leaned down and kissed her on the cheek and it had been obvious that the gesture was unwelcome. "So that day, with Jeremy on the boat. Berger had been in your cabin?"

She nodded without raising her head.

"Did he do anything to you?"

Lifting her head she said, "No, he is not interested in me now." She held her hands on either side of her belly. "He was there to tell me that later, after the baby is born, if I need money, he will pay. He treated me like a whore and he enjoyed it."

"I'm sorry, Catalina. You should have told me."

She nodded at the white box, the medal, and the chain. "He would do something like this. He takes pleasure in others' pain."

"I'll see if I can find this Danish woman. I'll check out his story. But you know, even if it does turn out that Berger had something to do with this, that would mean it was him—not you. You can't take this on yourself. You're not in any way to blame for what happened to Nestor." I stood up, preparing to go, and she looked up at me with those huge dark eyes sunk so deep into her face.

"You will find out for me, yes?"

I took her hand and squeezed it. "Yes, I promise."

I turned the key a third time and listened to the Jeep's engine struggling to catch. I clicked the key off and sat in the front seat feeling the street's quiet settling around me. I didn't need this just now. I stared at the silhouette of the Jesus statue on the dash. In daylight, the thing was bleached nearly white, but now, on this unlit street, only the black outline was visible against the white hood. Time had changed the look of it. In fact, most people who rode in my Jeep no longer recognized what it was. But me, I still saw the familiar features that time had long since worn away.

Come on, Lightnin', you can do it. When I gave it one more try, she coughed to life. Fearing she was going to stall again, I revved up the engine and let out the clutch, making my tires squeal on the pavement as I took off.

Fortunately, at this time of night Davie Boulevard had little traffic and I nursed the Jeep down the deserted street, coughing and sputtering all the way. I kept my eyes on the few cars around me, watching for a tail; while in the rearview I could see the smoke coming out of my exhaust, the streets were almost empty.

It wasn't until I'd crossed into Rio Vista, my neighborhood, that I saw a pair of headlights in my rearview mirror. Because I expected the engine to stall, I slowly coasted through the stop signs, fearing what would happen if I came to a halt. The lights behind me did likewise, keeping a distance between us of just over a hundred feet.

I was about three blocks from home when the engine stalled and I drifted off the road onto the swale to allow the vehicle behind me to pass. I sat still, eyes on the mirror, watching the lights that did not move. I unzipped the side window and stuck out my arm, waving him past. Still the lights did not move. I couldn't see anything behind the glare, but judging from the height of those lights, it was a big, high vehicle, like a truck. The idling engine rumbled softly as the driver tapped lightly on the accelerator, and I reminded myself to breathe as my heartbeat doubled its rate.

Moving slowly, I took the strap of my shoulder bag and slung the bag diagonally across my chest, shoulder-to-hip. I gauged the distance between my Jeep and the cul-de-sac ahead where I could cut out to the seawall and follow it through the two lawns that would eventually lead me to the Larsens' place. I figured I could cover the distance in less than thirty seconds at a dead run. My hand closed around the door handle lever.

I hit the street running and heard the squeal of the tires spinning on the pavement behind me as the driver failed to release the brake before the engine's RPMs had climbed the dial. When the tires caught, I was halfway there, watching the familiar homes on either side of me pass in a watery-eyed blur. My breath felt like sandpaper in my throat as I pumped my arms and heard the big engine growing louder, eating up the few hundred feet that separated us like a crazed Pac-Man.

I hurdled the hedge that rimmed the Martinez property and threw my body at the wooden fence surrounding their backyard. It's amazing what adrenaline can do. These arms of mine, which usually struggled to do a single pull-up, grabbed the top of the fence and pulled my body up with them. I got one leg over the top, rolled over the edge, and fell to the ground on the other side, crushing a bed of impatiens. Dusting the dirt and flower petals off my hands, I put my eye to the gap between the boards. The vehicle was gone.

I made my way out to the seawall and walked across

the backyards of the Larsens' neighbors. The houses were dark, and other than landscape lighting, they looked abandoned. When I got to the Larsens' yard, I whistled softly for my dog. She came running, surprised and delighted to find me arriving from the wrong direction.

I squatted in the bushes, scanning the yard, looking for anything out of the ordinary. What had that been about? I hadn't actually been trying to look at the vehicle—I'd been intent on getting over the fence—but from the periphery of my vision, I had the impression that it had been a dark-colored SUV. A vehicle very much like the one that had tried to run Cat down in Key West.

Relieved as I was to make it home, I was reluctant to enter my cottage alone. Did the owner of that vehicle out there know where I lived? Had he followed me from the Sparkses' house? I hadn't seen a tail, but then it would be easy for someone who knew where I was going to follow on parallel side streets.

Someone had already been inside my home, and I didn't know who. How'd they get in? Like lots of people, I hid a spare key to the place not far from the front door. It was a bad habit I'd picked up from my parents—they so rarely locked the house at all that when they did, we kids often didn't have our keys. They hid a spare key under a flowerpot. I wasn't quite that bad. At least I'd graduated to one of those plastic fake rocks and I kept it hidden under a bougainvillea bush. When I'd checked it this morning, the key had been there, but there was no way to tell if someone had used it the night before.

Nothing looked disturbed as I crossed the yard, Abaco trotting at my side, nosing my hand and asking me to pet her. My cottage looked unchanged. I squatted down and saw that my fake rock was resting there, looking as real as ever. After unlocking the front door, I sent the dog inside first. She disappeared and didn't make any noise, no barking, no sound of running doggy nails on the Dade County pine floors.

I pushed open the door and reached in for the light switch. The lamp on the end table switched on. The place was so small, I could see it all from the doorway, since the bedroom door was standing open. Unless he was hiding in the bedroom closet, there was no bogeyman in my place. The living room, kitchen, bedroom—all looked just as I had left them that morning. Abaco was sitting on the couch smiling her doggy smile, her tongue hanging out one corner of her mouth.

I dialed the nonemergency number of the Fort Lauderdale Police Department and was greeted with the robotic voice telling me that if I knew my party's extension I could dial it at any time; if I wanted the detective bureau, please press one, if I wanted robbery, press two, homicide, press three. I tried several numbers, hoping to get a human being. Finally, I did.

I told her I wanted to speak to a Detective Collazo. She told me there were no detectives there.

"But you're the police department," I said.

"Yeah, but it's almost midnight."

"Okay, but isn't that when the bad guys usually come out?"

She sighed. "If this is not an emergency, you'll need to call back during regular business hours."

"But someone followed me home."

"Are they still there?"

"No."

"And you are inside your home?"

"Yes."

"Would you like me to send a patrol car out to your residence?"

I was beginning to feel like some weenie whiner. I had no proof that anything had happened, and I didn't know how I would explain to a police officer the fear I had felt running in the street earlier. Somebody came into my home and washed the dishes. Someone entered my friend's room and left her a necklace. Everything I had to report went against what the cops would see as a usual crime. They didn't vandalize, they cleaned. They didn't steal, they brought jewelry. None of it made any sense. "No, I guess not. I'll call back during regular hours tomorrow. Thanks."

After I'd double-locked the front door, checked the closet and windows, and got ready for bed, I couldn't get over a general creepy feeling. Was it just my memory of the fact that someone had been inside here, or had it happened again? When I climbed into bed, I patted the covers and let Abaco jump up on the bedspread, an unusual treat for her. Her warm body resting against mine, I turned out the light and lay in the darkness staring at the ceiling, scratching the scruff of her neck, my eyes wide open. I was tired, but I knew that sleep would not come. It was going to be another very long night.

XX

BACO reminded me, as I was drinking my coffee out on the bench in front of my cottage on Tuesday morning, that I had promised her a dinghy ride and swim, and I had not yet lived up to my word. There are those who would call me crazy for thinking that my dog was giving me some kind of message, but anyone who was watching her run over to the dinghy davits, stick her rump up in the air and whine for my attention, then return and paw at my hands would have gotten the message as clearly as I did.

The rain and wind from the previous day had cleared out. Though there was a light five-knot breeze out of the west and the temperature was down in the fifties, this morning had cast off Florida's notorious humidity and the air was so clear and freshly washed, even the blue roof of the Larsens' new pagoda sparkled. Thoughts of random night visitors and dark threatening vehicles seemed to lose their weight in the bright sunlight.

After the dog had made her third hopeful trip over to the davits, I decided I could accomplish two things at once by taking her along on a dinghy trip to see the *NautiBoy* at Hillsboro Inlet.

I stood up and stretched. "Okay, girl, you talked me into it."

She began leaping and gyrating and wagging her tail

so violently, she made a truth out of that saying about the tail wagging the dog.

Inside the cottage, I heard my phone ringing, and I began the usual search to find the portable. This time it was under my sweatshirt on the couch.

"Hello. Sullivan Towing."

"Miss Sullivan, this is Detective Lassiter from Key West."

"Hey. I'm surprised to hear from you. What's up?"

"I'm sorry to bother you like this, but I thought you'd want to know. I kept thinking about what she said, you know, Ms. Frias, and I decided to make a phone call or two. I learned something, and maybe you can pass the word on to her."

"I'm not sure I'm following you, Detective."

"The last time we talked, Ms. Frias told me to ask an expert. About the windsurfing thing. That kept bugging me. So I did it. I called a guy I used to do some off-duty work for, back when I was still on patrol. The guy's got a place, a guest house, here on the island, but he used to do that windsurfing shit."

"Okay. What did he tell you?"

"I'm getting to that. I called you. It's my dime. He told me what he thought and he gave me the name of another guy who's still doing it. *Both* of them said the same thing. Said it couldn't happen that way. Said that if that rope was wrapped around his wrist that way, there's no way he was flung into the mast. I even showed my buddy the pictures. He laughed."

"That's really interesting, Detective Lassiter, but you're not telling me anything I don't already know."

"Yeah, but see, now I know it, too."

"Is it enough to get you to really investigate Nestor's death as a homicide?"

"Officially? No. On the side? Yeah, I'm gonna be looking into it. I thought Ms. Frias would like to know."

"Thanks, Detective. I'll tell her. We'll take whatever we can get at this point."

After I hung up, I just sat on the couch. I supposed the thing I should have done was tell him some of the things I had learned, and some of what I was guessing. The problem was there was lots more guesswork than solid knowledge at this point. Maybe if I asked around, found a little more evidence to support what I thought Pinder was doing, I'd be able to take it all to Lassiter, turn it over to him, and go back to figuring out what I wanted to do with the rest of my life.

Slipping on boat shoes and zipping up my sweatshirt, I grabbed my handheld VHF radio and then headed for the door. It wasn't even eight AM yet, but I'd been up for a couple of hours after finally abandoning the tossing and turning that had plagued me through the night. As soon as the sky had shown a light gray through my window, I'd been up and trying to read, then trying to paint, successful at neither. I'd needed to do something, and now that I'd decided on a course, I quickly lowered the dinghy into the water and set off downriver.

Early as it was, I wondered if my grandmother, Faith, would be peering out from behind the blinds when I passed her house. As I rounded the corner I saw the heart-shaped stern of the yawl *Annie* docked in front of her house, but there was no sign that anyone was up and about at that hour of the morning.

Hillsboro was about ten miles north on the intracoastal waterway, and other than a small section of woods near the historic Bonnet House, the banks of the waterway were crowded over their entire distance with high-rise condos, a few older low-rise apartment buildings, restaurants, and private homes. Mile after mile I saw evidence of the older homes and buildings being torn down and gigantic replacements going up in their places. When a three-bedroom ranch-style home with generous yard sold, it was replaced with a three-story, six-bedroom, eight-thousand-square-foot home built right out to the property line. A small boutique hotel with shuffleboard court would get bulldozed in favor of a thirty-plus-story condo tower with parking and retail on the first several floors. At one point, I was able to see seven construction cranes at the same time. The new joke was they'd become the state bird of Florida.

The worst part of it all wasn't that twenty years from now an airplane passenger looking down at this town wouldn't see any grass or trees, only shoulder-to-shoulder red-tile roofs. The part that made me really sad was that they all looked so similar, and they were never going to be anyone's home. The condo complexes, the McMansions, were all being built in a pseudo-Spanish style with arches and towers that made them all look alike so they could appeal to investors hoping to turn over the property to other investors. The old retiree apartment buildings with their slapping dominoes and leathery pool ladies or the quirky, individual homes with their pink lawn flamingos that once lined the streets and waterways of my hometown would all soon be gone in favor of these monstrosities that will sit empty most of the year as their owners jet off to Newport or Nice. Lauderdale would become a hollow town with empty stores and vacant schools. These developers think they're just making money, but really they're gutting the heart right out of my hometown.

I stopped briefly in Lake Santa Barbara after the sun had climbed higher and the air had warmed into the upper sixties. Retrieving an old ratty tennis ball out of the Whaler's forward compartment, I cut the engine, let the dinghy drift, and threw the ball as far as I could for my quivering companion. She launched herself off the bow of the boat and happily swam off in search of her treasure. Each time she retrieved it, I pitched it back out across the blue water again until finally, I started to see her slow. I lifted her forepaws onto the bow and heaved at her collar. Then, once she was aboard, I tried to put at least five feet between us before she started her shaking.

"Now are you happy?" I asked out loud, watching her rub her wet face against the sweatshirt I'd discarded in the sun.

Out beyond the dog, I recognized the familiar yellow-green of an Ocean Towing boat that had been making its way southbound down the waterway, but had now diverted into Lake Santa Barbara and was heading directly at me. It looked like a boat of about thirty feet, and its semi-displacement hull was throwing up quite a wake at the speed it was traveling. I could see the outline of two men at the console, but I couldn't make out anything more about them. There were a couple of seconds there when I started to get a little nervous with them heading straight for me, thinking about the dark vehicle of the night before and getting that *Oh shit, here we go again* feeling in my gut. I was about to turn the key in the Whaler and move the hell out of the way, but at the last minute he turned aside, his wash rocking and splashing into my boat.

I was just trying to ride out the wake without putting the gunnels under when I recognized the dreadlocks and realized that one of the men was none other than Quentin Hazell. The other man was the guy he had referred to as Brian at the symposium the day before, and they were both wearing matching neon green shirts.

"Thanks, guys."

"Sorry about that," Quentin said.

"Yeah, you look really sorry." They were both looking at me in my soaked jeans, and then turning their heads away and laughing. "This should be a no-wake zone. It's manatee season."

"We just wanted to say hello when I recognized you over here in your dinghy. I wanted to tell you my news," Quentin said.

"It's not exactly a secret considering you're wearing one of their shirts. I take it you talked to Pinder and got the job?"

"Yes. Brian is going to be training me."

"I'm happy for you," I said. I looked at Brian watching us from his seat at the helm. I got the feeling—from the way he looked away and pretended he hadn't been watching—that Brian wasn't thrilled about Quentin being friendly with the competition. "Just remember that even though towing work might look easy, people do get hurt in this business. I want you to be careful, you hear?" I knew I sounded like his mother, but I hoped he was reading between the lines.

Quentin smiled and nodded, bouncing his dreads. "I hear you."

"Hey, man," Brian said. "We've got to get going. Boss doesn't like us wasting time."

Quentin handed me a slip of paper. "They gave me a cell phone so they can stay in touch with me. This is the number."

"Thanks. I'll see you soon?" I said, hoping to remind him of his commitment to work for me the next day.

Quentin winked at me, nodded once, and let go of my dinghy.

I pushed off and floated free of the blindingly green hull. "See ya," I shouted again, but my words were drowned out by the roar of the engines as they took off across Lake Santa Barbara.

It wasn't difficult to find the *NautiBoy* along the intracoastal close to Hillsboro Inlet. There were no large marinas in the area, and knowing that the vessel was about seventy-five feet long narrowed the possibilities even further. As it turned out, she was on a side tie with her stern pointing south, and I recognized the name before I could assess the size of her. Just for politeness' sake, I tried calling him on the handheld VHF first, but I wasn't surprised when no one answered. They probably had cell phones, landlines, and satellite phones on board, so the VHF wouldn't be on at the dock. I tied the Whaler off on the dock just astern of the yacht, told Abaco to stay in the dinghy, and walked down to their gangplank.

"Hello, anybody aboard?" I shouted.

A young man wearing the usual khakis and white Polo shirt appeared on the aft deck. "Can I help you?" he asked. He looked like he was barely out of his teens.

"I hope so. Are you the captain?" I expected him to say no and to offer to take me to the captain, but he surprised me.

"Yeah, that's me. What can I do for you?"

If the captains in this industry got any younger, I thought, they would be boat drivers before they got their driver's permits for cars.

I told him who I was, adding that I was in the towing and salvage business and wanted to talk to him. He replied that he had grown up in town and knew *Gorda* by sight. He invited me aboard. I was glad to get inside the boat and out of the wind with my wet pants. We settled on vinyl chairs in the galley after I told him that I didn't want to get salt water on the fancy upholstery in the main salon.

"Can I get you something to drink? Coffee or water or anything?"

"No thanks. I just want to ask you a few questions about the incident last month when you went aground.

I hope you won't think I'm prying," I said, "but I'm trying to do some research into yacht groundings."

"I don't mind." He reached into a big industrial-size refrigerator and took out a bottle of water. "Shoot."

"Okay. Did you guys have a towing contract with Ocean Towing before the accident occurred?"

"Yeah, we did. Just signed it not too long before."

"Did you go to them or did they come to you?"

"I just brought the boat down from Annapolis this winter for the first time. The owner flew in over Christmas for a couple of weeks, and one night he had some guy from Ocean Towing over for drinks. I guess he'd met him in a bar a couple of days before."

"Was that guy Neville Pinder?"

"Yeah, I think that was him. He's a white Bahamian dude."

"That's Pinder. Did he look at your navigation equipment at all?"

"I don't think so. Why?"

"Well, I don't know if you've noticed, but there have been several big yachts that have gone aground in the past couple of months. We've been thinking that if there was something similar in the equipment, a cause we could isolate, like the same brand of GPS for instance, then maybe we could discover a technical cause and correct it."

I assumed he would have to go look, but he surprised me again. "We have Raymarine units at both inside and outside steering stations, and I have an extra Garmin handheld of my own as backup."

The *Power Play* had contained all Furuno electronics, so the idea that maybe there was some kind of glitch in the equipment already wasn't panning out. "Can you tell me what happened the day your vessel grounded outside Hillsboro? What were the conditions?"

"First off, it wasn't day, it was night, or almost. We were coming back from Bimini and we had cut straight across to Miami, then we were hugging the coast coming north trying to stay out of the Gulf Stream. It had been a rough trip, wind out of the northeast, and we were tired. The owner was aboard and he was anxious to get home. I was on the helm, and even though I had a visual on the coastline, the buildings, and the lighthouse, I was watching the GPS because it's hard to estimate exactly how far offshore you are with just a visual."

"Were you using radar?"

"It was clear, and we could see any ships for miles. The little boats would just get lost in the sea clutter, so no. Once we got across the Gulf Stream, I'd turned it off."

"And according to the GPS, you should have been okay?"

"Yeah, we should have rounded the outside sea buoy at least a hundred yards off."

"I admit I don't know a whole lot about electronics, but I worry when I think about helmsmen looking at a screen rather than out the window."

"I agree, and I've learned my lesson. I was relying too much on the electronics. The GPS was off by way more than they say—and since it happened, I got on the Net. I've read where you can get interference from boat-mounted TV antenna amplifiers, from sunspots, even from the ship's refrigeration system. But, you know, shit happens."

I thought about Nestor and how devastated he was when he put *Power Play* on the rocks. "You don't seem too upset by it."

"Not my problem. The owner's not going to fire me over it. He figures that's what he's got insurance for."

"And if it makes his premiums go up?"

"It's chicken feed to this guy."

"What do you and the owner think about Ocean Towing charging you for a salvage instead of a tow?"

"Again, not our problem. The owner says that's between Ocean Towing and his insurance company. He'll let them work that one out."

ON the way south, as I was passing Bahia Mar, almost to the mouth of the New River, I heard a whistle and saw George Rice, a broker friend of mine, with his lovely little varnished launch tied to the stern of a motor yacht named the *Savannah Jane*. He waved me over.

I doubt that George had ever been to England—I'd heard he was really from a small town in Alabama—but he had the best fake English accent I'd ever heard. It was a known fact in the yachting business that women often had the final say as to whether or not their husbands could buy their dream boats. George, apparently, figured that since women really went for men with English accents, he would get more women on his side if he talked like someone off *Masterpiece Theatre*. He wound up sounding like *Fawlty Towers* set in Mobile Bay, but he did sell lots of boats—he had to in order to pay for the expensive hair and nail work he had done at a Las Olas salon.

As I pulled alongside, he leaned down and petted Abaco on the head. "Aren't you just the most precious little girl?" he sang out in a voice nearly an octave higher than mine.

"How's it going, George?"

"I just had to call you over to find out if it's true. You know I have always loved *Gorda*, and there was that one time that your brother teased me, led me on, and made me think that your lovely little boat was going on the market. I was devastated when I found out it wasn't true, but now a little bird told me that things have changed. That you are ready to sell. I thought I would just let you know that I would be happy to be of service to you."

"What the hell are you—" I started to light into Rice when I remembered. Pete. Last night at the Downtowner. "Goddammit. You can't tell anybody anything in this town without everybody knowing it by the next day."

George rubbed his hands together. "So it's true? You really might sell?"

"I just said I was thinking about it."

"Well, I know there are a lot of brokers in this town, but your father and I went way back."

"George, Red couldn't stand you."

"But we'd known each other for years, and your father was just a surly fellow. He treated everyone that way. Why, I just know that if he were alive today—"

"If he were alive, he'd never sell that boat. But it's true, I am giving it some thought." I pushed away from his launch and put the outboard in gear. "Give me a call in a few days, okay? We'll see how I feel then."

"Oh, absolutely. I'll call you Friday. Ta ta."

XXI

B.J. was sitting cross-legged on the seawall in front of my cottage when we came around the bend in the river.

"Boy, am I glad to see you," I said after I cut the outboard.

"And I'm always glad to see you."

He took the dinghy painter and pulled the boat under the davits.

"Lightnin' was acting up last night," I said as I took the two snap shackles and secured them to the dinghy's lifting eyes. "And I don't have time to get into it, to try to figure out what's wrong, but I need to get over to Arlen's. Can you drive me?"

Sitting next to him in the cab of his truck, I told him about Neville Pinder and my suspicions. "This guy has only been in this business a little over a year and all of a sudden he's even getting more work than Sea Tow. Nobody knows where he's been getting the money to expand like this, and his luck at being the first on scene at wrecks is just a little too uncanny. The captain of the *NautiBoy* told me that Pinder had been aboard shortly before they went aground. I guess my next step after Arlen is to find out if he or someone who works for him had been aboard the *Power Play.*"

He parked in front of Molly's house since he was

going in for another of their marathon study sessions, while I headed across the street to the Sparkses' house.

Catalina answered the door. She wasn't looking much better than she had the day before. "Hi, Cat, is Arlen here?"

"Yes. He just got back from a morning running errands. He is right out there on the porch—where his equipment is."

"Okay. I have a message for you from B.J. He wants you to go over to talk to him and Molly. They're over there now. It has something to do with this project they're doing. You're going to be their project pregnant lady."

"But if Mrs. Sparks wakes—"

"If she wakes up, I'll be here. Don't worry. They've been getting along without you all these months. They can manage for a few hours."

In fact, B.J. had told me to get her out of the house just so she could get a breather from living here. It wasn't easy caring for a terminal cancer patient, and B.J. and Molly were going to see to it that Catalina got out of the house at least every other day.

The Florida room on the back of the Sparkses' house had probably been a screened-in porch at one time. Now French doors along the far wall of the living room opened onto a glass-enclosed porch. Tinted glass and bimini shutters prevented the space from growing unbearable in summer, and the shafts of sunlight shining through the cracks in the shutters gave the room a cool tropical feeling. A ceiling fan turned slowly overhead. Arlen Sparks sat at a long table covered with tools and radio equipment, his head bent forward, almost resting on his chest.

I knocked on the French door, and he jerked his head

up as though he had been dozing. "Hi, Arlen, you got a minute?"

He drew in a deep breath and ran his hand over the top of his head, smoothing his comb-over from left to right. "Sure, come in. Sit down." His eyes were bloodshot; when he moved to face me, I smelled his sour body odor.

"Thanks." I pulled a wicker chair closer to his work area, but not too close. "Catalina just went across the street to Molly's for a little visit. How're things working out with her?"

"Great," he said. "Sarah likes her, and it has taken some of the load off me. I'm able to get out more." He moved his head from side to side as though trying to work out a crick in his muscles.

"That's good. You should really try to get some sleep, though. You look tired."

He blew out air through rounded lips. "I've got a lot on my mind these days. It's hard to know what's the right thing to do sometimes." I smelled cigarettes on him, too. I didn't remember him smoking when I was a kid.

"I know. Boy, do I know. I mean, the stuff I'm dealing with isn't nearly as bad as you, but still, it's tough dealing with somebody who's sick. I remember when I was taking care of my dad just before he died."

"That's right. You do know."

"Arlen, if you don't mind, I came here today to talk to you about something else. I wanted to ask you some questions about electronics."

"I don't mind. What do you want to know?"

"Did you ever do any work with GPS?"

He rubbed his eyes before he answered. "GPS? Not really." He pointed to the ham radio equipment on the table. "At Motowave, I worked primarily on radio equipment."

"Do you know much about GPS?"

"More than the average layman, I'm sure, but it's not my specialty."

"Okay, well, you surely know more than I do. Here's what I want to know. Would it be possible to mess with another boat's GPS?"

"Well, sure, if I can get into the guts of any electronic equipment, I can mess with the signals."

"Okay. Do you think you could put something in a boat's GPS that would make it go off course when it reached a certain location or something?"

"I'm not sure I understand your question."

"And I'm not sure how to ask because I have no idea what's possible. I know this sounds kind of like science-fiction stuff, but I mean would it be possible to, I don't know, point a ray gun or laser or something at a boat from another boat and send a signal that would make their GPS go out of whack?"

He narrowed his eyes as I was talking, and when I'd finished he barked out a laugh that turned into a coughing fit.

"Do you want me to get you a glass of water?"

"No, no, just give me a minute." He cleared his throat a few more times. It sounded like he had a huge wad of phlegm in there.

I wished he'd excuse himself and go spit somewhere. Maybe he'd been smoking longer than I thought.

"Sorry about that. I've had a cold." He coughed again. "It's been so long since I've laughed I've forgotten how."

"I know it sounds crazy and far-fetched, Arlen, but the way I see it, our government has got to be working on something like this. I mean in desert warfare, everybody is navigating now with GPS. Surely they're working on a way to screw with the enemy's equipment, right?"

"If so, Seychelle, I don't know a thing about it."

"From what you do know, though, don't you think it's possible? I mean, I've heard that GPS on a boat can get screwed up by being too close to other electronics or even refrigeration. So if that stuff can mess it up, doesn't it stand to reason that somebody could invent some kind of thing that would purposely aim interfering energy waves at a boat that would cause it to go off course and go aground?"

He reached forward and patted me on the knee. "You've got a good imagination, honey." Then, leaning back in his chair, he said, "Of course, anything's possible. That's what we scientists and inventors have to believe."

"But you've never heard of anything like that?"

He shook his head. "Sorry. Why are you asking?"

"It's a long story. Just a theory I had. I've been doing some digging around, trying to figure out what's going on with a recent rash of boat groundings."

"Are you certain there really has been an increase? Lots of times we perceive an increase in the number of events around us, but our perceptions are skewed. For example, if you have a loved one injured or killed in a plane crash, you'll likely think there's an increase in the number of plane crashes over the next few months because you'll be predisposed to notice. Just as you are predisposed to notice the number of groundings now that you work on your father's tugboat. Do you know that there really have statistically been more wrecks?"

"No, you've got a point. It's just seemed that way to me. I mean, I have been at this over three years now full-time, and before that I often crewed for Red."

"I suspect you're seeing a problem where one doesn't really exist."

"In a way, I hope you're right. Maybe I should go talk to the Coast Guard and see what the numbers say."

"Why is this so important to you?"

"Well, for one thing, this is my industry. I don't like the idea that there might be crooks in it. I believe we need to police ourselves, report anything that's illegal. But the real reason is Nestor. To Catalina, it's about his honor and integrity. Nestor was convinced someone had messed with the GPS on his boat. He believed someone got aboard and messed with the equipment, causing it to malfunction. And according to you, it sounds like if it happened, that was probably how. If somebody did do something like that, it would mean he wasn't an incompetent captain who ran that new multimillion-dollar yacht on the stones. That matters to lots of people, but most of all to his wife."

"I can see that."

"So I promised her I'd check it out for her. There's a guy I know, he's working for this towing company now, and hopefully, within a few days, I'll have something solid to take to the police. Then they can try to figure out what's possible and what isn't."

CATALINA excused herself immediately when I walked into Molly's living room. The three of them were sitting around the coffee table with books and papers spread out on the table and floor and, as usual, B.J. was sitting at the computer. She said she didn't want to leave Sarah Sparks alone. Arlen had been gone more than he'd been home ever since she had moved into the house, she added, and much of the time he didn't even tell her he was leaving.

I gave her my arm to help her off the low couch. "He

told me having you there has made a big difference in his life. He's able to get out and do the things he'd let pile up."

"It is working well for us all." She squeezed my hand. "Thank you, again."

After she left, Molly closed the book on her lap, leaned forward, and placed it on the coffee table. "Seychelle, sit down. You don't look well. What's going on with you?"

I flopped down into an armchair and smiled at my friend. "I'm tired, that's all. I haven't been sleeping very well."

"Have you eaten anything today?"

I tried to remember. Food just hadn't tasted good lately. I had no appetite. "Not really."

B.J. stood. "Afternoon tea, coming right up."

"So what's eating at you?"

"Molly, I feel kinda lost these days. This morning I saw George Rice, the broker, and he asked me if I wanted to sell *Gorda,* and I told him I'd think about it."

"What? You're joking, right?"

"No, I'm not. I'm not having much luck figuring out what happened to Nestor. It seems like every time I get an idea, I get the door slammed in my face. And then I told you about the lawsuit against me. We go to court Thursday."

"You told me about it, but I thought he was just some jerk taking a slip-and-fall con to the next level."

"Yeah, but see, his daughter almost drowned in the process, and I keep thinking—"

"Sey, listen to me. Stop your thinking. From what I heard she wasn't breathing and you revived her. Would that have happened if it had been Perry who'd gotten to her first?"

"I don't know."

"Yes, you do. You are damn good at what you do, and don't you dare go into that courtroom and look and act like this."

"But I'm not so certain that I am good at this anymore."

"Don't do something that you'll regret. And for God's sake, don't let a weasel like this Burke guy push you around. When you go to court, I want you to squash his revolting little lawsuit. And promise me you'll think long and hard about selling *Gorda*."

So many people were extracting promises from me lately. I was about to complain to her that I couldn't keep track of them all when B.J. walked in with a tray containing three steaming mugs and a plate of oatmeal cookies and I felt a hollow rumble in my belly. Maybe I could eat a couple.

B.J. and I left Molly's house in his El Camino around four in the afternoon, and as we pulled out onto Davie Boulevard, I was digging into my shoulder bag looking for the slip of paper Jeannie had given me. I looked up as we passed Andrews Avenue and noticed a bright green truck pull onto Davie behind us.

"Do you think we could make a little side trip?"

"Sure, where do you want to go?"

"Just a sec." I rummaged through the old gas station receipts and crumpled gum wrappers at the bottom of my bag, and finally found the folded sheet of notebook paper. "Here it is." I looked around for the green truck— gone. So much weird stuff was happening, I was getting paranoid. I unfolded the paper and read the address aloud to him. "Molly's right. Let's just see what kind of condition this guy's in."

Melvin Burke lived in a small two-story apartment building off Las Olas on a street called Isle of Venice, one of many isles between downtown and the beach. It had been a street of small apartment complexes built in the late 1940s and early 1950s for the snowbirds who came down and vacationed from the Northeast. The canals behind the buildings were lined with slips filled mostly with live-aboard sailboats. Many of the older buildings had a distinctly art deco style, but today they were dwarfed by the newly built Mediterranean-style five-story condo complexes, with unit prices starting at one million. The way property values were rising all over South Florida, the owner of the Sea Nymph Apartments must have been holding out for the highest price before selling the land for a teardown. And judging from the condition of the place, he wasn't doing many repairs while he was waiting.

As B.J. drove slowly past, I said, "Doesn't look like any place to raise a kid." Trash littered the courtyard, and the railings on the upper landing streaked rust down the outside walls. Several windows were missing their awnings.

"When these buildings are just waiting for demolition like this, the rents get pretty low even though they're on the water. It's usually waiters and bartenders, guys who do boat work. Not a bad crowd."

We parked a ways up the street from Burke's building; B.J. backed the truck into a spot and shut the engine off, but left the CD player playing a soft reggae tune. There were six parking places across the way in front of the two-story building. The name SEA NYMPH written in a curly neon aqua-colored script was partially covered by an overgrown palm tree. All the parking spaces were occupied.

"So what are we doing here?" B.J. asked.

I pulled the camera out of my bag. "According to Jeannie, we're here to document that the gentleman suing me is not incapacitated by his post-traumatic stress."

B.J. looked at me with one eyebrow arched way up. "You are going to sit here and wait until the gentleman in question does something you can photograph."

"Yeah."

"You?"

"What's so funny about that?"

"This is going to be interesting. You usually can't stand waiting for a bagel to toast."

"Well, you've got to admit, they take forever."

He lifted his hands in a gesture that I took to mean he agreed with me. Then he crossed his arms over his chest and closed his eyes.

There are some things I don't do very well, and one of them is waiting. But another thing I don't do well is admit such things to my friends. I knew that B.J. wasn't asleep. He was sitting there waiting for me to get tired of waiting, and he was thinking that he wasn't going to have to wait very long. I *really* wanted to prove him wrong.

I checked my watch. It was four twenty-five. I reckoned we'd been sitting there for about ten minutes. It felt like an hour.

A few minutes later, I heard the ragged growl of an older truck engine. When I looked toward Las Olas Boulevard, I saw a rusted-out white pickup headed our way. It was easy to recognize the bald head through the dusty windshield.

"Heads up, sleepy. Here comes our guy."

B.J. opened one eye and watched as Burke pulled the truck up behind several of the cars that were parked nose-in to the building. He jumped out and disappeared into the courtyard.

"Surely he won't be gone long. He's blocking those

other cars. When he comes back out, we'll follow him, right?"

"Let's see what happens."

Burke soon appeared again, this time holding on to the end of a couch. His daughter was holding the other end, and she kept having to stop for breaks. Her arms, less than half the diameter of his, weren't strong enough for the weight. At that distance, we couldn't really make out the words, but it was obvious from his gestures that he was getting more and more angry with her.

I snapped a couple of pictures of him loading the couch into the back of the truck before the two of them disappeared into the courtyard again.

The next person to emerge from the Sea Nymph Apartments wasn't Melvin Burke. This guy wore jeans, boat shoes, and large Polaroid glasses. He wasn't a big guy, but his white Guy Harvey T-shirt did little to conceal the enormous beer gut that hung over his belt. I didn't need to be Nancy Drew to peg him as a fisherman. When he came around the corner and saw the truck that was blocking his Ford Explorer, he started cussing, and I had no trouble at all hearing him.

Melvin seemed destined to have bad timing. He came out of the courtyard walking backward, his meaty hands grasping one side of a Formica dining table.

"Are you the fucking asshole blocking me in?"

"Who the fuck you calling an asshole?"

Burke dropped his end of the table and assumed a stance with his legs spread shoulder width apart, his hands balled into fists.

Within seconds they were almost belly-to-belly and their verbal exchange had been reduced to the word *fuck* used as noun, verb, adjective, and a few other parts of speech I couldn't remember from high school. When they'd yell at each other, they'd rise up on their tiptoes, tilting their heads from side to side.

The fisherman was the first to take a swing, and then they were down in the dust and gravel, fists flailing, for the most part ineffectually.

I paused for a moment from snapping photos to glance at B.J. "You going to go break it up?"

"Not unless the little girl gets involved."

I shook my head. "Not likely. I think she's enjoying it as much as we are."

XXII

MORNING light works best for painters. After another night of fitful sleep, I rose in the dark, collected my supplies, and carried my easel out into the Larsens' yard just as the sky was starting to go gray. I'd been working for a while on a painting of my cottage. I had a photo of a great blue heron I had seen one morning on the seawall, but I wanted to paint it the way it looked in the first hour after sunrise. Painting helps me clear my mind. It blows out the fog and allows me to see what's there without looking directly at it. I felt as though some answer to all my questions was right there in front of me, like that elusive spot in your eyes that comes from staring into a bright light. The more you try to look right at the spot, the less you're likely to see it.

By eight o'clock, I decided to take a break and I went inside to make some coffee. The real stuff, not the powdered kind I usually resort to. I felt good for a change, and I was even beginning to think about eating some breakfast. I was on my way back out the door when I heard Abaco bark once. By the time I got outside, she was bounding over to greet Ben Baker as he rounded the side of the big house.

"This is a surprise," I said. Ben was wearing a royal blue jogging suit, and his hair was still damp and slicked back. His face flushed from exercise, he looked like he was ready to model for an ad for men's cologne.

"I decided to drop by on my way home from the gym."

"How did you find me?" I tried to make my voice even and natural.

"It wasn't hard. Seems half the folks in this town know where you live. I asked in the Downtowner last night and three guys gave me three different sets of directions." He walked up behind me and examined the painting over my shoulder. "Nice."

I, too, was staring at the painting. It was nearly finished, but something wasn't right yet. There was something I wasn't seeing. "I thought you'd left yesterday."

"Change of plans. Something came up." He jingled the keys in his jacket pocket. "I remember watching your mother paint. Before she—" He stopped, apparently unsure how to phrase it.

"It's okay to talk about it," I said, turning away from the painting and facing him. "You were going to say before she died. Before she killed herself. It's okay. It was a long, long time ago."

He smiled that big toothy smile and I swear, if I hadn't had a job in the next couple of hours I might have asked him to pose for me. He looked great.

"I am leaving this morning, though, and thought I'd stop by and make one last stab at getting you to join me for a meal. You look like you could use it. I don't suppose I can get you to join me for breakfast at Lester's Diner?"

I laughed. "Like old times? Just me and Glub?" In high school, Molly was the first one of us with a car, and she used to take us out to Lester's sometimes before school in the morning.

"Yeah, like the old days. When we were buddies."

I liked that. I figured it was his way of telling me that

even if I was with B.J. right now, he and I could still be friends. I wasn't ready to close this door just yet. "I'm afraid not, Ben. I've got to work this morning. Gotta be at Bahia Mar at ten to pick up a tow."

"Too bad. You keep turning me down and I'm going to get a complex. I was even going to pop for mimosas."

"Yeah right, at Lester's."

"Then I guess I'll have to eat all alone before my long lonesome drive."

"Nice try. At least you're driving."

"What do you mean?"

"My Jeep. It's been acting up."

"Oh yeah? What's wrong?"

"Coughing, sputtering, stalling. I don't know if the problem is with fuel or air. I haven't had time to deal with it. And I don't know when I *will* have time. By the time I finish this job today, it'll be too late to take it anywhere. I have to be someplace for dinner tonight at five."

He opened his mouth as though he was going to say something, then looked at his watch. "If I didn't have a charter this afternoon, I'd offer to take a look at it myself. Not that I'm much of a mechanic."

"That's okay."

He snapped his fingers. "Why don't you take it out to Gramps. Seriously. He'd love to help you out, and there isn't a better mechanic in South Florida—especially when it comes to older engines like yours. Not only that, he's open twenty-four hours."

"I don't know."

"You'll be doing him a favor. He gets lonely out there. I'll call him on my cell on my way out of town. He'll be expecting you. No matter what time you get there."

"Thanks," I said, and I turned back to face my canvas.

"So I guess this is good-bye again." He stepped behind me to look at the painting one last time and placed his hands on my shoulders. When he spoke he was so close I felt his breath on my ear. "I think you're a better painter now than your mother was."

I wasn't seeing the painting or the river anymore. I closed my eyes and tried to slow my breathing because I wanted to say something and I didn't want to make a fool of myself. "Thanks, Ben." My voice was low and breathy. I cleared my throat. "I wish I'd known her better. I remember her as this tall, beautiful woman who seemed to shine with inner light."

"Yeah," he said over my shoulder in a whisper. "You're very much like her, only better."

I didn't say anything at first. Then I realized I'd been holding my breath and when I exhaled a faint moan escaped from deep inside. This wasn't right, I knew it, but there was a connection between us that was growing harder to ignore.

"You know," he said. "We have something else in common now, too."

"What?"

"Our mothers. We've both lost our mothers."

"That's right. You told me that in Key West. I'm sorry, Ben."

"My mother was a suicide, too." I felt his fingers tighten on my shoulders as he said the words.

I didn't know what to say to that. That it didn't surprise me? That she was probably better off? You can't always say the things you're thinking.

"Your mother didn't have an easy life, Ben."

He turned me around to face him and stared at me through narrowed eyes. "It wasn't what you thought. What you saw that night. I knew you were there. I saw you. But it wasn't what you thought." He paused and held his breath as though he were on the verge of doing something explosive. Then he turned around and stalked off toward the Larsens' gate.

To his back, I said, "I didn't think anything, Ben. We were just kids."

He paused at the gate then half turned. When he spoke, his head was lifted as though he was examining the side of the Larsens' house. "Everyone always blamed him. But women—" He paused as though searching for the words. "They get away with stuff." Then he was gone.

I thought back to that night and played the memory through, trying to see it from an adult point of view. We'd both been fourteen years old, that age of rapid growth and raging hormones. As a girl, I had matured faster and I'd already reached my adult height of five foot ten. Ben was about five inches shorter and his voice was still high and soft. I had been sleeping that night when I heard tapping at my bedroom window.

"SEYCHELLE!"

It's Ben and he's crying.

The screen is permanently off my window, as Molly and Ben and I frequently use this method of entering and exiting to stay under our parents' radar. I slide up the window, and Ben props his bike against the wall and climbs through.

He tells a story that's grown familiar to me. His parents are fighting again, he says, and he doesn't want to go home. He says he wants to protect his mother, but his father is too big, too strong. As he says this, he wipes the snot from his nose on the back of his hand and he tells me he knows that his father will kill both him and his mother someday. He asks me to help him run away. There's something about this night that makes it different from all the others. There's an urgency in Ben that frightens me. He makes me promise that I won't let his father kill him and I promise, knowing full well that Mr. Baker scares me to death.

Ben is acting crazy. He's pacing the floor of my room talking to himself. I consider asking him to spend the night on the floor of my room when the window slides up and out of the darkness Junior Baker's voice speaks a single word.

"Come."

I've never seen such terror in a kid's eyes. Those eyes are begging me to do something but I can't breathe, much less speak or move. As Ben crosses the terrazzo floor, I see and smell the trickle of urine that follows his footsteps. I want to grab his shirt and pull him back because I'm afraid I'll never see my friend again. Then Ben's father reaches through the window and grabs one of his son's pant legs and mumbles, "Fuck," as he pulls the wet denim out the window.

When I can feel my limbs again, I cross to the window, but they are gone. I run down the hall and awaken my father, telling him that I am afraid for Ben, afraid that his father is going to beat him, maybe kill him. My father tells me to go to bed. He says that I am exaggerating, and we cannot intervene. He tells me again to go back to bed, that Ben will be fine, and I know that this time my father is wrong. When I return to my room and see that trail of pee, I pull on clothes over my pajamas and climb out the window.

The street is quiet, the houses all dark. Bugs circle in the cone of light under a street lamp. I move slowly down the walkway that leads to the backyard gate and to his window. I don't hear any shouting or any crying, and this surprises me.

His room is dark, the window still open. A shaft of light from the streetlight shows the big lump in his bed.

"Ben," I whisper.

The lump shifts. Two heads pop up. I duck back behind the wall, my heart pounding loud, but not so loud I can't hear Ben's mother say, "Ben, who was that?"

I run all the way home.

I hadn't thought it then, and I wouldn't have been thinking it now if he hadn't brought it up. Was it possible? What had I thought back then? That his mother was comforting him after his father had beat the crap out of him. Could it have been something else? I couldn't stop thinking about it as I motored down the river. I'd always thought I'd had it tough with my mother, with her bad days and over-the-top manic hysterics. But if what I now suspected was true, what was happening inside Ben's house explained a great deal about his not ever wanting to go home.

I got to Bahia Mar and tied up *Gorda* in an empty slip close to *Wild Matilda,* a Ron Holland 43. The owner had been using my family to look after his boat since Red used to run the business. The owner was an engineer who lived in DC and used the sailboat as his Florida vacation home. He didn't like to have to come down and waste his precious free time seeing to haulouts and maintenance, so he hired me to get the boat up to the yard and to keep an eye on it over the next three weeks while the guys at River Bend Boatyard got all her systems back in top working order. Most years, I would just show up and motor the sailboat to the yard under her own steam, but this year the engine had been overheating at the dock when I'd just been doing routine maintenance, so rather than risk losing power on the river, I was going to tow her up.

At quarter after ten, I was beginning to get upset with Quentin. I wanted to get up the river while the tide was still running out so it would be easier to maneuver the two boats when we had to wait in the tight spaces between the bridges. I had already rigged the towline on the bow of the sailboat and readied the dock lines and fenders to make it easier to cast off. I'd also run the engine a few minutes to make sure it would start in case we needed it. I was just waiting on my crew.

By ten thirty, I had shifted from mad to worried. Where the hell was he? Had he gotten lost? Bahia Mar was a huge place; maybe he'd forgotten the slip number and the name of the boat. He'd always seemed to have no trouble getting around without a car, but if he was relying on the bus, there was no telling what time he might show up. If he didn't come soon, though, I'd have to risk running upriver with the tide behind me or cancel the trip until tomorrow or the next time I could schedule a haul at River Bend.

I paced the dock. "Shit," I said aloud when I tripped over a cleat and nearly went into the water. I thought about the last time I'd seen him up in Lake Santa Barbara. I had told him to be careful. And then I remembered him giving me the number to his new cell phone. I ran back to *Gorda*, jumped aboard, and grabbed my bag out of the wheelhouse. I slid the door closed and headed down the dock at a run. One of these days, I was going to have to give in and buy myself a cell phone. I was postponing that moment as long as possible, but on days like this I regretted it.

Over by the pool, I found a pay phone, and after the damn thing rang almost ten times, a male voice—with no lilting Caribbean accent—answered the phone.

"Hello? Is Quentin there?" I was breathing hard from the running.

"He's not able to come to the phone right now. I can take a message."

There was something familiar about that voice. I was

going through the voices I knew that were connected to Ocean Towing and I was drawing a blank. "This is Seychelle Sullivan. Quentin Hazell was going to work for me today. I need to speak to him."

There was a long silence on the other end of the phone. I was beginning to wonder if the call had been disconnected, when the man spoke. "Miss Sullivan. This is Detective Collazo. I'm afraid I have bad news for you."

I closed my eyes and for several seconds all the sound in the world seemed to recede into the distance, then stop.

"Miss Sullivan, are you there?"

His voice sounded as though he were at the bottom of a deep well. Then it grew louder.

"Miss Sullivan?"

I knew what it meant if Collazo was on the scene, and part of me hadn't even registered the words when he told me what he was looking at. I didn't want him to hear the sound of my pain so I had covered the mouthpiece. No, no, not again. Not Quentin.

"Miss Sullivan?"

I uncovered the phone. "I'm here," I said, though the words came out at a barely audible level. I was leaning against the wall alongside the pay phone, the tears beginning to slide down my cheeks. I tried again to speak. "I'm here, Detective. Sorry." I wiped my face with the back of my hand. "What happened?"

Collazo and I had a history. This wasn't the first time he and I had met up because someone who knew me had turned up dead.

"I'm over here on Sistrunk," he said. "Behind a chicken restaurant. Employee found the body out by the Dumpster when he came in to work this morning. Single blow to the head."

The body. That beautiful man with a smile that could

just knock you out was now being referred to as *the body*. Oh, Quentin. What have I done to you?

"Sistrunk?" I said. That was a predominantly black, high-crime neighborhood in the northwest section of town. "What was he doing over there?"

"Same as most. This looks like a drug deal gone bad."

"Quentin? Drugs? Not unless he was scoring some ganja, and he could find that on the docks."

"And you know this guy."

I told him the story of our meeting in Key West and how he had crewed for me on the trip north. "I just saw him yesterday. He had found a job with Ocean Towing." He had been so eager to help me, I remembered. What had he done? Why did I ever ask him to help? Oh, Quentin. "Collazo, I think I need to talk to you. There's more to this."

"Miss Sullivan. I understand you are upset, but this looks pretty straightforward."

"Collazo, I get what you're seeing. A black man, worn clothes, dreadlocks. But you aren't seeing Quentin Hazell."

"Repeat his name."

I spelled it out for him, and I could picture Collazo writing it in his notebook in that neat hand of his. "So his wallet is gone?"

"Like I said, it's pretty straightforward."

"You're not looking at it right. Collazo, think about it. When was the last time you ever heard of a drug dealer who left a cell phone behind?"

I sat on the sidewalk under the pay phone, leaning my back against the wall, trying to understand how this could have happened. I didn't believe for a minute that Quentin's death had been a random killing. He didn't have any reason to be in that part of town, but whoever had done this counted on the cops not asking too many questions about a dead black man on Sistrunk. What happened? And why had I encouraged him to do anything? If I had just kept my mouth shut, Quentin would probably be alive. Thinking about that actually hurt; it caused a physical pain in my chest like I was going to collapse inward. I rested my head on my bent knees and cried again.

I wasn't aware of the passing of time. When I raised my head and looked around, I realized it could have been five minutes or an hour since I'd first heard the news about Quentin. The whole world seemed askew. Time wasn't working properly, and good people who should live long lives were dying.

I felt something shift inside me. I could breathe easier, the tightness in my chest gone. Two good decent young men were gone. And the son of a bitch who did this was going to pay. I'd told Collazo that I would be in to speak to him in the afternoon. And there was still the matter of the *Wild Matilda*. It was time to get moving. I stood up, reached into my bag for more change, and dialed a number I knew by heart.

"Hi, Mike," I said when he answered. "I could really use a hand if you're free."

XXIII

MIKE Beesting was a retired Fort Lauderdale cop who lived aboard his Irwin 54 *Outta the Blue* and ran occasional day charters—more out of his need to be social than a desire for income. After losing the lower half of one leg in an incident considered the line of duty, his severance package with the city had been generous. Mike had never been a boater before and he loved gear, so he'd loaded up his Irwin with too many toys that drained his batteries and too many fancy gadgets that frequently malfunctioned. Our friendship had started with me towing him in the first two or three times he couldn't start his engine. From then on, we rarely went a week without seeing each other.

Thirty minutes later, he was pulling up in his hard-bottomed inflatable dinghy.

"Thanks for doing this for me, Mike." I held the painter to his dinghy while he crawled out onto the dock.

When he was sailing his own boat, Mike hardly ever wore his prosthetic leg, but today, with his worn blue jeans, he had both boat shoes on. Navigating the metal-runged ladder to climb onto the Bahia Mar dock was a challenge for anyone, but crawling on hands and knees presented different challenges for Mike. After he got to his feet, he wrapped me up in a big bear hug.

"It's good to see you, my friend. Now tell me again

what sort of trouble you've got yourself into this time. Start at the beginning, 'cause I couldn't hardly understand a word on the phone."

"Come on aboard the *Wild Matilda* here, and I'll tell you while I show you around the controls." I tied his dinghy off on one of the sailboat's stern cleats.

Mike had known Nestor and had heard about his death already. He didn't ask me many questions, the way some people had. In his life as a cop on the streets of Fort Lauderdale, Mike had seen enough bloodshed. He didn't need to hear any more grisly details. As I pointed out the engine controls, the fancy chart plotter, the depth sounder, and the VHF radio, I told him about Nestor's belief that someone had sabotaged his GPS, Catalina's certainty that someone had killed Nestor, and all my experiences since with Neville Pinder.

"Even the detective who worked Nestor's case down in Key West has come around to thinking that there might have been foul play, Mike, but Key West has closed the case. Accidental death by drowning. We don't have enough evidence to open it up again, yet. And now this morning I find this out about Quentin."

"And who is Quentin again?"

I gave him a brief overview of how I'd met the man and how he had come to be working for Ocean Towing. Several times I had to stop and swallow down the ball of emotion that was trying to crawl back up my throat. "Mike, Quentin wouldn't have had any reason to be over in northwest Lauderdale. No way this guy was into crack or heroin or anything like that. He was staying on the *Power Play* while it was hauled out, and once he got a paycheck or two, he was going to try to rent a room in a crew house. I'm sure his death had something to do with Ocean Towing."

"That's probably going to be a hard sell to the cops."

"I know. You want to get away with murder? Just make sure your victim is poor and black."

"That's not fair, Seychelle. There are lots of good cops in this town."

"Dammit, I know it. But you have to admit there's some truth in what I'm saying. I could use your help when I go talk to Collazo. Maybe he'll listen to you."

"Maybe. It's not like we were old chums, though."

"All right. You'll go with me then?"

He nodded.

"Great. But right now, this tide isn't waiting for us. Let's get this boat up the river and we can talk more afterward, okay?"

I had been a little bit leery of asking Mike for help with the tow, because he wasn't the most experienced captain. On the other hand, I needed his help with the cops and I figured I could keep him out of trouble on the water. We stayed in touch via the VHF and traffic was light on the river, so he never even had to fire up the Holland's engine until we were right off the boatyard there at River Bend. I held my breath as he drove her into the slipway. He went in a little too hot but threw the engine into reverse, and, spewing black smoke out her exhaust, she stopped just before hitting the wall. I tied *Gorda* on the outside dock and headed for the office to take care of the paperwork.

"You had me a little nervous there, hotshot," I said to Mike when he came in.

"I knew what I was doing."

In reaction to that, Charlie, the yard foreman, who'd come into the office for a stop at the coffeepot, choked and nearly spewed coffee all over the papers I'd just finished.

"Careful," I said, smiling.

He pointed to his throat. "Just finding it a little hard to swallow."

"Charlie, I've got a question for you. Would you say you've seen an increase lately in boats with damage from accidents?"

"There's always enough assholes out there to keep us plenty busy."

"So you wouldn't say you've noticed any change?"

"What are you getting at?"

"Nothing. Just kind of thinking out loud."

"Haven't really noticed any change here."

" 'Course you don't handle the really big megayachts here, either, do you?"

He shook his head and walked around from behind the counter. "Go upriver for that." He had one hand on the door when I thought of one more question.

"Charlie, if I was to ask for the top expert in town on GPS, who would you recommend?"

He didn't answer right away. "That's not really my thing, you know. Ask me about wood, fiberglass, bottom paint, I'll have an answer for you. But there was one boat in here that was having trouble with their GPS, and they brought in this old guy. I think he's retired. Had a funny name. Give me a minute, I'll think of it."

The answer he finally gave me made my stomach turn sour.

"Sparky. That's it. Don't know his real name, but the owner called him Sparky most of the time. Said he was a real expert in GPS. You know, some kind of rocket scientist—worked on the guidance systems for missiles or some shit like that."

I knew I should be asking him more questions, but my brain was having difficulty processing what he'd just said. Sparky. Arlen? It had to be him. He *had* worked with GPS at Motowave. He'd lied to me.

The door closed behind Charlie, and I grabbed my bag and followed him outside. "Charlie, when was that? When was this guy here in the yard?"

The yard foreman rubbed his chin and looked up at the slab side of a dark blue motor yacht on the hard. "Must have been last summer. Yeah. August. Before the hurricane. Or rather hurricanes."

"Thanks." I was standing there staring, but not seeing, when Mike walked up behind me.

"You want to tell me what's going on?"

"Do you know Arlen Sparks?"

He shook his head.

"He lives on the street where I grew up. He was a friend of Red's. Shit, Mike, I've known this guy all my life."

"Okay, and? He's some kinda expert with GPS and this is a problem?"

I looked across the basin and saw an Ocean Towing boat pulling in with a small cabin cruiser in tow. "Go get your dinghy and meet me at *Gorda*. We need to talk this out."

When we were settled in the wheelhouse, in a place I was confident we could not be overheard, I told Mike about my visit with Arlen Sparks.

"The guy told me point-blank that GPS was not his specialty. That he didn't know much more than the average layman. Now, according to what Charlie said, he lied. According to Charlie, that was his job at Motowave, it was his specialty."

"Maybe he was exaggerating his expertise to his friend. You know, guys do that sometimes."

I gave him a look that said *duh*. "Listen, Arlen told me that he got laid off last summer in July. He was here in the yard after that. After he got laid off. It makes sense. When he was working at Motowave, he was a real company man. I couldn't see him troubleshooting a GPS installation in a boat in his spare time in those days. He didn't have any spare time. But after he got laid off, he needed the money. He was trying to figure out what to do. But he didn't get really desperate until his wife got sick again."

"You lost me there."

"His wife survived one bout with breast cancer, but the cancer returned this last fall. The doctor wanted to do some kind of treatment that Medicare denied and Arlen desperately wanted to get the money for it."

"So?"

"Mike, I am convinced someone is deliberately causing some boats to go aground and then conveniently showing up to tow them off the shoal or reef and filing a salvage claim. The company that seems to be first to the wreck every time these days is Ocean Towing. It's almost as though they know the boats are going to wreck. Well, they would if they were causing the wrecks."

"And what kind of magic are you thinking they're using?"

"Not magic. Some radio waves or something. I'm not sure about the science of it, but I'm thinking they've figured out a way to selectively jam the GPS using, I don't know, some kind of directional antennas. I realize it sounds like something out of a comic book, but think about it. It makes sense. We've been fighting wars in the desert for some time. With GPS, you know exactly where you are, and if you can mess with your enemy's navigation system, you really have an advantage. Our government's got to be working on something like this, don't you think?"

"Yeah, in fact I've heard something about this. On the news."

"I thought so. I hate the fact that Arlen was able to convince me so easily that I didn't know what the hell I was talking about. I just figured he was the expert, and I gave up on the idea as soon as he said it wasn't possible. Besides, it was Arlen Sparks, my neighbor, a man I've known as long as I can remember. I think I'm going to have to give in to all these goddamn electronics and learn some more about computers and stuff. I shouldn't have been so gullible."

"It's about time, Sullivan. You've been a goddamn Luddite for too long."

"Speaking of which, could I borrow your cell phone? I want to call B.J."

Mike chuckled and pulled a tiny flip phone out of his jean pocket. I looked at the odd-shaped device in the palm of his hand. I was embarrassed to admit the thing frightened me. I'd seen kids barely old enough to go to school using the little phones, but I'd only made a couple of calls on them before, and I'd never called on one that you had to open. "Can you show me how it works?" I asked.

As expected, Mike roared with laughter. "You have got to be kidding me, sweetheart." Then he saw the look on my face. "Or maybe not. Look here, just open it up and push these numbers."

I dialed Molly's house first. I put it to my ear. Nothing. "It's not working," I said.

"Did you push *send*?" he asked, then rolled his eyes as he took the phone from me and pushed a button before handing it back.

"Well, you don't have to get snotty about it." When I put the phone to my ear, this time I heard a voice.

"Get snotty about what?"

"Oh, hi, Molly. It's me. Never mind. Is B.J. there?"

"Sure. Hang on."

"Hey," he said a few minutes later, his voice deep and gentle. "I was just thinking of you."

"Really?" I still found it hard to believe that a man like B.J. could be around petite, curvaceous Molly day after day and continue thinking of me. I turned my back to Mike and said in my best attempt at a throaty, seductive voice, "Well, I was just thinking of you, too."

Mike groaned. "I have things I need to do, Sullivan. I don't have time to sit here and listen to you make lovey-dovey noises into my phone."

I put my hand over the phone. "Give me a break, will you?" I said to Mike.

"What?" B.J. asked.

"Nothing. I was talking to Mike. He's giving me a hard time. The reason I was thinking of you is because I need someone who can look something up for me on the computer."

"I'd be happy to do it for you. What do you need?"

"I want you to try to find something about this GPS idea of mine. See if you can find out whether or not they—like the government, or some corporation—have developed the ability to mess with somebody's GPS signal. Not to just jam it, but to actually make it give a false readout. I'd also like to know if Motowave has been doing any of the R and D on systems like that."

"I can do that. Give me a couple of hours, tops."

XXIV

WE decided to take Mike's car to the Fort Lauderdale Police Department, so after securing *Gorda* to my dock we took his dinghy back to his boat. As we pulled up to his dock, I noticed a small, domelike new antenna on the arch that held up his boom.

"Another toy, Mike?"

"Yup. A satellite phone. Now, I've got communication capability worldwide."

"But you never go farther than ten miles offshore."

"Yes, darling, but you never know when I might. And now, if I do, I can call you and leave a message on your goddamn cottage phone 'cause you don't even own a cell phone."

"Okay, already. I'll get one. I will. I promise." I just didn't say when.

It turned out that having Mike along speeded up the process of getting into the inner recesses of the Fort Lauderdale police station, but once there, our progress toward Collazo's desk slowed considerably. Mike knew everybody, and they all had to stop and shake his hand and ask him how he was doing while trying to hide their furtive glances down at his leg. I knew my way and got tired of waiting for Mr. Popularity, so I abandoned him in the corridor and made for the detectives' bullpen where I found Collazo sitting, squinting at a screen, and doing two-fingered typing on a laptop.

My relationship with Detective Victor Collazo dated back a couple of years to the time my ex-boyfriend, lover, significant other—whatever you wanted to call Neal Garrett—had gotten himself involved with a Fort Lauderdale sleazebag who was trying to smuggle his ill-earned cash out of the States on rust-bucket freighters. When a stripper, Neal's new girlfriend, ended up dead, Collazo had suspected me, so we hadn't exactly started off as buddies. But we had achieved a state of grudging tolerance, and now especially, watching him struggle to type on the computer, I felt a kind of kinship. Pinder had called it: people like Collazo and me were Old School.

"Detective, how's it going?" I reached out and shook his hand.

Collazo had more body hair than any other individual I'd ever met, and because of that he always wore long-sleeved shirts. He never rolled up his sleeves or unbuttoned his collar—which was unfortunate because he also had a tendency to sweat. When he reached out his arm, there were already big wet circles under his pits, and his hand felt damp in my grasp.

"I got a ride here with Mike Beesting, but he's out there swapping lies with his old buddies."

"You said you had information to add concerning the Hazell case."

"Detective, don't you ever ease up a little, take part in the social niceties of life? You know, like say hello to a person for example?"

"Hello, Miss Sullivan. You don't think Hazell's murder had anything to do with drugs."

"Right. That's why I came. Collazo, have you ever been to Key West?"

"I can't see how that would pertain to this investigation."

"Oh, it does. Did you know that Key West was built by the wrecking industry in the the nineteenth century?"

"This is going to get to Hazell, eventually."

"Yes, just give me ten minutes to explain it to you."

"Five minutes."

"Okay. It's economics, supply and demand. In my business, the marine salvage business, when a boat goes on the reef, the salvage company that gets her off more or less in one piece can make a claim, which translates to a percentage of the value of the boat. Here in Fort Lauderdale, fifty years ago, most boats or yachts were relatively small, both in size and value. Today, if your yacht is under a hundred feet or worth less than two million, you're small potatoes. You know that even five percent of a million dollars is a nice piece of change. This has become a huge business, but as the yachts grew in size, more and more people jumped into the business. Then, with electronic navigation like GPS, not as many boats were having accidents. The end result is that today there are too many salvage boats and not enough wrecks, so somebody has decided to *make* wrecks happen, and I believe it's such a lucrative business that they have now killed two people to keep their scam from being discovered. Quentin was number two. The first was Nestor Frias in Key West last week."

"And you have proof of this."

"Well—" I started, but I was interrupted by Mike's arrival.

"Hey, Vic, old buddy, old pal, how's it hanging?" He plopped down into a chair he pulled over from an empty desk.

Collazo merely looked at Mike and bounced his head

in one curt nod. As a rule, everybody liked Mike. Collazo, however, wasn't everybody.

Mike said, "And I'm just fine, thanks for asking, Vic." He turned to me. "Seychelle, I see you're getting the warm reception I predicted."

"Mike, he's listening to me. Right now that's all I'm asking because he's right, we don't have any proof. It's all just speculation." I turned back to Collazo. "Quentin crewed for me on my tug on the trip I just made coming back up from Key West. We spent three days and two nights on my very small boat. He was never anything other than a good crew and complete gentleman. He was from a poor little island in the Caribbean, Dominica, but he had ambition. He was up here to make enough to go back home and buy his own boat. The man I knew wouldn't have been over there making some drug deal, Detective, I'm sure of it. Not Quentin. But the person who did this doesn't have a very high opinion of the Fort Lauderdale cops."

When Collazo narrowed his eyes, Mike cut in. "Seychelle thinks that they killed him and then dumped him over there because the cops won't pay much attention to another black dude getting his head bashed in along that stretch."

I forged ahead as though Mike had not spoken. "Quentin had just been hired by Ocean Towing. The company is owned by a guy named Neville Pinder whose main offices are in Key West, but he has branch offices all over. Including here. He's from the Abacos, and the way I hear it, the Bahamas don't want him back. Nobody knows where a guy like Pinder suddenly got the money to finance an operation like his."

Collazo reached for the notebook on his desk and flipped to a new page. He wrote the name *Neville Pinder*.

"The guy in Key West who was killed was named

Nestor Frias, and the Key West detective you should talk to about that is Lassiter."

"I should talk to," he said, repeating it just as I had, with no questioning inflection in his voice. Collazo never asked questions, he just made these maddening statements all the time.

"Detective, this is big. This is not just some guy getting mugged on Sistrunk. That guy, Nestor Frias, the one who died in Key West? He was the captain of Ted Berger's yacht. I'm sure that's a name you've heard of."

Collazo's dark eyes met mine in a quick glance before he slowly wrote the name in his notebook.

"I'm not sure where Berger fits into this thing, or if he even does. But he was with me in Key West when we found the body down there. Anyway, Quentin knew that I suspected Ocean Towing of causing these wrecks, and he said he was going to look into it and see what information he could get for me. He must have found out something, or else he was about to, and whatever it was got him killed."

The detective looked at his watch. "Your time is up, Miss Sullivan."

There was more that I wanted to tell him, but I was afraid that if I brought up the black SUV in Key West and the idea that perhaps the same vehicle had been the one that followed me Monday night, it wouldn't help swing his viewpoint on Quentin. I didn't want him thinking I was just some crazy paranoid female.

Collazo set the notebook down on his desk and returned to his computer keyboard as though we weren't still sitting there.

"I think we've been dismissed," Mike said.

XXV

BY the time Mike dropped me off back at my place, I barely had time to shower and change before heading down the street to try to reclaim Lightnin' from where I'd left her. As I was about to fly out the door, though, I noticed the red light blinking on my answering machine. The display told me I had two messages. I pressed the *play* button; the first message was from B.J.

"Seychelle, not only is it possible, but the technology was all developed at Motowave. I'm printing out all the information you'll need. I'll drop it off at your place later tonight."

The voice on the second message was nearly as excited. "Seychelle, dahling," George Rice began, "I know yóu said that you were only going to think about it, but I put out some feelers and got a strike right away. I have a buyer for you, cash in hand. This is a solid offer for the boat and the business." He went on to tell me what the offer was, and I had to hit *rewind* and play it again to make sure I'd heard it right. With that kind of money, I could travel, buy my own home. Heck, I could even go to college, major in art, start a whole new life.

It took four tries this time, but the engine finally caught and I went roaring off toward US 1—but not without noticing another bright green pickup in my rearview mirror.

* * *

THE house on the Colee Hammock side of the river looked a whole lot different than it had the first time B.J. and Molly's Gramma Josie had dragged me over there. Back then, the place was unkempt and overgrown, but my brother Maddy had paid to have the whole house re-landscaped. Now Faith had a service that came in twice a month to take care of the yard. They were working under her direction, and slowly the place was starting to look less like a suburban tract home's lawn. She hadn't wanted to hurt Maddy's feelings, but straight-lined hedges and red-mulched flower beds were not her style. Now ninety-two years of age, our grandmother had first arrived in Fort Lauderdale when it was little more than a frontier town, and when she said she liked native plants, she was one of the few people left who really remembered what they looked like.

I let myself into the house as she'd told me I should. "Hello, Faith?"

"Out here, dear, in the kitchen," she called.

The house was filled with the sweet aroma of baked ham, and when I found her in the kitchen, she was stirring a pot that held simmering candied yams. "Wow, it smells great." I came up behind her and touched her on the shoulder. She turned and presented her cheek to be kissed. "How have you been this week?"

"Just fine," she said. "The city tried to push through approval for another five hundred units downtown this week, though. I just don't know where it's going to end."

"Did you go to the hearing?"

She reached into the freezer and dropped three ice cubes into her glass. "Of course." For the last fifty years at least, my grandmother had been hounding the local government, attempting to keep them in line. Single-handedly, she had brought down various local politicians and tried valiantly to rein in their rampant development. "Help yourself to a beer. Let's go outside."

On her way outdoors, she stopped in the living room and made herself a gin and tonic. I followed her out onto the wooden deck that overlooked the river. This had become our routine: drinks until six, then dinner inside.

"I missed you last week, and we really didn't get a chance to talk the other night. So tell me more about this trip to Key West." We settled into the two weathered wooden chairs. The yawl *Annie* with her varnished spruce masts lay at the dock to our right, and we had a great view down the curving river to our left. Upriver, the sun was settling between the tall buildings; a crescent moon hung not far behind, ready to make her westerly descent.

"Oh boy, so much has happened. I feel like I'm a different person than I was a week ago. Guess what? I'm thinking of getting out of the salvage business. Someone has offered a lot of money to buy me out—and I'm thinking about taking it."

"Why? I thought you loved working on your river."

I leaned back in the chair and sighed. "Yeah, there have been some good times. But you know how much the town is changing. My business is changing, too."

"Be careful what you wish for, dear."

"When Red died, I decided to take over Sullivan Towing and Salvage, in part because it was a way I could keep a part of him alive. But I also got into this because I wanted to *help* people. Now it's all about the money." I took a long deep drink, and the cold beer slid down my throat, chilling me from within. The air was cooling as the sun dropped lower in the sky, and I pulled up the zipper on my sweatshirt. "Grams, you remember the stories about the days when wrecking was a major business along this coast, don't you?"

"Of course. When I was a child, I heard many adults lamenting that the wrecking business was fading into the past."

"Well, I'm afraid somebody's trying to resurrect it, and as a result two young men I know have died. Murdered—over money, I think. By somebody in my business. One of them left behind a widow eight months' pregnant. You met her at my house the other night."

"Men," she said, and then she sniffed in disgust. "Even though I buried two good husbands, both of whom I still miss, I know that for them, sex, money, it's all the same in the end. It's about power."

Despite her advanced years, Faith had not lost any thing in the spit-and-vinegar department.

"Women," she said, "are more decent. They care more about children and making a home."

"I don't know if I can agree with that, Faith. I never intend to have children and I like being in charge. And there are some vicious, money-hungry women." I remembered the woman who had married Molly's ex-husband. She also had him murdered.

"No babies, Seychelle? For heaven's sake, why not?"

Why was everyone in my life so concerned about having babies all of a sudden? "That just isn't meant to be for me, Grams."

"You don't know what you're talking about. Women are meant to have babies. *All* women."

"Not me. I'm defective in that department."

She placed her hand flat against her chest at the neckline of the simple cotton blouse she wore. "Oh dear, what's the matter? Is it something physical? Did you have to have a procedure?"

I opened my mouth to make a wisecrack, something

about still having all the equipment, but the only thing that came out was a strangled sob. Once again it had crept up on me, surprised me. It had been years since I'd felt the grief this fierce, this fresh. It was those words, *a procedure,* that brought it all back. That was what the nurse at the clinic had told me to do. To have a procedure done, to take care of the "problem." The memories that I usually managed to push back into the darkness broke loose and a wave of black pain washed over me, nearly drowning me. I leaned forward with my teeth gritted, my chest silently heaving, my nostrils contracting as I struggled for air.

Grams slid her chair closer to mine and placed her veined hand on my knee. She didn't try to stop my tears; she just stayed with me, and her presence helped me ride the storm in a way I never had before. When my sobs had quieted and I finally lifted my head to look at her, wondering what I was going to say, she was the first to speak.

"Was it a boy or a girl?" she asked, and with those words I almost went under again. She grasped my hand. "Hold on. You can get through this." Her words were barely more than a whisper.

"How did you know?"

"Oh dear, you know your mother came to us late in life. I told you that. What I didn't tell you about was the two miscarriages I had before her."

"Two? Oh my God."

Faith had taken the beer bottle from my hand when I'd collapsed. She handed it back to me. "Here, now, take a drink. So what happened, dear? Can you tell me?"

Could I? I wasn't sure. I did as she asked, took a long swig. It helped. "I've never told anyone."

"I think you'll find it helps."

I took a deep breath and tried to make my muscles relax. "I was twenty." I gave a dry laugh. "That was over ten years ago but at moments like tonight, it seems so fresh, like it just happened. I only slept with him once—didn't even know how to find him after. Not that it mattered. It wasn't his problem."

I stopped, not certain I could go on. To tell it would mean I would have to see it again. It would mean letting a little light shine on those images that most of the time I had successfully kept in the dark. Successfully? If that had been the case, then why did I still suffer from these crying jags?

"When I was late, I just figured I would go, have an abortion, no big deal. Only it was. A very big deal. When I went to the clinic and they started on about *the procedure,* I couldn't stand the sound of that word. I left. Walked out to my Jeep and never went back. I intended to. I told myself I wasn't going to keep it, no way, but I kept putting it off. My body was changing and even before it made any sense, I could feel the life in me."

"I know what you mean. I always knew I was pregnant even before there were any real signs."

I nodded. "I was working as a lifeguard on Fort Lauderdale Beach back then, and I worried that it might start to show. But it was winter and I wore my sweats to work most of the time. I could see my face and body softening, rounding out a bit, but no one else noticed. There never was anything bad—no morning sickness or anything. In fact, I felt great, you know, strong and healthy. There were weeks when I let myself forget all about it. I guess they'd call it denial.

"Then one morning I felt it move. I couldn't believe it. I hadn't been paying any attention to the time flying by and I was still not intending to carry this thing to term and then it moved inside me.

"It was that night I woke up around two in the morning in the worst pain I have ever felt. I lived in a little apartment then, over off Sunrise Boulevard. I had a phone on the nightstand and I called 911, but it took them forever to get there. When the paramedics arrived, I was on the floor in a pool of blood holding my dead baby. She was gray. She never took a breath. Tiny. Oh God, she was tiny, but she had all her fingers and toes."

"Oh, Seychelle. You poor dear. I never saw them. Your grandfather took me to the hospital and in those days, they knocked you right out."

"I didn't want to let her go. I fought the paramedics when they tried to take her from me. At the hospital, I asked them not to call my father. I was twenty years old, after all. They released me the next day and I went home and cleaned up and told the world I had a bad case of flu. I needed to stay home for a few days. I told myself to forget it ever happened. But I knew at that point, I knew for certain, that I would never live through that a second time. No more babies for me."

The sun was gone but the sky still glowed a bright pale blue. Lights were starting to wink on in the homes across the river. The current had stilled with the tide. It was slack water. On our side, upriver and fairly close to the dock, I saw an upwelling of water; concentric rings appeared and grew. Four feet farther down the river, there was another bump in the water, and another batch of rings began to widen.

"Grams." I pointed upriver. "Manatee."

We both stood and walked down the steps to the sea-wall. She was so deep we could only follow the path of water rings made by her pumping flukes as she slowly swam downriver. She passed outboard of the *Annie,* and then she glided right in front of us, at the surface, her gray bristly nostrils blowing out air, poking through pale water the color of the sky. The whole long ten feet of her mottled body was visible, covered with scars. One long white slash creased her back for a stretch of more than two feet. The wound looked fresh.

"Looks like she's been hit by a prop recently," I said.

"I used to see them passing all the time on winter evenings. Now, more and more, if I see them at all, I see that. Bad scars. But her wound is healing. She'll be fine."

"Yeah. Just so long as she doesn't get hit again."

I stayed and helped Faith with the dishes after our meal. I had eaten too much ham and felt bloated. While we sat at the formal dining table, she'd regaled me with tales of my tomboy mother who shocked the clerk at the Woolworth's toy counter when she tried to trade in a brand-new tea set for an Erector Set. She was always making a spectacle—even before the age of ten.

"I wish I had known her longer. I was too young back then, I didn't appreciate her, didn't really know her."

"She always reminded me of a butterfly. Such an unearthly, brilliant, yet fragile thing flitting around, but oh so easily damaged. She was my own daughter, but she frightened me. I didn't understand her, either. I wanted to tame her and she fought me hard."

"It's an illness, Grama. She couldn't help being that way. Maybe aging would have helped her. Made the dark times easier. Besides, today, they have great medication for people who are bipolar."

She folded the dish towel in half and hung it on the oven door. "We'll never know now, will we?"

"No," I said. "We won't." I stepped over to her and took her hand. We weren't quite comfortable enough around each other to make lots of hugging possible. "Thanks. For everything."

She patted my hand. "You go home and get some rest. I should think you'll sleep well tonight."

I looked at my watch. "It's only eight o'clock, and I

was thinking of driving out to a place to get my Jeep looked at."

"Lands sakes. Who's going to work on a car at this hour?"

"I have a friend—a guy who used to live on our street over in Shady Banks. We've been friends since we were little kids. His grandfather has this place out on Highway 441. It's called Hubcap Heaven."

She placed her hand flat on her chest and chuckled. "Are you telling me Old Ben is still alive?"

"You know him?"

"Of course. Everybody knew everybody when he first showed up in town. It was just after the war. My second husband swore by him, wouldn't take our cars anywhere but Hubcap Heaven for tires or simple mechanical work." We left the kitchen and headed for the front door.

"My Jeep has been acting strange lately and I need a dependable vehicle. My friend, that would be Old Ben's grandson, Ben Baker the Third, told me he would call out to his grandfather, tell him to expect me this evening. I guess he stays open twenty-four hours."

"That's just a ruse, but it appears it's been working if the man's still out there. The folk who live around his place have been trying to get rid of him for years. They think all those tires, car parts, and hubcaps are an eyesore."

I picked up my purse off the console table by the front door. "Can you blame them?"

"They've sent Code Enforcement to cite him for storing all that junk, but Old Ben insists it's inventory and it's for sale. He's outfoxed the county for going on forty years now."

"I met him the other day. He seems like quite a character. But if he can figure out what's causing my Jeep to cough and splutter, I don't care what he is." I opened the door. "Thanks again, Grams."

"Seychelle, I'm going to say something to you that I wish I'd said to your mother. Never had the chance. Not that it was anyone's fault but my own for being such a stubborn old fool. Dear, you are not defective. There is no such thing as a perfect mother. Lord knows, I made more'n my share of mistakes. So did your mama. So will you one day. If you give yourself a chance."

I nodded once at her and then turned and half ran to my Jeep.

XXVI

THERE are places you know exist, that have been part of the landscape you recognize as your home turf, but which you've never visited and never really looked at. Hubcap Heaven was a place like that for me. I knew how to get there, more or less, but when Lightnin' stalled the second time at the corner of Broward Boulevard and 441, I couldn't remember how many miles south I was going to have to go. I was hoping it wasn't too far, because I damn near couldn't get the thing to start this time.

At its best, up by the new Seminole Casino, the corridor along Highway 441 is purely commercial, but down where Hubcap Heaven was located, near Crazy Jim's strip joint and the Miami–Dade county line, it was a pretty rough area. Bars, peep shows, warehouses, pawn- and auto body shops gave the area its industrial theme. When I pulled onto the dirt outside the chain-link fence that surrounded the place, mine was the only vehicle parked in front of Hubcap Heaven, and if this was supposed to be a business that was open twenty-four hours, there was no indication of it other than a hand-lettered sign on the gate that said, *ring bell*. Next to it hung a tarnished brass bell. Once I shut off my headlights, the only illumination came from a streetlight in the next block.

I reached under the driver's seat and pulled out a baseball cap. I threaded my ponytail through the gap in the back and tucked the loose hairs up inside, away from my face. Shoulder bag across my chest, keys still in my hand, I approached the gate and rang the bell. The sound was so loud in the quiet night air, I felt like I was announcing to the surrounding neighborhood, *Hello, woman with a purse here, come rob me.*

I thought about Ben's grandfather cupping his hand behind his ear that afternoon at lunch. There probably wasn't any point in continuing to ring the bell.

It was difficult to see much through the fence, as nearly every square inch of it was hung with hubcaps on the inside. Strips of plastic sheeting covered the gate. I could make out some mounds of tires and what looked like car seats scattered around in a half circle just inside the gate. Whatever was beyond those tires was off in the shadows where it was too dark to see.

The seconds dragged by and, though I was straining my ears to listen, I couldn't hear the slightest noise on the other side of the fence. The only sound was the buzz of the traffic on the highway behind me. It was too dark to make out the numbers on my watch, but I figured it couldn't be past nine o'clock yet. I should just leave. Come back in the morning. But Ben had said he would call and tell his grandfather to expect me—no matter what the hour. I tried turning the latch on the gate, and it was unlocked.

"Hello?" I called out as I stepped inside and looked around. I wished I'd thought to bring a flashlight. "Mr. Baker?"

From the street, the lot hadn't looked so big, but here inside, piles of junk stretched out into the darkness in all directions. Immediately behind the group of car seats, I saw a mountain of tires. At the top was a flagpole that supported an American flag big enough to make a tent.

It hung limp, the lower corner grazing the tires. Paths led off around the tires and through the random piles of junk cars, engines, and auto parts. To my left, a path led along the fence toward the back of the lot, while to my right, a space led along the inside of the front fence. I could see what looked like a shed in that direction, so I turned right and followed that fence. The collection of hubcaps and wheels that hung on the fence, especially in that low light, looked like some crazy Warhol collage.

I kept thinking that I heard some faint far-off music. I couldn't make it out exactly; nor could I tell what direction it came from.

I had hoped the shed would be inhabited, but as I drew nearer, I could see that it wasn't. Where there should have been the fourth wall, the building was open. Inside was what appeared to be a broken-down riding lawn mower. The engine cowling was folded back, and several parts and bolts rested on a board in the dirt.

Turning away, I started to walk down a path that led toward the back of the yard when I heard the screech of metal scraping on metal. I froze. After all I'd been through the last couple of days, I wanted to be certain it was somebody friendly before I announced myself. Glancing down at my body, I realized my navy sweatshirt and dark jeans would be difficult to spot in the darkness, but I knew that despite my hat, my pale face would reflect the light. I reached back and slid the sweatshirt hood up over my hat, placing my face more in shadow.

There. From the periphery of my vision I sensed movement. I squinted into the darkness, trying to see what had attracted my attention. I didn't think it was my imagination. Maybe it was only Old Ben Baker, but for the moment I wasn't going to assume anything. Then I saw a shadow flit between two piles of tires. If it was the owner, why was he hiding, creeping around his own property?

Slowly, I lowered my body to a squat. The farther away from the highway, the higher the piles of dead cars grew, but where I was standing I felt exposed. Like anyone could see me, could be watching me.

There it was again. That music. It sounded like a woman singing in a very high voice. It was unlike anything I would expect to hear in a bar or a strip joint or any of the places located around Hubcap Heaven.

Although there were stacks of wheels, rusty engine blocks, and an engineless chassis with only the backseats in place, there was nothing around me big enough to hide behind. Nothing except that shed. I tried to gauge the distance between the wooden walls and me. I figured I would have to cross about fifteen feet of open area, just dirt and weeds, before I could slip into the darkness of the old building.

I placed my hands palms-down in the dirt and began to crab my way across the open space. Although it only took me a few seconds to cross, halfway there my hand hit a sharp piece of metal in the dirt and my breath hissed in an involuntary gasp. When I rounded the wall at last, I dropped my butt into the dirt and leaned my back against the wall of the shed. My heart was racing. I reached into my jean pocket to reassure myself that the stainless bosun's knife I always carried was there. The cold steel gave me comfort, though I couldn't imagine ever really using it on a human. I held my left hand close to my face, and the blood on my palm looked black in the semi-darkness.

Footsteps. There was no question about it, I heard the sound of feet hitting ground, running, coming this way. I jumped to a stand and peered around the edge of the wooden wall. I could barely make out a figure dressed all in black coming from the direction of the main entrance gate and running straight for the shed. Any hope of hiding was shot. He'd seen me and he was coming.

When it's been a question of fight or flight, most of my life I have chosen flight. I grew up with two older brothers, after all, and I knew that if they caught me, they could usually beat the daylights out of me. I rounded the wall and took off toward the back of that lot sprinting and screaming my head off. If somebody was going to take me down, I hoped to attract the attention of witnesses, at least.

As long as I stayed to the dirt corridors between the piles of junk, I could hear his breathing getting closer, so I turned into the maze of junk and began knocking over pillars of tires and hurling pieces of metal behind me, trying to block his path. A mountain of sheet metal appeared ahead, boxing me in, and I started to climb, my bloody hand grasping pieces of bumpers and hoods and pitching them over my shoulder. I heard him grunt right behind me when I heaved a chunk of rebar, and then I saw a growing black shadow from the corner of my eye, and I didn't see anything else.

WHAT woke me was cold steel pressing against my cheek and a bright light shining in my eyes.

"You're not a boy, are you?"

I knew the voice. I wanted to tell him he knew me, too, but I was having a hard time getting my circuits to fire right. It felt like things had been shaken loose in my head. There was a big difference at the moment between wanting to talk and figuring out how to get my mouth to move. And somewhere, that damn woman was still singing. It was louder now. I could tell it was opera, and I hated opera. Then I realized that the cold steel that kept prodding at my cheek was the barrel of a gun.

"Seychelle," I tried to croak out.

"What's that you say?" The gun barrel poked my shoulder this time.

My arm felt like it was wrapped in lead clothing, but I dragged my hand to my head and pulled off the hat and hood. The hair from my ponytail fell across my shoulder.

"I'm Seychelle. Old Ben, we've met."

The flashlight came in closer on my face. It was so close I felt the heat from the bulb on my skin. It felt good. The bright white light made everything else disappear.

"I do know you. You're that girl grew up with my grandson. What the hell are you doing running around out here screaming bloody murder?"

Good question, I thought, as I tried to heave myself up to a sitting position. The metal shifted under me, and I felt like I was going to vomit. He was waiting for an answer and I was trying to get my pounding head to work. I'd been running from someone, I remembered. Someone dressed in black. I looked up at Old Ben. He'd lowered the flashlight to his side, and it made a circle of light on the ground next to his boots. Where the light spilled onto his body, I saw he was wearing jeans and a flannel shirt; in his other hand he held a shotgun, the barrel now pointing at the ground as well.

My body was resting on top of that pile of sheet-metal hoods and fenders. I ran my hands over my head, feeling the tender spot on the right side just above my ear. Luckily, I didn't seem to be bleeding anywhere except on the palm of my right hand. As I held it up to examine the wound, Old Ben spoke up.

"That looks nasty. Better come inside and clean that up." He offered me his hand.

I took it. I don't think I could have risen to my feet without it.

After following his flashlight through the mounds of discarded wheels and tires, I discovered that *inside* was the interior of an ancient Airstream trailer parked in the back of the lot up against a cinder-block wall. The trailer was also the origin of the opera; by the time we entered, the volume made the music almost painful. Ben crossed to a boom box on a bunk and pushed a button, stopping the tape in mid-aria. After all that noise, the silence dropped on us with a tangible weight like the atmosphere in an elevator speeding to the ninetieth floor. I closed my eyes for a second and took a deep breath.

"Not a fan, huh?"

I shook my head. He chuckled.

"That was Kathleen Battle. I can't never remember the names of the songs but damn, that lady sings like an angel. I like to play it loud so I can't hear the traffic out on the highway."

At that volume, he wouldn't hear it if the frigging space shuttle landed in his yard.

He led me to the sink, telling me to hold my hand under a stream of cold running water in the tiny kitchenette while he rummaged around in the head. I held on to the counter to keep the floor from swirling me off my feet. He emerged in a few minutes with a shoe box and placed it on the Formica settee table. The trailer reminded me of a boat with the compact galley and built-in furnishings, but the entire interior was covered with a film of combined grease and tobacco residue. I was certain that a sponge on any surface in the place would have come away brown. Other than that, and the overflowing ashtray on the table, the interior was fairly neat, the bunk made and the dishes upended in a dish rack.

He told me to sit on the Naugahyde bench. He sat on

the other side of the table. Soon my hand was wrapped in clean gauze.

"Wanna tell me what happened out there?" Old Ben swiped a thick wooden match on the side of the box and held the flame to the bent cigarette in his mouth.

"I was hoping you could tell me. You were supposed to be expecting me."

"Why the hell would you think that?"

"Your grandson, Ben. He told me this morning he was going to call you to ask you to work on my Jeep. He didn't call?"

"Nope, I ain't heard from Ben since we ate lunch on my birthday."

"I've been having trouble with my Jeep and Ben told me to bring it to you. He said he was going to call. Tell you to expect me."

"Ah hell, he musta got busy and forgot," the old man said. "He does that. Don't matter." He dragged so deep on his cigarette, I thought he was going to be spitting strands of tobacco out of his mouth.

I touched the tender knot on the side of my head. "So what the hell happened out there? Who knocked me out?"

"What are you talking about?"

"There was a man out there. Dressed all in black. He chased me and I screamed, then he hit me with something. Next thing I remember is you poking me with your shotgun."

"I heard your screaming. Took me a bit to find you after you quit. I didn't see no one else. I figured you'd tried to climb up that sheet metal and took a bad fall. Sometimes the shadows play tricks on ya in this yard."

"He was real. No doubt about it. You must have scared him off when you showed up. I guess there's no point in calling 911 if you don't even believe me, though."

"What would some fella be doing in here?"

"Maybe he followed me in off the street. I was out there ringing that bell and announcing to half the neighborhood I was here. And your neighbors aren't exactly winning property beautification awards."

When the old man smiled I could see the yellow of his tooth enamel; deep in the crevices, his teeth were dark brown. I wondered if it was just stain from years of smoking or if they were rotted.

"Sometimes women git scared. Think they see things in the shadows. I think you fell and hit yer head."

"Shadows, hell. I know what I saw whether you believe it or not."

"I can see why young Ben's always been so taken with you."

"What do you mean?"

"You've got spunk. Baker men have always admired women with spunk."

"Ben and I were friends as kids. Nothing more."

"You know better than that."

"What do you mean?"

"My grandson followed you around like a puppy. I wasn't around much, but I was out there often enough to see that. And there ain't no human alive who deserves the kind of love a dog gives. That day you gave him that nickname? That day he just about wanted to die. He hitchhiked out here to stay with me. Told me he was running away from home. Wouldn't tell me what happened, but from that day his own daddy called him Glub and the boy was never quite the same."

"It wasn't meant to be mean," I said, knowing that I wasn't being entirely truthful.

"And one more time I'll tell you—you know better than that. The boy never would tell me the whole story. He was in some kind of raft race or something? Why was it so goddamn important?"

I didn't know the answer to that. But he was right—I had known better.

"We were just kids," I said, starting to try to make an excuse. But really, there was no excuse. And the worst of it was that I hadn't really felt bad at the time. It was only later that night at his house—and now, now that he was a handsome, successful man—that I felt really bad for the way we'd all teased him. Now that I wanted him to like me. "Ben got teased a lot when he was a kid."

"*You* were supposed to be his friend."

"I know. Now, I do. I can tell you the story behind the name. They used to hold this race every winter. It was called the New River Raft Race. Clubs or businesses or individuals could build their own rafts and we'd race down the river. The people on the banks of the river would cheer and throw water balloons at the racers. The folks on the rafts would splash each other. It was lots of fun, goofy fun. One year when we were in ninth grade, all the kids in our neighborhood decided to build our own rafts to compete in the race. My friend Molly and I built one together. My two brothers built one. And Ben built one all by himself."

Old Ben snorted. "That was Benny. The other kids never cut him a break."

"Because it's a lot easier to do certain stuff if you've got two people, our rafts were built better. Ben's raft sank. But not before we splashed him, threw water balloons at him, and someone on shore nailed him with a fire hose."

"Nice bunch."

"It was all supposed to be in good fun. We were all splashed and hit by water balloons. But we all didn't have our rafts sink under us. We all laughed when he sank. We thought he'd be laughing, too. I was the one who called out 'Glub, glub, glub.' "

"That boy never could take folks laughing at him. It happened too often."

"Well, Ben swam to shore and I guess he walked home. There was a cookout and party afterward, but he didn't show. I asked somebody, I don't even remember who, if they had seen 'Glub, glub, glub' around. It got a good laugh and the name kinda stuck. I didn't see him until the next Monday at school and everybody had started calling him Glub. It was just a stupid kid thing. I can't believe he even still remembers it."

"Why not? Folks like you keep reminding him of it every time you call him that name. He's a man now but that kid, the social outcast, is still in there."

"All kinds of kids have nicknames in high school."

"But they're not all connected to something the kid sees as a humiliation."

"I didn't realize he felt that way about it. That makes it an even bigger deal, I guess, that he was able to rise above all that childhood teasing and make his life into the success it has become."

"I never seen anybody work as hard as that boy."

"It shows. It really does. And the amazing thing is the way he makes it look effortless. He looks like this relaxed boat bum, but when you see his boat, the work shows. Now that he's put all that kid stuff behind him, he should feel very proud of himself."

"Ben? Nah. It does something to a kid to grow up with parents like that. He's been told he's a piece of shit so many times, it don't matter what he looks like. Best thing his momma ever did was to die and leave him money to buy that boat."

"The *Hawkeye*'s a beauty, that's for sure. I know he's proud of her."

The old man shook his head. "You are something else."

"What do you mean?"

He didn't say anything for a while as he lit another of his unfiltered cigarettes and dragged the smoke deep into his lungs, his head turned away from me. "So why was it Ben told you to come out here?"

I'd almost forgotten the reason I was there. "My Jeep. It's parked out front. It's been stalling, not wanting to start. It's a 1972, and Ben said you were great with the older engines that don't have all the computerized stuff in them."

"I'd be happy to take a look. Is your head okay? Can you drive?"

"I'm fine," I said, knowing that I was making a habit of telling half-truths to this man.

He told me how to find my way to an alley that ran behind the lot. He said he would open the gate to a con-crete pad where he had a garage with his tools and lights and everything he would need. Half an hour later, Old Ben straightened up from where he'd been leaning under Lightnin's hood and wiped his hands on a red cloth rag.

"Somehow, you got a shop rag or some kinda cloth stuck in your intake manifold. The valves been chewing and burning it up, but it been causing your loss of com-pression and the black smoke you been seeing. You had any work done on this machine lately?"

"No, not for several months."

"Hmm. That is odd. It ain't like you could pick this up driving on the street."

I thought about my Jeep parked for over an hour in the dark parking lot behind the Downtowner. "Are you saying someone tampered with it?"

"Sure looks that way to me."

XXVII

THE sight of B.J.'s El Camino in front of the Larsens' place was a pleasant surprise when I parked my Jeep in the driveway just after eleven. My head hurt and I was tired, but not too tired for a little naked wrestling with my Samoan friend. Mr. Magic Fingers had a way of making all my hurts go away.

I made enough noise closing the gate that I expected my dog to come running, but there was no sign of her. I imagined she was taking advantage of those magic fingers at this very minute. When I got to the end of the walkway alongside the big house and stepped out into the open yard, I could see two people sitting on the bench in front of my cottage. The smaller of the two got up as soon as I started across the lawn and ran toward me, my dog at her heels.

"Seychelle," Molly said, the alarm apparent in the way she said my name. "Thank God you're home." She linked her arm in mine and pressed her head against my shoulder as we walked over to where B.J. sat. "We've been sitting here for hours, worried sick that maybe something had happened to you, too." She hugged me as though I had been gone for weeks.

She was talking so fast, I was having difficulty keeping up with her.

When Molly took a breath, B.J. said, "I really wish

you would get a cell phone. At times like this, it's hard not knowing if you're okay."

"Why wouldn't I be? What's going on?"

B.J. stood. "Let's go inside," he said. "We'll talk in there."

I unlocked my front door and led the way inside. When we were all settled in the living room, B.J. explained that he had been over at Molly's earlier that evening when they had decided to turn on the TV and watch the evening news. They had seen the report on Quentin's death, and B.J. recognized the name. Although he wasn't sure it was anything other than the drug-related killing that had been reported, the news of it made him uneasy.

Then he turned to Molly and said, "Now tell her exactly what you saw."

"It was a little after eight. B.J. had just left. We'd been studying for almost four hours, and I just wanted to climb into bed, read a novel, and relax. I was in my nightgown when I remembered that I hadn't checked the mail. I stepped out onto the porch and I heard what sounded like a cry down the street. When I looked toward the Sparkses' house, I saw Arlen leading Catalina by the elbow out to his car. She was struggling, trying to get away from him. I couldn't hear what she was saying, but it was obvious she was arguing with him. He opened the back door and practically shoved her in. He was being so rough! In her condition!"

"Did they leave? What about his wife?"

"Well, that's just it. I started running over there when I saw what was happening, but he jumped into the front seat, backed out of the driveway burning rubber, and took off down the street. I could see Mrs. Sparks sitting slumped in the corner of the front seat."

"He shouldn't be moving her."

"I know! That's just it. I ran down the street after them, but I was barefoot and in my nightie. I couldn't catch them. I saw Catalina's face looking at me through the back window when they drove under the streetlight, though. She looked terrified. He's gone completely off the deep end."

I stood up and began pacing the room. "Shit, I should have done something. I probably could have stopped this. At least, I should have warned her."

B.J. said, "What are you talking about?"

I told them about my tow up to River Bend and the conversation I'd had with Charlie, the yard foreman. "I think Arlen must have been at the center of the R and D that Motowave was doing with GPS."

"From what I read on the Internet," B.J. said, "they've developed systems that will spoof or send simulated GPS signals in addition to jamming. When the GPS receiver is working, it locks on to four or five satellites at a time. These spoofers fool the receiver into locking on to them instead of one of the satellites, and they've developed the tables to determine how far off and in what direction the GPS unit will deliver an inaccurate fix."

"Geez, B.J., what's all that in English?"

"It means the boat's GPS receiver will look like it's working properly, but it's producing a false or intentionally manipulated fix. While Motowave has been at the forefront of this research, I did find one website where an anonymous author had posted directions on how to build a homemade jammer."

"I don't believe that Pinder is smart enough to figure out how to do this on his own even if there are instructions on the Internet."

"It is pretty complex," B.J. said. "And there are two different types of receivers, one for the military and one for civilians. Just building the thing wouldn't be enough.

To carefully set these boats on a wrong course, somebody would have to know a lot about the locations, orbits, and frequencies of the satellites. That was what the engineers at Motowave were working on recently. Their anti-jamming work was aimed mainly at preventing terrorists from using this on a commercial airliner or a huge oil tanker. It's scary stuff."

"And Arlen Sparks was one of those engineers. But for some reason, they laid him off shortly before he got his full pension."

"I didn't do all the research on who owns Motowave, but lots of these companies, these defense contractors, are owned by a few major corporations. They're into squeezing maximum corporate profit out of the American military infrastructure. Paying out lots of money in pensions won't result in maximum profits."

"So there's Arlen," I said. "Left dependent on Medicare—no supplemental insurance—when his wife's cancer returns. He's desperate to get the money to fund this new treatment the doctors are dangling in front of him. And somehow, he teams up with Pinder and they come up with this scheme to cause a few convenient wrecks."

"But if he'd sold the idea outright, he would have had his wife in treatment by now," B.J. said. "We went over to visit Cat this morning when I first got to Molly's. We saw Mrs. Sparks, and she looked very ill. What's he been doing with the money?"

"He probably hasn't seen any of it yet," I said. "Pinder wouldn't be able to pay him up front. It doesn't work that fast. Lots of these salvage cases go to arbitration or wind up in court one way or another. It would be months before they get paid. And then you'd have to assume that Pinder *will* pay out. I wouldn't trust that man—"

"So you think Nestor and Quentin were both killed over this?" Molly asked.

"This scheme could be worth millions. That's a lot of motive. I can't see Arlen doing the killing, though."

"Do you have any idea where he might be headed?" B.J. asked.

"Arlen? My best guess would be Key West. He's got Sarah with him. He needs to get her settled somewhere. And Key West is where Pinder is. When I was there last week, I saw Arlen go into Pinder's office. I didn't put it together at the time. I figured he was just a customer since he's got a waterfront house down there. But why would he leave Lauderdale in the first place? I can't see him being a part of anything that would hurt Catalina."

"All I know is that Catalina could go into labor at any time," B.J. said. "I don't like this at all. I'm her labor coach and I promised her I would be there when she delivered." He glanced at his watch. "What is it, a three-, four-hour drive?"

"What are you thinking?"

"I want to go down there. Now."

"Tonight? That's a long dark road for one thing, and these people have killed twice already. I don't think that's such a good idea."

"Whatever it is that has made Arlen panic, I'm not connected to it. They wouldn't see me as a threat to anyone there. I just want to stand by for Catalina in case all this excitement pushes her into labor."

"I'd go," Molly said, "but Zale's got school."

"And I've got that stupid court date tomorrow. I'd give anything to miss it, but Jeannie would kill me."

"Then it's set, I'll leave now."

"I'm worried about you driving all night," I said. I contemplated telling him about what had happened to me out at Hubcap Heaven, to warn him, but I decided against it. B.J. was always on guard, and I didn't want him distracted and worried about me.

"What are you going to do once you get there? Just drop by for a visit? And how are you going to find the Sparkses' house?"

He put his hands on my shoulders. "Hey, when you go running off to save the world, I have to trust that you know what you're doing. I don't try to stop you or tell you what to do, do I?"

I had to admit he had me there. He never played the macho male. He never tried to save me from myself. "You're right. Sorry. Call me as soon as you get there, okay? I don't care what time."

"I will. Listen, I don't intend to contact them at all. I'll watch from the street, and unless it looks like she needs me, I won't step in. I've got my MacBook out in the truck, and there will be places with free wireless in Key West. Everything I need is on the Internet. I'll find the address, don't worry."

I had no doubt he would.

XXVIII

ABACO'S whiskery muzzle rubbed against my hand. In my half-awake dream state, I was rubbing the day's growth of beard on Ben Baker's face. The dog started whining and even though I knew it was just a dream, I lay there for several seconds trying to bring it back, to see where we were and what we were doing. I had the strange feeling that I had been dreaming of making love to Ben, and some perverse sense of curiosity prodded me to try to bring back those images.

The second time the dog whined, I sat bolt upright in bed. I looked at the clock on the nightstand and saw that it was after seven.

He hadn't called. I was supposed to meet Jeannie for breakfast at eight o'clock at Lester's Diner, and I hadn't set an alarm because I was certain B.J. would call me between four and six in the morning.

I leaped out of bed and searched my living room for the cordless phone. I dialed his cell, but the damn thing went straight to voice mail.

"B.J., where are you?" I said after the beep. "You promised me you'd call. As soon as you get this message, call me."

*   *   *

JEANNIE was already seated at a table sipping coffee when I hurried into the diner. "What happened to you? You don't look too hot."

I slung my bag on the back of the chair and slumped into the seat. When I'd gone into the bathroom to shower earlier, I'd found dark circles under my eyes—probably a result of the blow to the head the night before. I had a small goose egg under my hair, but I'd blow-dried some volume into it to try to cover the bump.

"Mostly, I'm worried about B.J." I told her the whole story about Arlen having worked with GPS while he was at Motowave, and how he must have partnered with Pinder. "Last night when I got back home around eleven, B.J. and Molly were at my house. Molly saw Arlen Sparks drag Catalina into his car and take off. His wife, who is in so much pain she's on a morphine drip, was in the front seat. We figure Arlen must have gone to his Key West house. B.J.'s supposed to be her birth coach and he doesn't want Cat down there with no one to turn to."

The waitress brought me a big white ceramic mug and poured me a cup of black coffee. She asked if we were ready to order, and I shook my head. I couldn't stand the thought of food at the moment.

"So he left," Jeannie said. "I'm surprised you didn't go with him."

"Believe me, I wanted to. But I had this damn hearing or whatever this is today. Jeannie, the thing is, he promised me he would call as soon as he got there. He left around midnight. He should have been in Key West by four or five in the morning."

"Maybe he just didn't want to wake you."

"I was home until almost eight. He knows I'm an early riser. Why didn't he call between seven and eight? I waited until the last possible minute to come here."

"Have you tried calling him?"

"Of course. I only get his voice mail." I twisted around in my seat to reach my shoulder bag and pulled out the digital camera, setting it on the place mat in front of Jeannie. "I'm sorry that I haven't been more help to you with this lawsuit. B.J. and I went by the guy's apartment. We took these photos of him moving furniture, getting into a fight. I didn't have time to print them."

"You're going after him, aren't you?"

"It's not like him not to call."

"Yeah, you're right. Don't worry about it. I'll handle this business this morning on my own. You should eat something first, though. You look like you haven't eaten in days. That's not like you."

"Food," I said, shaking my head. "No, something's wrong. I've got to go. If I get hungry, I'll stop along the road and eat while I drive. He's in trouble or he would have called."

I swung by my cottage and threw a bunch of clothes and toiletries into a duffel. Jeannie had agreed to keep an eye on Abaco while I was gone, but I still kneeled down in the middle of my living room and crooked an arm around her, burying my face in the fur at her neck. "You be a good girl while I'm gone, okay?" She licked at my ear and gave one short whine. She didn't like it when I left, but she had learned to live with it. Besides, if I knew Jeannie, she'd be bringing her meat bones from the butcher and cooking her scrambled eggs.

The drive down to Key West gave me plenty of time to think. Lightnin' roared down the turnpike, the engine having not so much as a single hiccup. Old Ben said that someone had stuffed a shop rag up the intake manifold. That was no accident. He'd cleaned it all out and gotten me back to running right, but the questions remained: who and why. The old guy said the Jeep should have quit—he was amazed that she had kept running at all. Someone had wanted my car to quit on the road that night that big vehicle had followed me. It had to have happened while I was at the Downtowner. Just like someone had broken into my home and rearranged things. Like someone had followed me to Hubcap Heaven and tried to—what? Knock me out? Again, I returned to why and who. All these near hits weren't quite believable. Nestor and Quentin had wound up dead, but it seemed that someone was just messing with me.

Involuntarily, my eyes flicked again to my rearview mirror. I'd been checking it compulsively ever since I pulled away from the Larsens' place. So far, I hadn't seen one single neon green vehicle, no black SUV; nor could I make any other vehicle following me. I wasn't a pro or anything, but I was watching pretty closely. I remembered the smirk on Pinder's face as he'd watched me across the bar in the Downtowner. Was it because he had just been messing around under my Jeep?

Late morning certainly isn't rush hour, but the traffic on the turnpike where it passed through the outskirts of Miami was miserable. Then there was an accident on the route between Florida City and Key Largo, and all the traffic was at a complete halt as the emergency vehicles cleared the mangled metal from the roadway. I switched on the radio I almost never used. The engine noise was usually too loud to hear it, but since we were stopped, I figured it would pass the time. I turned the dial trying to find a station with news and weather.

Outside, the sky had gone slate gray and the temperature was rapidly dropping. I hadn't listened to the Coast Guard marine weather in a couple of days. I'd been too distracted, but I could tell by the look and feel of the air that a low-pressure area was sweeping in over us and we were going to be feeling some nasty wind by nightfall.

Right now I guessed it was only blowing five to ten knots out of the northwest, but once the front really moved through and the cold descended on the area, the wind would pick up and blow out of the northeast like a witch.

I finally found a station that reported the weather at the top of the hour. I had to sit through ten minutes of a radio-team routine about today being Groundhog Day. Their stupid one-liners made me realize that I wasn't missing much by doing without the radio in my noisy vehicle. It might have taken me three days to make this same Keys trip by boat, but I found myself getting more and more frustrated the longer I sat in the stalled traffic. The guys in the truck ahead of me had taken out their poles and were fishing in the lagoon off to the side of the road.

The traffic had just started moving at eleven when the weatherman reported essentially the same thing I had already figured out—a cold front was moving through. The only real point of interest he added was that a second stationary front over the Bahamas was going to squeeze the air; the winds would be stronger than normal starting tonight and running through Saturday. He promised his listeners that by Sunday we'd see the sun again, but for the moment even that was hard to believe. The sky was solid gray flannel.

When I drove over the bridge from Stock Island and found myself on the island of Key West at last, I decided to head straight to the police department and try to find Lassiter. I'd left him a message on his cell phone, but I hadn't received a call back. First I had trouble finding a space to park—Key West had been much easier to navigate on foot. Once I got there, the receptionist told me it was Lassiter's day off. She wanted to know if another detective could help me. When I told her no and asked for Lassiter's home address or phone, she gave me such a withering look that I simply thanked her and left.

I stood next to my Jeep in the motel parking lot where I had finally found a spot to park and tried to decide what to do next. The weather was worsening. I could see whitecaps on the water off Garrison Bight. The few tourists walking the streets wore faces of grim determination. The weather wasn't cooperating for water sports, but they weren't going to sit in their hotel rooms.

Maybe I'd be lucky and the Sparkses would be listed in the telephone book. I crossed the lot and asked for a directory in the motel lobby. The man behind the desk, whose muttonchop sideburns made him look as if he'd time-traveled from the 1850s, told me that I could find one in my room. I leaned across the counter.

"Look, I'm not staying here yet. I'm trying to decide what kind of customer service you offer. If you can loan me your phone book for just a minute, I might consider taking a room."

He replied that regulations did not permit him to loan out the front desk telephone books. While he was talking, he stared at his computer monitor, his fingers tap-tapping on the keys. He never even looked at me.

I pushed my way out the door. As I was walking to Lightnin', I saw a maid with a cart working outside a room. Under her blue pinafore uniform she wore what looked like a home-sewn dress, and her hair was tied up with a bandanna. I guessed she was Haitian. She responded to my question with a shy smile and invited me into the room. When I sat on the bed, I had a nearly overwhelming urge to climb in and pull the covers up over my head and hope the world would go away. I shook it off and reached into the nightstand drawer for the telephone book. I didn't find anyone with the last name of Sparks, but I tipped the maid five bucks. She deserved it—especially since she was probably working under the management of the asshole in the lobby.

I hopped in the Jeep and turned back out onto Roosevelt. The rain started falling as I headed for Key West Bight Marina. The only other person I knew to turn to was Ben. Maybe he knew computers like B.J. did and would be able to find Sparks on the Internet. I parked in the lot behind the Turtle Kraals Restaurant and cut through the gap next to the Waterfront Market, my baseball cap pulled low over my eyes to keep out the rain.

Out on the dock by the Schooner Wharf Bar, I was able to see the empty dock where Ben's boat was usually tied up. Most of the other charter schooners were still in their berths, all charters canceled due to the nasty weather, but on Ben's dock I had a clear view of his fishing boat, the *Rapid*. Wouldn't you know he'd be the diehard sailor, taking folks out on a charter with *Hawkeye* no matter the weather? I could picture him telling them about his great-great-grandfather as he squinted into the rain and wind. I was wearing my rain slicker, but my pants were getting soaked. Damn. I was standing there cursing out loud when I looked down the dock and saw the stringy-haired fellow with his bike and dog, the same one we had seen that first morning I'd come ashore and had brunch with Nestor and Catalina. He was watching me swearing aloud to myself. Maybe he thought I was a kindred spirit of some sort.

"Excuse me," I said, walking closer to him. "Do you know the guy who runs that black schooner that usually docks out there?" I pointed out to the empty pier. "The one called *Hawkeye*?"

"Most people don't hear the voices like we do." He seemed to be talking to someone sitting on my right shoulder. "They don't understand that when the man says it is time to go, you have to go."

"That schooner, *Hawkeye*, do you know when he usually gets back?"

"Alien abductions occur right under the noses of everyman. It happens all around us and we don't even see. They walk right by and people don't see the fear and the pain when the man is telling them it's time to go. Go to the big mouth, he said. Stare into the precipice. Only the dark one has the courage to look you in the eye. Do you hear what I'm saying?" He reached out and grabbed my arm. "Do you hear what I'm saying?"

"Sorry, man, I've got to go." I tried to shake him loose, but his grip was strong.

"The man says fuck you, and none of the others dared to look in the eyes of the damned."

"Shit," I said as I twisted my arm free and began to trot back to the Jeep. I could still hear him hollering after me.

"The dark one has eyes that look through to my soul. You must find him in your dreams."

Way to go, Sullivan, I thought as I slid behind the wheel of the Jeep once more. You ask for information from crazy people and you expect rational answers. Not only did that guy not know what I was talking about, but I'd been asking a man who didn't even live on this planet.

There was only one other thing to try. It was risky, but it might work. I had seen Arlen go into the offices of Ocean Towing that day. I turned up Simonton Street and headed for Fleming.

XXIX

THE girl with the pierced nipple was sitting on top of her desk when I walked in. She was wearing a black hooded sweatshirt that had D.A.R.E. TO KEEP KIDS OFF DRUGS written across the front, over white Capri-length pants and red Converse high-top sneakers, and she seemed to be holding some sort of yoga pose with her arms up high over her head, her fingers laced together.

"Hi," I said, not caring if she thought me rude to break her concentration.

She didn't look at me but she began whispering, "Forty-seven, forty-eight, forty-nine." When she reached fifty, she lowered her hands and started shaking them as though she were trying to dry them off. "Sorry," she said, only it came out *shorry,* and I was reminded of her tongue stud. "Nobody was in here so I decided to try my stretches. I have to hold that one for fifty counts. It drains all the blood out of my hands, though. Totally pins-and-needles time."

I wanted to ask her why she did it, any of it—the piercings, the exercises—but after my experience with the man on the docks, I decided it might not be such a good idea.

"I was in here a little over a week ago. I don't know if you remember me."

"Sure I do. The boss was really pissed off after you left. What did you do to him?"

"Nothing. Really. I don't know why he was mad. Anyway, today I have a favor to ask. When I was in here last time I met an old friend right outside. He came in after me. His name is Arlen Sparks."

"Oh yeah, Sparky. I know him. He's a cool old dude."

So far so good. I'd come in here hoping I could get what I needed without crossing paths with Pinder. "Well, I'm trying to find Mr. Sparks. I've known him since I was a kid up in Fort Lauderdale, but I don't have his Key West address. I was wondering if you could give it to me."

"I don't know about that. We're not supposed to. I'd better go ask."

"I'd rather you didn't," I said, but before I could say or do any more she twisted her body and yelled in a surprisingly loud voice.

"Boss! Somebody here to see you."

I contemplated running for the door. The fact remained, though, that this was my last hope of finding out what was going on, of finding Catalina and B.J., and the desire to know overrode any concerns about my personal safety. Well, almost. I backed my way to the door and noted the busy Chinese restaurant across the street as a possible escape path.

"Oh shit. What're you doing here?" Pinder said when he appeared from the back office. His hair was disheveled, his clothes wrinkled, his eyes bloodshot. He looked like he was still hung over from a long night's revelry. Judging from the look on the girl's face, he didn't smell too great, either. He didn't give me a chance to answer. "One time you took a job from me. It was fucking pocket change. You're like all the mainland chicks. So fucking superior."

"I just came here to see if you would give me Arlen Sparks's phone number and address."

"Who the hell is that?"

"Mr. Pinder, don't jerk me around. You know who I'm talking about."

Pinder looked genuinely baffled. He glanced at his secretary, who was in the process of unbending her legs and climbing down off her desk.

"You know him," she said. "Sparky, the sweet old guy with the really bad comb-over who sometimes delivers envelopes here for your partner?"

"Oh yeah, that guy. What do you want with him?"

Neville Pinder must have made a hell of a con man judging from his acting ability. "You know, I could almost believe you," I said. "You're good."

"What the fuck are you talking about? You're some crazy bitch. I don't have time for this." He turned to the girl, waving his hand in a dismissive gesture. "Give her what she wants." He turned back to me. "Then you get out of my office and stay out. You're like a pimple on my ass. You're yesterday's news. I heard you're selling out. About time. Like they say, don't send a woman to do a man's job." He gave a couple of dry chuckles before he turned and disappeared down the hall.

The girl extended a tentative hand, holding a sheet of paper with an address and phone number scribbled on it. "He always says stuff like that to me, too."

I took the paper and left the office, but as I walked back to where I had parked the Jeep on Simonton, I thought about how the girl had misunderstood my reaction to her boss. I wasn't mad. I didn't care if a twit like Pinder insulted me. The look on my face had been one of astonishment. If Neville Pinder really didn't know anything about Arlen, who did?

The address she had given me was for a place on a street called Venetian Drive. I drove out of Old Town and headed back over to the commercial district along Roosevelt, where I pulled into a touristy shop that promised to sell me tickets for the Conch Train and various boat and snorkel trips. I checked out the free maps in the rack of brochures by the door but couldn't find one that showed a Venetian Drive, so I wound up buying a detailed street map. I found the street located on the other side of the island, over by the airport. Ten minutes later, I was pulling to the curb in front of a small pink, boxy-looking house with a white-tile roof. The day had grown dark with the low clouds and slanting rain, but no lights illuminated the interior of the house. Arlen's car was parked in the carport; farther up the street, I saw the familiar black lines of B.J.'s El Camino.

No one answered my knock. There was no doorbell. The knob would not twist in my hand. I tried going around into the carport where there was another door, this one with jalousie windows that probably led to the kitchen. My knocks there weren't answered, either. I decided to try this knob. It was unlocked and turned easily in my hand.

The kitchen looked clean and tidy except for the fact that one of the chairs by the little eat-in kitchen table lay on its side. Through the arched passage, I could see into the living room, where a lamp lay on the floor. My wet boat shoes squeaked on the linoleum in the kitchen. I considered calling out, but decided I didn't want to announce my presence.

From the kitchen doorway, I could see the front door and entry to my left, the living room mostly off to my right and the hall to the bedrooms straight ahead. All the doors were closed. It wasn't until I was in the hall proper that I began to hear the sobs.

I put my ear to the first door. Nothing. I turned the knob and found a bathroom on the other side. The next door was shut also. It led to what looked like a sewing room. I wondered how long it had been since she'd last worked in there. The second bedroom looked like a much more extensive radio room than the one he had at home. The equipment looked newer, too. A wooden workbench ran the entire length of the room, and conduit snaked up the wall to a four-outlet box above the table.

I knew even before I went into the radio room that the sobs came from the last room on the hall. It had to be the master bedroom. Hearing the depth of the anguish should have spurred me forward to try to help, but something told me it was too late. There is a sound to grief. I was afraid to go through that last door. I was searching for people I loved and in this moment for me they were alive still.

But postponing the knowledge wasn't going to change what was. I stood with my hand on the doorknob, took a deep breath, and walked in.

Arlen lay on the bed spooning around the still body of his wife. Sarah's mouth hung open, her cheeks sunk so deep the skin showed the outline of her teeth. The eyes, though open, were dry and dull, no longer the eyes of the woman I once knew. She was dressed in a pink nightgown, but the arms and legs that the garment did not cover looked like mere bones draped with a loose-fitting yellowish cloth.

The smell of death will always be tinged with the odor of the sea, for me. It is an organic earthy smell, as though whatever it was that once made that person live has gone to ground. I remembered a line from a poem I had read in high school. *The force that through the green fuse drives the flower.* I didn't know about God or heaven or hell, but I believed in that force. Life. And when it fled the body and drove back into the earth, it left behind a dry husk and a smell that was distinctive over and above the odors of sickness and disinfectant and urine that so often accompany death.

I leaned against the dresser next to the door. Where most women might have had a jewelry box or a collection of perfume bottles, the dresser here held a collection of miniature art books. Sarah Sparks had been a fixture from my childhood. Like a beloved aunt, she had watched over us and made us feel safe in our world on that little cul-de-sac by the river. For Sarah, as for my father, death had come as a welcome release. But how well I knew that it didn't make it any easier for those of us left behind.

I crossed the room and touched Arlen's shoulder. "I'm sorry," I whispered.

When he looked up at me, I had to turn away. The pain pouring from those eyes was more than I could bear.

WE stayed like that for a while, and then he got up and left the room. I followed him to the front door. His face was so swollen from crying, I might not have recognized him if I'd passed him on the street.

"Leave," he said. "Leave me with her."

"Arlen, I came here looking for Catalina. Where is she?"

He put his hands to his face and ran his fingers up over his forehead and through his hair, pushing the long strands off his bald crown. "I don't know."

"You brought her here. You must know something."

There were those eyes again. I tried to hold his gaze. This time he looked away.

"All I wanted was the money. He told me no one would get hurt. But now she's dead." His eyes were filling with water again, and he was staring off as though he was looking at something far in the distance.

I grabbed him by his upper arms and tried to make him focus on me. "Who told you, Arlen?"

"I believed him. But she's gone and now it doesn't matter."

"Arlen, I know Sarah is gone. But what about Catalina?" The fear that clutched my gut was making me dizzy.

"I didn't know he was going to kill anyone."

"Who did he kill?" I was nearly shouting. I squeezed his arms tight and gave him a single brisk shake.

It seemed to have an effect on him. His eyes returned to focus on my face. "I didn't know before today. I never would have been a part of it if I'd known he was a killer. He told me there were others. He said it was getting out of control. He said you were the problem. That you'd always been the problem. Ever since you were children."

I'd like to say I had some inkling—that his statement didn't catch me totally by surprise. But that would be a lie.

"Ben? Ben Baker?"

Arlen nodded.

I let go of him and walked away a few steps before turning back. "He's the one behind all this?" I threw my arms out. "I thought it was Ocean Towing."

Arlen sighed. His shoulders sagged and his eyes were still shiny with tears, but once again I saw the light of intelligence there, tinged with resignation. "Baker *is* Ocean Towing. When his mother died, he came into a lot of money."

Pieces started fitting together as a new picture formed in my brain.

"Ben is the partner Pinder talked about?"

Arlen nodded again.

"Of course, why didn't I see it?"

"Neville hasn't got the intelligence to run an operation like this," Arlen said. "He still hasn't figured it out.

The man thinks he's just lucky, that he's got some sixth sense for the business of finding wrecks."

"Okay," I said, trying to adjust my thinking to fit this new reality. "So you still haven't told me where Catalina is."

"He took them."

"Them?"

"Catalina spotted your friend B.J. parked out on the street early this morning. She asked him inside."

"What does he want with them?"

"He's using them. To get to you. He thought *you* would follow Catalina when we left last night. He's waiting for you. He said it's always been about you. Even the *Power Play* and Nestor."

I turned my head aside as though I'd been struck. I didn't have time for this now. I shoved the guilt and hurt back into a corner of my brain and looked back at Arlen. "But I went by the dock and *Hawkeye* is gone."

"He's got them. He didn't say where he was going. He told me he wants to make you come to him for a change. That you'd better be smart enough to figure it out." Arlen reached down and picked up an envelope on an end table. "He told me to give this to you. He said you would understand."

I reached for the envelope. "It feels like there's a key in here." I tore open the paper. That was it. There was a key—but no key chain, no lettering on the key itself, no note, no indication of what the key would fit. "This is insane."

"I know it sounds that way, but I've never seen him even raise his voice before today. He gets tense, yes, but he doesn't act like a crazy man. He always seemed so normal. I knew what we were doing was illegal, but I needed the money. For Sarah. Then yesterday he came by the house in Shady Banks and told me I had to bring

Catalina down here. Right away. I couldn't leave Sarah alone." He ran his hands over the top of his head again. The long strands of hair now hung down, touching his shoulder. "I was such a fool."

"You were, but I can understand why."

"Not Sarah. She couldn't understand. He came here this morning and took Catalina while she was sitting on my wife's bed. The girl struggled and Baker hit her. Sarah just looked at me. She expected me to do something more. When I didn't, she turned her back to me and faced the wall." His voice grew hoarse with emotion. "I couldn't take it. I left the room." He covered his eyes with his hands. "When I came back to her, she was gone."

I pulled a hand away from his face. "Arlen, you've got a boat here, right?"

He shook his head. "It's too small for the ocean. And there's not much fuel." He turned away and walked across the living room.

"Do you have any idea where he might have taken them? Charts, do you have any charts?"

He kept on walking back down the hall, pointing to his radio room as he passed, then entered their bedroom and closed the door.

I ran into the radio room and began searching the shelves. I finally found a box near the top of the closet with half a dozen rolled-up charts sticking out of it. I tucked them under my slicker before I ran out to my Jeep on the street. I slipped the key I'd taken from the envelope into my jean pocket. I had an idea where I could find a boat.

XXX

THE plastic zippered windows on Lightnin' didn't do a very good job of keeping out the rain, and with all the moisture inside the vehicle, the plastic was now completely fogged over. I was parked behind the Waterfront Market with a chart of the area surrounding Key West spread out across the steering wheel.

Ben Baker had told Arlen that he wanted me to come to him for a change. That meant he wasn't hiding. He was someplace he hoped I would find him. And though there were lots of banks and keys within a twenty-mile radius of Key West, there weren't many anchorages that could accommodate a boat like *Hawkeye* with her seven-foot draft. Depths in the anchorages and over the banks looked like they averaged about three to five feet.

The other consideration was that he would want to be left alone. There was no way he had just followed a channel to the tourists' favorite anchorage. Even if the weather was likely to keep most boaters away, he would not want to be someplace where a swim and walk ashore would lead to civilization. Ben wasn't insane. He may have killed and kidnapped, but he knew exactly what he was doing.

I considered and rejected the islands in Florida Bay to the northeast. The Bluefish Channel, the Bay Keys, or the Lower Harbor Keys all had areas with enough depth for the big schooner, but the approaches were all too shallow. Due west from the entrance to Key West, however, was a string of islands: the Barracouta Keys, Woman Key, Ballast Key, and Boca Grande Key.

As soon as I saw the name on the chart, I remembered that evening aboard his schooner. Ben had told me that he wanted to take me out to Boca Grande Key someday. The last of the Florida Keys out at the edge of the stream where his great-great-grandfather had once anchored. Once upon a time, Boca Grande Key had been a jumping-off spot for the wreckers on their way out to Cay Sal Bank. Wreckers' Key.

I stopped at the pay phone outside the public restrooms and tried the Key West Police Department. I found myself in voice mail hell again. Press one if you want to report a traffic accident, press two if you would like to speak to a detective . . . After pushing several more numbers, I got Lassiter's voice mail. Frustrated, I launched into my explanation of the death at the Sparkses' residence and a suspected kidnapping aboard the *Hawkeye*. I had just started to explain what I intended to do when the machine clicked and hung up on me. I glanced at my watch. It was already four o'clock and darkness would be here in less than two hours. I dug in my bag for the change for one more call. At Jeannie's house, I also got her answering machine. I tried to leave a more succinct message and got most of it out. This time it was my money that ran out. I had no more change. It was time to go.

A momentary lull in the rain had been filled by an increase in the strength of the wind. I figured it was blowing more than twenty knots now, and the noise of the flapping flags and banging halyards was nearly as loud as the whistling in the rigging. The docks were deserted except for my friend and his dog. He still stood at the head of Ben's dock, his poor soaked dog shivering in the wind. I had to squeeze around him to get down Ben's finger pier, but I didn't want him to grab hold of me again, so I tried not to make eye contact.

"You see," he shouted almost making me fall into the harbor. "I told you so. Find the dark one in your dreams."

Wet wooden docks are treacherous—many a sailor has been on his back before he knew it—but I didn't care. I broke into a run.

The *Rapid* was a Conch 27 with a single 227-horse-power Mercury outboard, and as I had guessed, the key fit the ignition. The engine fired up at the first crank of the starter. I flicked on the instruments switch, and what had looked like a panel of dark glass just forward of the steering wheel lit up with the colors of a GPS plotter. I'd seen a radar dome resting on the hardtop; while I wouldn't need it right away, when darkness came it might be my only way to find the *Hawkeye*.

I threw off the dock lines and pulled away, trying to get a feel for the boat. Immediately, a gust of wind pushed me way off course. It took a few minutes for me to learn how to correct for the growing wind.

Outside the harbor entrance, I pushed the throttles forward and put her up on a plane. It was a hell of a bouncy ride; my wet pant legs felt like they'd turned to ice in the wind. I reached up and turned on the VHF radio that rested in a rack just under the hardtop. No digital numbers appeared on the channel readout screen. I double-checked to make sure I had turned the radio switch on at the panel. Damn. That meant Ben had disabled the radio. I wished I'd checked it out before leaving the harbor.

The boat's motion changed significantly when I lost the protection of the island and entered the open ocean. I was forced to slow way down in the six- to eight-foot

seas that rolled out of the east, to where I was only making about six knots of progress. Visibility was almost
nonexistent, and I didn't know how I was going to spot
the schooner—assuming I had even guessed right and
was heading in their direction.

I'd been closing my mind to thoughts of them and
what they might be going through out there, but in that
moment I pictured them bound, injured, or worse, and I
felt the panic start to rise in my chest. My breathing
grew fast and shallow; I was going to make myself dizzy
by hyperventilating if I wasn't careful. I forced my body
to slow the breathing. I closed my eyes for a couple of
seconds and tried to picture something that would calm
me down. I saw B.J. looking straight into my eyes and I
could almost hear his voice telling me I could do this,
that it would all turn out all right if I would just think it
through. *Think*, he said again. *Think*.

I opened my eyes and remembered the crazy man on
the dock. He was right. I'd found the dark one in my
dreams. I laughed out loud then. Despite the cold and
the rain and the fact that I was chasing after a man who
wanted to harm me, for me there had always been something exhilarating about steering a boat in rough seas.
My legs were planted shoulder width apart, and I bent
my knees to compensate for the motion of the boat until
the movement was totally natural and I felt as though I
had become one with the waves.

My brain began repeating other phrases the man had
said, and some of it began to make sense. He'd muttered
something about abductions—that they can happen right
under our noses. Maybe he had seen something and some
part of him was trying to tell me about it. He'd said only
the dark one looked him in the eye, and I knew that if B.J.
was being forced to do something and passed a stranger,
he would have looked him in the eye. He would have to

tell him with his eyes the story of what was happening to them. And maybe it took someone living, not on another planet, but maybe on another plane, to understand his message. What else had that guy said? Something about going into the precipice and seeing a big mouth?

When it came to me, I felt like an idiot. Of course. I'd only had one year of college Spanish before I quit—both college and Spanish. But living in South Florida, you're bound to pick up a bit of the language every few days. *Boca Grande* translated into English meant "big mouth." B.J. had been trying to leave a message for me. He was alive.

Boca Grande Key had a channel that ran alongside it through the flats. Though the current would be fierce, once the anchor set, you'd only have to worry about the changing of the tide. There would be protection from the wind in every direction. And in weather like this, you'd have the place all to yourself. It was more than ten miles out from Key West, and given my slow speed I wouldn't get there before dark, but that was probably better anyway. I didn't have any weapons and he was expecting me.

I hatched one plan as I rode over the waves out there, but I never got a chance to try it out. It was a good thing. It might have worked for Johnny Depp in *Pirates of the Caribbean*, but I really wasn't looking forward to swimming out to that schooner with a knife in my teeth. I was going to pass between Woman Key and the Barracouta Keys through a narrow channel, but as I neared the island, putting my faith in the GPS unit, I realized that the reading I was getting was way off. The current was pushing me toward the banks at a speed I would never be able to fight while swimming. I tried a direction I thought would put me in the clear and soon realized I was heading straight for the shore of Woman Key.

Ben must be playing with his GPS jamming toy. We were going through some kind of battle of the wits here, and he was determined to show me that he was now the stronger of the two of us. The poor fat kid whose boat sank under him all those years ago had become a fierce competitor and a good boatman. He was trying to make my boat sink under me this time.

Okay, so I'd learned a couple of things. Don't leave the boat and don't rely on GPS. I made another pass at the channel, but this time I shut off the GPS, using the boat's radar and a handheld spotlight. With the lamp, I could make out the water color, but it ruined my night vision when I turned it off. Halfway through the cut, the rain started up again, and visibility closed down to near zero.

The cold rain stung my face and blurred my vision. I kicked up the outboard, took it slow, especially fighting the current as I was. The hull ran aground on the soft bottom a couple of times, but it was easy enough to back off. By the time I made it through, the tide was running off the bank at full speed, exactly as I'd hoped.

He wouldn't be expecting me from the north. If Ben had anchored the *Hawkeye* where I was thinking, in the old wreckers' lair in the channel alongside Boca Grande Key, he'd expect me to approach him from the open ocean on the south side. His anchor would be up inside the pass, with his boat pointing northeast into the current and the wind.

I cut the engine on my boat long before I spotted the schooner. The sound of an engine travels through the water, and I didn't want him to hear me coming. On the way out, I'd searched the boat for any useful weapons or tools. Though I had my rigging knife in my pant pocket, that straight-edged blade would have little effect on a thick nylon anchor rode. I'd found a paddle strapped to the gunwale on the port side; under the bench seat was a fishing knife in a scabbard with a long serrated blade. With Ben's knife in the pocket of my jacket, I positioned myself on the bow with the paddle and peered into the rain.

There was no anchor light on *Hawkeye,* but faint lights shone from her portholes and reflected off the dark water. The current ran fast and deep in the channel, and the fishing boat rode through at a fast clip. At times I had the illusion that the boat had stopped drifting because the water around me looked still. Occasionally, through the veil of rain, I could see the banks on either side of the channel where the surface of the water was broken by wavelets in the mangrove shallows. When I got too near, I used my paddle to steer the boat back to the center of the channel.

From the moment the masts appeared against the night sky, I had about twenty seconds before I was on the anchor line under the bow of the schooner. I dug the paddle into the water and pulled the boat across the current. When my fingers closed around the anchor rode, I could not believe the speed I was traveling, and I feared I'd get pulled right out of the boat. I gripped the anchor line in one hand and held tight to the *Rapid*'s bowline with the other. The stern of the *Rapid* swung around and nudged the black hull. I hoped the bump was not loud enough to alert anyone below.

I crooked my elbow round the anchor rode, took the fishing knife out of my jacket pocket, and began to saw at the nylon. The knife's serrated edge was sharp, and the anchor line parted with little work. I pushed the *Rapid* free and paddled across the current. The big schooner was adrift.

XXXI

To reach that inner anchorage off Boca Grande Key in the best of circumstances requires quite a bit of maneuvering through a minefield of shoals. With daylight and a working GPS, it's easy enough; fishermen do it on a daily basis. In the driving rain, though, and adrift with the wind and current pushing her around, I predicted that *Hawkeye* would grind aground within minutes. While it was easy enough to back off when I went aground in the light little *Rapid,* putting a seventy-five-foot schooner on the reef was another story.

The spreader lights blinked on, and I saw a man on deck. Ben had probably set an anchor alarm, which sounded when the boat moved outside its charted position. I heard the big diesel engine start up at the same time I saw the masts begin to lean over at an odd angle. Over the noise of the surf and the shriek of the wind came the creaking and grinding of a wooden hull hitting a hard bottom and coming to a fast stop. I was still sculling the *Rapid* in the current, and I could see now how fast *Hawkeye* had been traveling as she ground to a halt and tilted over at a thirty-degree angle.

Despite the wind, I heard his voice amplified by the boat's loud-hailer.

"Pull alongside, Seychelle. I won't mind giving her the same treatment I gave her husband."

I started the outboard and idled up to the spot where the black schooner lay on her side. When I touched the transom, I could feel the vibration through the hull as she lifted and pounded down on the reef with each wave. Ben had a small black gun in his hand. Neither of us spoke. I climbed over the boomkin and tried to stand on the sharply tilting deck. Ben took the powerboat's painter and tied it to a midship cleat. In the darkness, the shape of Boca Grande Key blocked out the horizon no more than a hundred feet off. The schooner was perched on the hard coral shelf that surrounded the island, and the waves were breaking over the slanting foredeck.

"Cutting the anchor line was smart. I have to give you credit for that one," Ben hollered. Then he told me to place the knife on the deck. I leaned down and placed his fishing knife so that it would not roll downhill. He pointed to the cockpit and the ladder that led below.

"Think you can get her off this shoal by yourself, Ben?" I shouted.

"Shut up," he said. "Just move."

I heard her over the noise of the weather and waves and engine before I got to the bottom of the ladder. She was on the settee, on her back, her hands and feet bound. She was grunting in pain. B.J.'s feet were lashed to the settee table base, her hands tied to a built-in bookrack over his head. His mouth was gagged with a red bandanna, but the eyes that shone in the yellow lamplight were not the eyes of my pacifist lover.

I rushed to Catalina's side and held her hand as she cried out in pain.

"Get away from her," he said. "Over here."

The noise of the grinding reef and the waves was even louder below, and the engine room, which was just aft of where we were standing, didn't seem to have much sound insulation, either. I had to shout to be heard. "Just what was your plan, Ben? Were you going to show me that you weren't a scared little boy anymore?"

He never raised his voice or sounded angry—just tight, like he was having trouble breathing. "I said, get over here. Down on the floor." He pointed the gun at Catalina, and I did as he asked. He told me to lie face-down, then hog-tied me. The line wound around my hands, then around my ankles. When he'd finished trussing me up like a farm animal, he sat on the cabin sole next to me. He spoke with his head so close to my ear I could feel the warmth of his breath.

"How does it feel?"

I said nothing.

"How does it feel to have everybody think you're crazy?"

"What are you talking about?"

"Did you try to tell the police that someone broke into your house? Tried to run you down? Why not? What about Gramps? Did he believe your story?"

"You're the crazy one. All this shit you've been doing, it doesn't make any sense."

His teeth glowed white in the lamplight. I wondered how I could ever have found that face handsome.

"Your dog loved me. She let me in anytime I wanted. I watched you sleeping."

A shudder shook my body more violently than the engine's vibrations or the pounding of the waves. I felt sick, violated.

"See," he hissed in my ear. "See how it feels."

I turned to look at Catalina, her face contorted with the pain. She wouldn't hear my words. "So how did you do it? At the Wreckers' Race? How did you get to Nestor?"

"Neville was out there with one of our launches, hoping to pick up some tourist chicks. I saw Nestor out on

the windsurfer and recognized him. I'd met him in Fort
Lauderdale at the Downtowner."

"You were at the Downtowner?"

"So were you. That was when it started. He told you he
was going to Key West. Like I told you, I was able to walk
right by people I'd known before and they never recognized me. You didn't. I wasn't the fat kid anymore."

"You haven't changed that much," I shouted.

"You have no idea how hard I've worked to get where
I am. Do you know what it takes to lose a hundred
pounds? Look at me," he said.

I kept my head turned away.

He grabbed my head and forced it around. His hands
were on either side of my face, squishing my cheeks, dis-
torting my lips so I must've looked like a fish.

"Don't you see what I look like now? All the other
women stare at me, talk to me. They all want to screw
me. You? You still look at me like I'm fat Ben, Old Glub,
the freak. The kid who pissed his pants."

He lowered his face and smashed his lips against
mine. It was crude and clumsy, like the kiss of an adoles-
cent boy.

I tried to wipe my mouth on my shoulder. I didn't want
the taste of him on me. "What did she do to you, Ben?"

"Shut up. She always hated you. She said you were
going to tell. She said it was my fault."

I moved my head to indicate Catalina and B.J. "Why
don't you let them go? If I'm the one you want to hurt,
then let them go."

He laughed. "You're so fucking predictable. Thanks to
you, I lost everything. My father hates my guts. The only
one I ever loved is dead. Now it's your turn. Now you'll
see what it feels like. You'll watch *them* die." He waved
the gun at Cat and B.J. "And when you're hurting so bad

you wish you were dead, when you've got no one left but me, I'll decide if I want to keep you."

"While you're down here talking, your precious boat is self-destructing."

"You're going to beg for it," he said. "For me."

He sat next to me for another minute or so, waiting for my response. When I didn't say a word, he climbed the ladder topside and began the job of trying to get the schooner off the limestone shelf she'd grounded on.

The engine roared and raced as he tried to work her off in reverse.

I squirmed my way downhill, across the floor to the settee that held Catalina. Her hands were bound in front so she could lie on her back. I rolled onto my side, and with my head against the settee, I worked an elbow under me. Then I inched my shoulder up the settee until I was in a sitting position.

"Cat, can you sit up?"

She was breathing like a horse that had just crossed the finish line. She nodded.

"Reach into the right front pocket of my jeans. I've got a knife."

Between contractions, she managed to reach down around that massive belly of hers and squirm her fingers into the front pocket of my jeans. She worked my rigging knife up and out.

"Just drop it on the floor. I'll get it." I heard the knife clatter onto the wooden floor. Cat collapsed back on the bunk.

I fell over on top of the knife and worked it to my fingers. First, I cut the line that connected my hands to my feet. Catalina's screams grew louder and she began crying out in Spanish, saying things I could not understand. I was able to bring my hands under my butt to the front, and once I could see what I was doing, it was no problem to cut the line on my feet. I cut loose B.J.'s hands before mine. Within a matter of seconds he had cut me free and he was at Catalina's side.

"What do we do now?" I asked.

He stood, and his eyes flicked up past my shoulder. I turned to see feet coming down the companionway stairs.

Ben pointed the gun at Cat as she let loose with another horrible scream. "Drop the knife or I'll shoot her."

I did as he asked.

"Where is he?"

I turned to look where B.J. had been standing a minute before—and he had vanished. The dark companionway that led forward was empty. Before I could turn back around, Ben's arm slid around my neck and he held me against his body, the barrel of the gun pressed to my head.

"You'd better come out or I'll shoot her," he yelled.

On deck we heard heavy footsteps. "He's going for the boat, Ben. You know that boat is our only chance of towing this schooner off."

He swung me around and pushed me toward the stairs. "Move it." I began to climb.

It happened before I had time to register that I was seeing someone. I stepped out onto the deck and something pushed me down. As I fell I heard a shot and the two men crashed down the companionway ladder. Then it went quiet. When I peeked down the stairs, I saw a dark shape on the cabin sole. He wasn't moving.

I inched carefully down the ladder. Over by the settee, B.J. was placing a blanket across Catalina's legs. The pants he pulled from under the blanket were dark and wet—with what, I couldn't tell. He gazed up at me, a blank look on his face I had never seen before. "I'll take care of her if you can see to the boat."

"What about him?" I pointed to Ben.

"He's done. Broken neck." He said it simply, without any emotion whatsoever, and went back to his preparations.

I tried the schooner's VHF radio, hoping for a helicopter that could fly her off and put an end to those screams, but Ben had disabled that, too.

Out on deck, I surveyed the situation. The wind was now blowing at more than thirty knots, pushing the water and waves and boat farther up onto the reef. With each bounce, she moved a fraction of an inch higher. When I'd cut her loose, her bow had blown around in the wind, and she now lay on her starboard side with greenie waves breaking all the way over her bow.

I began digging in his lockers, making my preparations with lines, blocks, and anchors. The gear on that big heavy old boat nearly did me in. I found a spare Bruce and a big old Fortress anchor in the aft lazarette and after dumping both of them, two sections of chain, and two three-hundred-foot coils of nylon line into the *Rapid,* I jumped down myself and motored forward.

Working on the bow was hell. Most of the waves just swirled around my legs, but the occasional larger swell would knock me off my feet and wash me into stanchions and hatches and rigging. My body was so bruised, I hurt with every movement, but rather than driving me to give it all up, it just made me angrier. Curses flying, I rigged a towline on the bow then used the *Rapid* as a tug to swing her around so I could have running room to increase her heel. I set one anchor a hundred yards off the starboard bow parallel now to the reef, and with that line tied to the main halyard running through a snatch block at the staysail stay, I used the anchor windlass and winched her over to a thirty-five-degree heel.

The pounding was worsening, and I hated to think of the effect on B.J. and Catalina below, but I had to get the boat on her side, off the keel, in order to slide her off the reef. I worried that I'd hole her before I got her loose, so I tried to work faster. Pulling with the *Rapid,* I dragged her to the edge of the ledge, and then an hour after I'd started, with me back at the helm and the engine screaming, she slid off the coral shelf. I threw off all the anchors. We could return and retrieve them another day. I set her on autopilot on a course for deepwater at the Key West Harbor buoy and went below to check the bilges.

I realized that the screams had stopped some time ago, only I didn't know when. Perhaps it was while I was out in the boat setting the anchor, or while the waves had been battering me on the foredeck. I paused in the shuttle hatch and took a deep breath of the fresh ocean air. I knew I was going back down to face Ben's corpse, and exhausted as I was, I wasn't sure I could handle it.

At the bottom of the ladder, it took several seconds for my eyes to adjust to the dark cabin. Either B.J. had turned out the lights or the electrical system had failed. With all the water that had poured below, the latter was likely.

I saw B.J. sitting on the settee in the dark. The front of his once white shirt was now mottled with stains. He held what looked like a bundled infant in his arms, but his head rested on the settee behind him and his eyes were closed.

Mounds of blood-soaked towels littered the cabin sole. On the opposite side of the salon, the blanket B.J. had used to cover Catalina's legs now covered her whole body. Her knees were no longer drawn up as they had been when I had last seen her. Now she was stretched out beneath the blanket that peaked over her toes and then stretched nearly smooth to the point of her nose. It took my exhausted brain several seconds to comprehend why the blanket covered her face.

"Oh no, God no." I rushed to the settee. When I leaned against the cushion, I realized it was soaked with blood. I pulled back the blanket. Her long dark lashes curled against the smooth cocoa-colored skin of her cheeks. I pressed my cheek to hers. "Cat, no, not you." I took her shoulders in my hands and started shaking her. "No, not now, you can't go."

Her body shook like a flaccid bag of bones. Her head rolled to one side. I pulled back my hands and stared at her, my vision blurred by the tears. Slowly I pulled the blanket up and re-covered her face.

I crossed to the opposite settee and slumped on the cushion next to my lover. His eyes remained closed. I watched his chest rising and falling with his breaths, and I reached out and touched his cheek.

He turned his head away as though burned by my touch. Finally, he sat up, pulling the bundle to his chest. For the first time he opened his eyes and looked down into the folds of the blanket.

With one arm he held the tiny bundle toward me. There in the shadows I saw blinking eyes and a tiny mouth opening and closing. "She told me we're to call him Nestor."

XXXII

FAITH gave us the keys to the place. She said the house belonged to some relatives of her second husband and that she had many happy memories of escaping there when the stresses and strains of their daily lives had grown too heavy to bear. The house, located on Lower Matecumbe Key, had been built in the 1960s in the shape of an octagon up on stilts, and because the place stood over six feet off the ground, it was possible to park several cars in the space beneath. Part of the interior was broken up into smaller bedrooms, but most of the floor plan consisted of the great room that was part living room and part kitchen. The view overlooking Florida Bay was spectacular on those clear blustery March days, but when we'd first arrived after all those hours with cops and in court, seeing judges, making statements, dragging out records, we'd been just too exhausted to notice.

We'd sailed Faith's boat *Annie* down, again at her insistence, cutting through the Channel Five Bridge and turning back north to make the short tack up around the point and into the bay off the house. The lovely old boat now bobbed in the boat basin, tied to the concrete seawall, and B.J. was out there daily keeping himself busy with new coats for her brightwork. He wasn't talking much these days, but at least he was keeping himself busy and out in the sunshine.

Once we'd arrived and moved into the house, neither of us went down below inside *Annie*'s cabin if we could avoid it. In the main salon, behind the dining settee, there were two white cardboard boxes that I knew we would need to deal with eventually, but we had plenty of time. We were having trouble enough dealing with the living, much less the dead.

So much had changed in the last month. Melvin Burke had dropped his lawsuit when Jeannie met him in the halls of the Broward County Courthouse, where he was wearing a cervical collar and walking with a cane. She showed him the photos I had taken, but the coup de grâce was the fact that she had met up with his daughter in the ladies' room and learned some very specific details about his boat—and how he had intentionally sunk her—in the exchange.

The deaths of Nestor Frias and Quentin Hazell were reclassified as homicides, the cases closed with the demise of the perpetrator. Ben's boats were both seized by the government, as was Arlen's house on the canal, but by the time the cops got there, Sparky and his little boat were long gone. They haven't found him since. I'd like to think that he's holed up somewhere out in the back-country in the Ten Thousand Islands waiting for the mess to blow over, but it's just as likely he put his boat on autopilot, set an easterly course, and sailed off on a last cruise to nowhere. I didn't expect to ever learn the outcome of that one. Arlen would remain one of life's mysteries.

The authorities discovered that Neville Pinder was in the United States on a tourist visa that had expired twelve years earlier, and the government promptly deported him. Since I knew he wasn't welcome back home in Man O' War, I wondered what poor little cay had wound up inheriting Neville.

And that left me and B.J. After what felt like weeks of talking into microphones, telling the story over and over again, they cleared B.J. in both deaths. In those first couple of days, when we were still in Key West, they hadn't allowed us to talk to each other very much, and I worried about him. Then Jeannie arrived, and once she'd swept in and taken over on the legal front, things started to go a little easier for us.

On our second day back in Fort Lauderdale, when Jeannie and I had been sitting in the hallway outside another office in the county courthouse, she told me she wanted to talk to me about all the consequences of Ben Baker's actions. She wanted to know how I was feeling, about where my future was headed.

Jeannie had, in her inimitable way, learned a great deal about the Bakers via courthouse and waterfront gossip. She'd learned that Ben had been the one offering to buy *Gorda* and that he did indeed own a black Lincoln Navigator. He had inherited a trust fund worth more than two million when his mother died, so for Ben, the whole GPS wrecking business had never been about the money.

As happens in many cities that are really just big small towns, Junior Baker had always gotten special treatment from the Fort Lauderdale police when they were called out to his house. He had been one of the jolly boys who ate breakfast at the Floridian with the mayor and the chamber president and the local developers. If he lost his temper with the wife and kid, the cops usually just drove him around for a while to calm him down and then took him back home to sleep it off. No one except me had ever seen any hint of what Ben's mother had done, where she had turned for solace when her husband left the house.

"You know what's strange?" Jeannie said, not really

expecting an answer. "Even as modern as we supposedly are today, as open and tolerant, males who are victims of maternal sexual abuse still have the toughest time finding help. It's one of our last and deepest taboos. I've never been one to excuse criminal behavior because somebody had a bad childhood—there are just too many survivors who make it through and are okay. But from what I've heard was going on in that house, that poor kid didn't have much of a chance. I guess his mother's death was the thing that nudged him over the edge."

"Jeannie, it seems like being a mother should be something that comes naturally. Look at you. You make it look so easy when you're with your sons. I mean, where did you learn this stuff? How do you know what to do? And why do so many of the rest of us screw it up so bad?"

"Sey, I don't think it's a question of mothering taking all that much talent. Really, I don't. It's a question of what kind of heart you've got. You know, there are good people and there are bad people in this world. The real heart of goodness is found in the ability to love unconditionally. To love someone else so much that you would sacrifice your life for his happiness. That's all it takes to be a good mother. And you already know how to do that. Women like Ben's mama? They only know how to think of themselves." She patted my knee. "Honey, that will never be your problem."

She only had to ask me once where I stood on the whole issue of motherhood and baby Nestor, and she wasn't the least bit surprised by my response.

I was right to worry about B.J. It didn't matter which he saw as worse, the taking of a life or the failing to save a life: he bore the responsibility for both like a coat of nails. There was no more lovemaking or laughter in our lives. He wouldn't talk, he barely ate. And I was the one who sailed *Annie* down to the Keys while B.J. slept on a settee belowdecks. Once inside the five-bedroom house, he'd chosen his room and come out only to work on *Annie*.

The third week in March, Jeannie called to say that my brother Pit was back from his delivery and Maddy had agreed to bring everyone down to the Keys. She told me that the time had come for us to open our doors to the world, hold the wake for those we'd lost, and move on with our lives. When I told B.J. they were coming, he unloaded some gear from the sailboat, including the two boxes of ashes, and then motored *Annie* out and anchored off the dock.

That afternoon, Maddy's sportfishing boat, the *Lady Jane,* arrived with Jeannie, Molly, Zale, Pit, and all the gang. They had brought a ton of food and CDs and soon the place was rocking with music and laughter. Maddy volunteered to take us all out to an island he knew on Florida Bay on the *Lady Jane* the next day. The time had come for Catalina and Nestor to find their last home.

As they settled into the big house, Jeannie walked out on the dock with me. She was carrying a special basket she had brought just for me. I'd been waiting for them all morning, pacing the dock, watching to see if B.J. was going to raise his head or show any interest in me or the rest of the world. There had been no sign of him.

"Seychelle Sullivan," she said. "You never cease to amaze me."

"Ah, Jeannie, come on."

She indicated the *Annie* resting at anchor. "I would have expected him to be the strong one and you to fall apart. Not the other way around."

"No way. I don't think any of us will ever fully understand what that day cost him. He's lost himself. It's been so hard standing by, feeling helpless to make him better.

He was the guy who caught mosquitoes and let them go outside the house. To have taken a human life—even if it was to protect the lives of himself and those he loved— cost him more than you or I can ever imagine. And then to lose his first patient. Jeannie, I'm so afraid I'll never get him back."

"You know, there's still a long legal road to walk here."

"Yeah, but I can never thank you enough for helping make this happen. He may not be getting the best deal offered, but it's what she wanted."

I climbed down the dock ladder and stepped into the dory. She handed me the basket, and I set it carefully in the bottom of the dink. I sat on the thwart, fitted the oars into the locks, and looked out at the *Annie* sitting at anchor not more than fifty feet off the dock. "Don't worry Jeannie. I'll take good care of him."

I rapped my knuckles on the hull. "Hey, sailor, you want to give me a hand?" I hollered.

B.J. appeared in the cockpit looking like he'd been fast asleep. His long black hair hung in dull tangles around his unshaven face. "Come on," he said. "Just leave me alone."

"Sorry, I need a hand to get our passenger aboard."

He ran a tired hand through his hair and looked more annoyed than puzzled. "What are you talking about?"

I lifted the basket and held it out to him. "B.J., this is Nestor. You two have already met, but I think it's time you got better acquainted."